SMILE AND BE A VILLAIN

*A Selection of Recent Titles by Jeanne M Dams
from Severn House*

The Dorothy Martin Mysteries

A DARK AND STORMY NIGHT
THE EVIL THAT MEN DO
THE CORPSE OF ST JAMES'S
MURDER AT THE CASTLE
SHADOWS OF DEATH
DAY OF VENGEANCE
THE GENTLE ART OF MURDER
BLOOD WILL TELL
SMILE AND BE A VILLAIN

SMILE AND BE A VILLAIN

A Dorothy Martin Mystery

Jeanne M. Dams

This first world edition published 2016
in Great Britain and the USA by
SEVERN HOUSE PUBLISHERS LTD of
19 Cedar Road, Sutton, Surrey, England, SM2 5DA.
Trade paperback edition first published
in Great Britain and the USA 2016 by
SEVERN HOUSE PUBLISHERS LTD

British Library Cataloguing in Publication Data
A CIP catalogue record for this title is available from the British Library.

ISBN-13: 978-0-7278-8629-3 (cased)
ISBN-13: 978-1-84751-733-3 (trade paper)
ISBN-13: 978-1-78010-797-4 (e-book)

All Severn House titles are printed on acid-free paper.

Severn House Publishers support the Forest Stewardship Council™ [FSC™],
the leading international forest certification organisation.
All our titles that are printed on FSC certified paper carry the FSC logo.

Typeset by Palimpsest Book Production Ltd.,
Falkirk, Stirlingshire, Scotland.
Printed and bound in Great Britain by
TJ International, Padstow, Cornwall.

. . . one may smile, and smile, and be a villain . . .
Hamlet, Act I
William Shakespeare

ONE

'**W**here's Alderney? For that matter, what is it? Sounds like an expensive school.'

Alan chuckled. 'I suppose it does at that. It's a small island in the English Channel, one of the Channel Islands. You've heard of Jersey and Guernsey?'

My English husband isn't always sure of what his Yank wife might know about my adopted land. 'Of course. Cows.'

'Also the islands famous for those cows. They're the two largest of the group. Alderney is the next in size, and then there are Sark and Herm, which are not a lot more than large rocks.'

'Oh! I've heard of the Dame of Sark. Isn't that island independent of England, its own little duchy or something?'

'Or something. Sark is feudal, but the governance of all the islands is a trifle complicated. They're Crown dependencies, which means that they owe allegiance to the Queen but are neither governed by, nor represented in, Parliament.'

He went on to further explanation, very little of which I understood. Actually, once he launched into history, William the Conqueror and 1066 and all that, I stopped listening. The political system of a small group of islands I'd never seen was not wildly fascinating.

'So I thought perhaps in late June. The weather's usually quite good then, and it's just before the mass influx of tourists.'

'Sorry, dear, I missed part of that. What about late June?'

'I thought it would be a good time to visit. A beautiful and very peaceful place, Alderney, and we've not had a holiday for a long time.'

The last one had been a trip to Orkney that we had both looked forward to. We'd intended to explore those remote and wonderful islands, and we did – sort of – but not until we'd become embroiled in the death of a wealthy but unpopular man. I was ready for a real vacation, and I'd learned to love islands. Except . . . 'How do we get there? I'm not an awfully good sailor.'

'Not to worry. The only practical way to get to Alderney is by plane from Southampton. A very interesting plane. You'll love it.'

The gleam in his eye should have warned me, I thought a month later as I walked across the tarmac to the toy airplane sitting there. Our plans had changed; we had visited friends in London before leaving for our vacation, and then on a Monday morning had taken the train to Gatwick airport, to fly from there rather than Southampton. That made it a two-stage journey, the first in a perfectly normal small jet to the island of Guernsey. There we boarded a craft called the Trislander.

It resembled nothing so much as the balsa wood models that were popular when I was a child in America. The wings sat atop the box-like fuselage. There was a propeller on each wing, and one on the high tail. I saw doors on either side. I was escorted to one door, which opened directly onto my seat. Alan sat on the other side, but in a different row. 'We're distributed by weight, you see,' he murmured. That thought did not increase my confidence.

There was no aisle, and no real cockpit. The pilot sat directly in front of the first row of passengers (there were seven of us) and turned around to give a brief report of flying conditions ('A bit bumpy in spots') and the obligatory safety announcement ('There are life vests under your seats'). Then we were trundling down the runway with a roar that sounded much louder in this tiny box than in a well-soundproofed jet, and finally off the ground. I wished Alan were close enough to hold my hand. I also wished I had eaten some ginger before we took off; it's my favourite preventive for motion sickness.

The flight was, however, very short and entirely uneventful. We picked up our bags (straight off the airplane to a small shed; no nonsense about a carousel and a long wait) and found a taxi to take us to Belle Isle, our bed and breakfast accommodation.

'No passport control or anything? Even though this isn't exactly part of the UK?'

'Not exactly, but very few formalities.' He clasped my hand. 'All right now, love?'

We've been married only a few years, after the deaths of our first spouses, but Alan knows me very well indeed. He had felt my panic on the flight.

I smiled at him. 'Fine. I won't mind, next time.'

'It's actually a reliable little plane, you know. Sturdy, despite its appearance.'

I decided not to comment on that.

There is one principal street on Alderney, called Victoria Street. (I later learned that the name dated from a royal visit a good many years ago.) Our lodging was about halfway up the street, in an attractive house dating, I guessed, from the Georgian era. We settled down in our room, which was a little cramped but had a lovely bathroom and two big windows overlooking the busy street below.

'Right,' said Alan after we had unpacked and settled in. 'What about a nice little walk to familiarize ourselves with the general layout?'

'I thought you'd been here before.'

'Not to Alderney, only Jersey and Guernsey and Sark, and years ago at that. I'm told this is the best of the lot. Better put on your hat; the sun is strong.' He gave me his arm. 'Shall we?'

I might as well say at once that I fell in love with Alderney before I'd been there five minutes. The weather didn't hurt. It was a perfect day: bright sunshine with just enough breeze to keep it from being too hot. There were flowers in hanging baskets, in window boxes, in tiny gardens. Many of the houses and shops were painted in cheerful pastel shades of pink or blue or yellow; one shop was pale yellow with window and door frames of bright turquoise.

Victoria Street is certainly a tourist's mecca. Just a few steps from Belle Isle was the Visitor Information Centre, where we stopped to pick up a map of the island and other information from the friendly staff. We found shops selling clothing and souvenirs, and several restaurants. But it was obvious, even on casual inspection, that this was also the main shopping area for islanders. There was a business-like hardware store, a pharmacy, a general store-cum-post office, a farm shop selling local meat and cheese and produce along with basic groceries. I peered into the bakery as we passed and saw not only delectable pastries, but good wholesome loaves of bread.

On a busy weekday afternoon the street was thronged with people. They gathered to chat in little knots of two or three, their shopping bags on their arms. Drivers stopped their cars in the (very narrow) street for conversation with friends, blocking the road completely. No one seemed to get impatient; no horns sounded in irritation.

We walked to the bottom of the street, 'bottom' in this case being an apt term. Victoria Street has a decided grade, as, I was to discover, is the case almost everywhere on the island. There are very few spots where the walking or driving is level for more than a few yards. 'Do you want to go on down to the harbour?' asked Alan, looking at his map.

'How far is it?'

'Half a mile or so.'

'Then I'd rather change my clothes first. And have a cup of tea.'

Which just goes to show how thoroughly I've adopted English ways since moving from Indiana several years ago.

We had our tea, and a couple of biscuits each, provided by the management. They came in little packets and were actually called cookies on the label. More and more Americanisms are creeping across the Atlantic, and I'm not at all sure I like it. Whatever they were called, however, they were good, and nicely filled up a corner that had been registering mild hunger. Then I got into jeans and sneakers, and we walked on.

If I thought Victoria Street was hilly, I soon learned that it had far steeper cousins. Braye Road wound its curvy way down to the harbour on a pretty good incline, but at one point I stopped to look at what seemed to be bougainvillea growing on a house off to the right. 'Alan, for heaven's sake. Look!' I pointed. The house, only a few yards from where I stood, sat at least ten feet lower. Its roof was at about the level of my shoulders.

Alan whistled. 'When we go out for real walks, we'd best take our sticks and hiking boots,' he commented. 'Looks like the terrain could get a trifle rugged.'

'Not much like the Cotswolds, is it?' Some years before, we'd taken a walking tour of the Cotswolds and enjoyed its gently rolling hills, but Alderney was, I realized, going to be a whole 'nother story.

The walk down to the harbour, though a bit steep, was very

pleasant. Homes on either side were sturdy, well-built and neatly painted. Some had tiny front gardens. Men and women were at work on many of the houses, digging, painting, repairing. They responded to our waves with cheery greetings. The traffic up and down the road was as good-humoured as that in the village; where there wasn't room to pass, one car would pull over to the side and wait for the other, with no sign of ill temper.

I was slightly winded by the time we reached the bottom. The slope had forced a faster pace than I would have liked, so I was glad simply to stop and look at the harbour spread out before me.

There was, of course, the usual clutter of any working seaport. Huge shipping containers littered the pier, along with the derricks used to unload them. Boats of every size and type from rowboats to pontoon boats to cabin cruisers to cargo ships were tied up at the dock or moored out in the water, along with sailboats ranging from simple sloops to full-fledged yachts.

But beyond the busyness there was the beach, a crescent of golden sand, and beyond that the sea, as sparkling and blue as the Mediterranean, and as beautiful.

I love the sea. I always have. Growing up in Indiana, with the nearest ocean something like eight hundred miles away, I had to content myself with the waters of Lake Michigan, where my family used to go for vacations. I thought it was wonderful until one summer we went on a long road trip to the east coast, and I saw the ocean for the first time. Heard the crashing waves, tasted the salt on my lips, watched the tide coming in. I was hooked forever. The big lake was still nice, but it wasn't the same.

Then, late in my life, my husband died and I moved to England. I've been told that at no point in England is one more than sixty miles from the sea. I don't know if that's literally true, but it can't be far wrong, and that, for me, is bliss. If I feel like watching waves, I can get in the car and go, even if Alan is busy with something else. I can take a few sandwiches and eat my lunch and listen to the cry of gulls wanting to share (or wanting it all) and still be home in good time for tea. The wind blowing in my face is a tonic, refreshing and invigorating.

I grasped Alan's hand and sighed with pure contentment.

However, I'm nearing seventy, and Alan has passed that milestone. After a while I got tired of standing, and the sun was getting a little too warm for comfort, even with my broadbrimmed straw hat for protection. Alan loosed my hand and stretched his neck and shoulders. 'Getting stiff,' he said. 'The old boy needs a rest. In other words, how about a pint?'

'That sounds perfect, but I don't know if I'm ready to walk back up that hill.' I turned around to look back. The hillside looked beautiful, covered with wildflowers on one side of the road and attractive houses on the other. It also looked even steeper than it had coming down.

'We don't have to, just yet.' He gestured with his head. 'I'm sure one of those pubs can provide good beer.'

We went into the Divers Inn, which was just beginning to fill up with customers, mostly visitors, I thought. We enjoyed our beer, laughed over the dummy in the corner dressed in full old-style diver's rig, helmet and all, and talked about dinner. 'I don't want to eat out,' I said. 'I'm tired. Couldn't we pick up sandwich makings somewhere and eat in our rooms? I'd like to sit and read the stuff we picked up about the island, and plan what we're going to do tomorrow.'

The barman directed us to a small but very nice grocery store where we bought materials for an upscale picnic supper: pâté and Stilton, smoked salmon, a couple of interesting salads, granary bread, and some fresh apricots and raspberries.

'Wine?' I asked the woman at the till.

'Are you staying at the harbour or in town?'

'In town.'

'Then you'll want the off-licence at the Coronation Inn. It's in the High Street, just at the top of Victoria Street. Look right and you'll see it.'

I groaned at the thought of walking up Victoria Street after the climb up Braye Road, but Alan took pity on me. 'Let's take a taxi back to Belle Isle, then I'll walk up to the off-licence.'

'You are a verray parfit gentil knight,' I said gratefully. 'You're on.'

So we had our picnic, with a nice bottle of some sort of Spanish white wine, and planned out our next couple of days. It had been a lovely day, quiet, leisurely – the perfect beginning to a holiday.

We went to bed well-pleased with Alderney, each other, and life in general.

If I had known what lay ahead, I would have lit out for home by the first plane.

TWO

The next day dawned clear and cool, perfect weather for wandering about the island. We lazed in bed until the last possible moment for breakfast, which was excellent: scrambled eggs with smoked salmon (both local, we were assured) and fruit. When we were sated, we thought exercise was in order, so set out for a proper exploration.

'Up or down?' asked Alan.

'Neither. The church is just across the way. Let's have a look.'

I have a great fondness for old English churches. This one, I guessed, was not particularly old, certainly not medieval, but it was a pleasant-looking building in grey stone, irregular in design, with an apse-like structure in front of us as we approached through the churchyard. Some scaffolding at the side encroached upon the walkway.

'Doesn't look as if any work is actually going on,' I commented.

'Probably the usual lack of funds,' said Alan.

The sun was already growing warm, and the interior of the church was pleasantly cool. As my eyes adjusted to the dimness, I saw that a few people were gathering in the choir stalls. 'I think we've walked into the beginning of a service,' I whispered.

'Yes,' said Alan imperturbably. 'I saw the notice. Morning Prayer. Shall we join them?'

A handful of women and the vicar were settling down. We asked, of course, and they graciously invited us to participate. There was a little bustle as they found prayer books and Bibles for our use, and we read and listened to the familiar, beautiful words of the Psalms and canticles for the day.

When the service was over, we introduced ourselves. The young man in the collar was not, it transpired, the vicar. 'The regular man is on holiday,' he explained. 'I'm a locum from a village near Canterbury. My name is James Lewison.'

'Alan Nesbitt, and my wife, Dorothy Martin.'

Older people sometimes blink at the difference in our names.

This young man didn't even blink. 'And did I hear a transatlantic accent during the Psalms?' he asked me.

'Yes, I'm American originally, but I've lived in England for some years. In Sherebury, virtually under the bells of the Cathedral.'

'Ah, yes, you recently acquired a new bishop, didn't you? And a fine man, I'm told.'

We chatted about our new bishop and church matters in general for a few minutes. 'So how long are you going to be here?' I asked.

'Only two more weeks. The vicar's been gone for a week, and he'll allow himself only three away from his duties.'

'I expect you'll be glad to get back to your family.'

He pulled a little face. 'Actually, it's been rather peaceful here. We have three-year-old twin boys, and—'

I laughed. 'You need say no more. In that case, I'm sure your wife will be delighted to see you again.'

'She's very capable, and seems to take the boys in her stride. She has brothers. I was an only child, and . . . well . . . it's been lovely to have a tranquil interlude.'

'Is there a large congregation here?'

'Not bad, for a village church. There's quite a lot going on, actually, but I've been fortunate to have help. A retired priest from America has been volunteering a good deal. He can't actually take services, because of course he hasn't been through the "safeguard" vetting procedure. But he's been quite happy to act as a lay volunteer in all sorts of capacities. It's freed up my time considerably.'

'And Mr Abercrombie is a real asset to our church,' said one of the ladies who had attended the service, as she finished putting the prayer books away. 'We're all hoping he'll be able to get through the vetting quickly, because he wants to be able to assist the vicar here, as a real priest.'

'He's planning to stay here in Alderney, then?' asked Alan.

'Yes, he's thinking of buying a house and making this his home. We all hope he will!'

I noticed another of the ladies, the one who had sat next to me and helped me find my place in the service, which was slightly different from the one we used back in Sherebury. We were standing just in front of the lectern, and she moved past me in the crowded space with a murmured apology. I noticed her expression, the frown, the pursed lips, and watched as she strode up the aisle and out of the church without a word to anyone.

Hmm.

'Will you be in Alderney for long?' asked Mr Lewison.

'Two weeks,' replied Alan. 'We decided to give ourselves a real holiday.'

'And it's such a lovely place!' I added. 'I do love islands, and this one is amazing.'

'Have you done any of the walks yet? My name is Sylvia, by the way, Sylvia Whiting. I volunteer at the Visitor Information Centre, and I'd be happy to help you find some of the points of interest.'

'That's very kind of you,' said Alan. 'We only just got here yesterday, and we've been down to the harbour, but nowhere else. And we do enjoy walking.'

'Well, then! Come to the centre any time. I'm going there now, but if you come when I'm not there, someone else will help.'

Alan and I looked at each other. 'Sounds good to me,' I said. 'And the centre's just down the street.'

'Almost everything's just down the street in Alderney, or up, as the case may be,' said one of the other ladies, laughing. 'Do enjoy yourselves.'

We left the church surrounded by goodwill.

There were, it turned out, seven planned walks in Alderney, designed to give visitors a good overview of the island and its more interesting features. It seemed there was plenty to see. Old fortifications from the time the islanders feared invasion from France, much newer ones built by the Germans when they occupied the Channel Islands during World War Two. Stunning views of the sea. Wildlife of all sorts, including rare sea birds and Alderney's pride, the blonde hedgehog.

'They're extremely rare everywhere else in the world,' said Sylvia, 'but we have a large population. They're not particularly shy, but you'll probably not see them in the daytime. They like to come out to feed at night. In fact, on Thursday evening we have a Bats and Hedgehogs walk, and we can almost guarantee seeing some then.'

I've never been able to get enthusiastic about bats, but I did want to see the hedgehogs, so Alan and I signed up for that tour. 'Now, for today, which walk would you recommend we start with?'

'My favourite is the Zig-Zag,' she said, pointing to one of the brochures. 'There's a steep bit, but you can always turn around and go back the way you came, and the views are delightful.'

The sun was shining. The cool breeze was bracing. I was feeling hale and hearty and ready for anything. 'The Zig-Zag it is,' I said with determination. 'Alan, let's go and get our sticks and boots, and we're off.'

The first part of the walk, up to the top of Victoria Street and then into an area of homes, was easy if not particularly interesting. We passed the pub and off-licence where Alan had bought our bottle of wine the night before, and another pub or two. 'Remarkably well-supplied with pubs for such a small place,' I commented.

Alan grinned. 'Alderney has a reputation. Unfounded, I'm sure.'

Then we left the town proper and approached the airport (rather a grand name for a very small facility), and set out into proper country. A signpost directed us to the Zig-Zag.

In America we call such a path a switchback. A series of not-too-steep tracks took us gradually down toward the sea. The cliff itself was very steep, but the pathway made it easy, and Sylvia had been absolutely accurate about the views. She hadn't mentioned the wildflowers and the butterflies, but I kept having to stop and admire them. 'There are so many of those adorable little blue ones!' I enthused.

'My dear, they're all over our garden in summer.'

'I know, but they're unknown in America, at least where I lived, and I still can't get used to them. Oh, and there's a red admiral! I do know those; we have them in Indiana, too.'

We encountered several people as we went on down the narrow path: a couple of obvious husband/wife pairs, then one lone man in a natty green-and-white jogging suit ('A dedicated walker,' I whispered to Alan). Then there were three giggling teenagers who sounded like Americans or Canadians.

'Ah, to be young again!' I said. 'Look how easily they climb.

But then I never was any good at anything athletic, even when I was their age.'

Diplomatically, Alan made no comment. He didn't even glance at the bulges of flab that I tried to hide with loose-fitting shirts.

I cleared my throat. 'Yes. Onward.'

We reached the bottom of the cliff and walked along a paved road for a bit, then Alan stopped and considered the leaflet guide. 'I think the walk goes this way,' he said dubiously, and pointed.

I was certain he was wrong. There did seem to be something resembling a path, or a track, leading up the cliff, but it must have been made by goats. It was so narrow it didn't seem as if it would accommodate two feet side by side, and it appeared to me to lead straight up.

'Alan, that can't be right.'

He looked back at the guide. 'It is, though. Look.'

He pointed to the contour lines printed on the little map. I hadn't noticed them before, and wouldn't have thought about their meaning if I had.

In case you've never followed a map with this kind of detail, let me explain. Contour lines mark elevation. They will curve around from one point to another that is at the same elevation. That is, if a given point is at an elevation of, say, a hundred feet above sea level, the line will run from that point to the next that is also at a hundred feet, and so on. Then the points that are, say, ten feet higher will have another line. In a flat area, the contour lines will be far apart. In an area that is steeply pitched . . .

'Oh, good grief!' The lines on the map of this path were so close together they almost touched. 'Alan, I can't possibly climb that!'

'We could go back,' he said, sounding somewhat wistful.

He was pining to climb that hill. That mountain.

I took a deep breath. 'Well, my stick has a spike on it, and maybe the hill isn't as bad as it looks. These jeans are good and sturdy. I could always get down on hands and knees if I have to.'

'I'm sure it's doable, or the walk wouldn't go this way. Suppose I stay behind you, just in case you slip.'

'And send both of us rolling down into the sea? No, you go ahead. That way you can give me a hand if I get stuck.'

The first few feet were hard, but then there was a stretch that wasn't quite so steep, though it was studded with rocks that could make me lose my footing. My sturdy boots helped, and Alan found small detours around the worst bits. I'd begun to lose my fear of the adventure and was scrambling up with some confidence when Alan stopped so suddenly I bumped my nose on the heel of his boot, and my hat fell off.

'Ow! You might have warned me. What did you find?'

'Dorothy, do you think you can manage to get back down to the road?'

Uh-oh. 'What is it? Are you ill?'

'No, I'm fine. But this chap isn't.'

He moved aside just enough for me to see the man lying on the path. His head was just beyond Alan's hand, lying in a patch of weeds. There was quite a lot of blood on the ground, and the man wasn't breathing.

THREE

I sat down. On a thistle, or something that was very uncomfortable. It didn't matter.

'Alan, I can't go down. I'd never make it. I'll be okay here, as long as you're here. He's dead, isn't he?'

'Yes. It looks as though he fell and fractured his skull on a rock.' He pulled his phone out of his pocket and punched in 999.

The sun was growing warmer and warmer. There were flies buzzing around the poor man's head.

'. . . on the Zig-Zag walk. Not on the Zig-Zag itself, but on the rather steep path back up the cliff, a bit farther on. Yes. Less than halfway up. We'll wait.'

There was nothing else for us to do, really, I thought as Alan ended the call. Even if we could, in conscience, leave the poor man, we couldn't get past him to go on up, and I, at least, could not go down.

'How are they going to get him out of here?' I asked. 'Surely no one could handle a stretcher here.'

'They'll have cliff-side rescue equipment, ropes and such.'

I became aware of my discomfort. 'Give me a hand, will you? I need to stand up.' It wasn't just the thistle or whatever I was sitting on; I couldn't bear watching the flies. 'Do you have a handkerchief?' I asked when I'd achieved a rather tottery stance. 'I forgot to put tissues in my pocket, and I want to cover his head. All right, I know it's irrational. He isn't worried about the flies. But I am.'

'Perfectly natural, love.' He produced a large square and spread it over the man's head, first shooing away the flies. 'Better?'

'Much.' I found a flat rock to sit on. It was too low, and I'd have an awful time getting back up, but I felt more secure in solid contact with terra firma. 'How long do you suppose they'll be?'

'They're here.' Alan, sitting a little higher than I, had been able to see beyond me to the sturdy form of a black-clad policeman toiling up the hill.

Alan stood. 'We're very glad to see you, sir.'

'You're the chap who reported the accident?'

'Yes. Alan Nesbitt, late of the Belleshire Constabulary. I'm happy to assist you in any way I can, but is it possible that someone could help my wife to get back to our B & B? She doesn't especially care for heights, and this matter has distressed her somewhat.'

'That shouldn't be a problem. The rescue squad can help her get down.'

'I don't think I can go down,' I said. 'I'm sorry, but the very thought makes me dizzy.'

'Not to worry, madam. These chaps are quite competent. They'll not let you fall.' He made a quick call, and then turned back to me. 'American, are you?'

'Expat. I've lived in England for quite some time, but I never seem to have lost the accent.'

'Ah. And I imagine this is your hat?'

'Yes, it fell off when Alan stopped suddenly and I bumped into him. Thank you. That sun's getting hot.'

He handed it back to me with a courteous little half-bow. 'And you, sir, you say you were with the police?'

'Retired for a few years, now, but yes.'

I piped up. 'He won't tell you, so I will: Alan was chief constable of Belleshire.'

The policeman said, 'Ah,' again, but with a different tone in his voice. Alan and I both recognized it. Since he's retired, he's often met with a somewhat bemused attitude when dealing with other police officers, an unspoken blend of 'I do hope you're not going to interfere' with 'I wonder if we could use your expertise.'

Before this man could make up his mind about his reaction, Alan said, 'I do assure you, I have no desire to become involved in this matter, except to help you in any way I can.'

'Yes, sir, quite. Do you have any reason to believe there is a "matter" to become involved in?'

'Only in the sense that any accidental death must be investigated to some extent – as of course you know. I've seen nothing to indicate that this was not an accident. It looks to me as though the man may have been coming down this path, somewhat unwisely, I'd have thought, and tripped and fell. Fractured skull and loss of blood, wouldn't you say?'

'Looks that way. You've seen no one else in the area?'

We both shook our heads. 'Nobody in particular. There were a few people climbing up the Zig-Zag as we were going down.'

'Yes, a lot of walkers like that path, especially on a fine day. Well, the rescue squad will tell us more about the cause of death, I imagine. I believe I hear them up top. As soon as they get here, ma'am, one of them will escort you down. I requested a man for just that purpose, and frankly, I'll be happy to have a little more room for them to work here.'

'I'll get out of the way, too,' said Alan, 'unless you'd like me to stay.'

'I don't think we need you at this point, sir, though we may need to speak with you later. Would you also like some help getting down the hill?'

'I think I can make it.'

Going down was, in a word, terrifying. Alan went first, to catch me if I fell, but even with him there I couldn't possibly have done it without the policeman's help. Where the path was very steep, I had to turn around and face it, feeling for footholds. All the time there was a strong arm to support me and encouragement to keep me going.

I was a wreck by the time we got to the bottom, hot, sweating, covered in dust and burrs, and trembling.

A police car was standing by the side of the road. Alan addressed the policeman who had helped us. 'Do you think, Mr . . . I'm sorry, I don't know your name.'

'Gering, sir. PC John Gering,'

'Mr Gering, do you think you could take my wife back to our B & B? I'm not sure she's up to walking.'

'Certainly, sir, and you, too.'

So we were driven back in comfort. Alan gave Mr Gering one of his cards, in case the police needed more information from us, and then I collapsed onto the bed.

'I'm going out to get you something cold to drink. And what

about some food? It's nearly lunchtime. I think part of your trouble is hunger.'

I didn't feel hungry, just hot and tired and shaky, but . . . 'You're probably right. Low blood sugar. I don't want to go out, though. Just get something we can eat here.'

While he was gone I mustered enough energy to strip off my filthy clothes and take a shower. Clad only in my nightgown I felt much cooler and considerably refreshed, but I fretted. I fear I'm rather an accomplished fretter. At the front of my mind was concern about the poor man on the cliff. I hoped they'd get him off soon. Not that it mattered to him now. I did know that, with my intellect, but my emotions wanted him to be out of the sun, away from the flies, to a place where he could rest in peace. Which was idiotic, so I turned to the concern at the back of my mind, which was laundry.

We hadn't been able to pack very many clothes, because of the weight limit for baggage on that tiny plane. And as I had no idea what laundry facilities might be available on the island, I'd carefully chosen shirts and pants that could be made to work, in various combinations, for two weeks. Now one of those outfits was out of the loop on the very first day. There was no question of rinsing out either garment in the bathroom basin. The dirt was ground in.

Well, that worry was idiotic, too, now that I thought about it. I'd just have to find a laundromat somewhere. Doing laundry wasn't the way I'd planned to spend my holiday, but needs must.

I had reached that conclusion when Alan came back with a couple of pasties from the bakery, along with lots of fruit and two cold bottles of orange juice. '*And,*' he said triumphantly, holding up a plastic-wrapped package, 'dessert.'

'Ooh! Looks lovely.' I took it from him. 'Lemon drizzle cake? Is that from the bakery, too?'

'No, from a small stand on the street. Up a few yards from here there's a wicker basket sitting on a little table, with several sorts of baked goods and a jam jar for the money. Two pounds, this was, and I'd say a great bargain, if it tastes as good as it smells.'

It did. Everything was wonderful, and I ate far too much, but I felt considerably better when I'd finished.

'There's enough cheese and fruit and cake left for our supper, if we don't want to go out.' I found an empty drawer where we could stash our food. 'It's cool enough that everything will keep.'

'I was thinking we might like to try the Indian restaurant up the street. Nellie Gray's, it's called. I had a look in the window and it seems pleasant.'

'Funny name for an Indian place, though. I wonder—'

Alan's mobile rang.

He answered and mouthed at me, 'Police.' The conversation was very brief and for me, listening only to Alan's end, not very informative. Alan clicked off and said, 'That was PC Partridge, the man we saw first. He wants to come up and talk to us. He's only a few minutes away, so you'd best hustle into some clothes, love.'

It doesn't take long to get into jeans and a tee. Alan and I went down to the little lounge to meet the constable.

He had some disquieting news for us.

'It seems, Mrs Martin, that the accident victim was an American. There are very few American visitors on Alderney just now. Well, at any time, really. Most of our tourists come from France or the UK. So I wonder if you might have any connection with him.'

I thought I disguised the little wave of unrest that swept through me, but Alan took my hand. 'You must remember that I've seen his face only covered with blood and—' I swallowed hard – 'and flies. I tried not to look. In any case I've lost touch with most of my American friends; it's been many years since I lived there. But I suppose there's just a chance. What's the man's name?'

'Abercrombie. William Abercrombie.'

Alan and I looked at each other. I swallowed again. 'Alan, wasn't that the name . . .?'

PC Partridge came to full alert.

Alan cleared his throat. 'I don't know anyone named Abercrombie, and I don't think my wife does.' I shook my head. 'But it's not a terribly common name, and we heard it just this morning in connection with a visitor to the island. If I understood correctly, he is a retired clergyman from America who has been doing a great deal of volunteer work at St Anne's. I don't think they mentioned his given name. You may want to talk to the chap who's filling in there for the vicar.'

'Mr Lewison, yes. Thank you. I'll speak to him right away. And you'll let me know if anything else comes to mind?'

'Of course. And, constable, I have a question if you don't mind. Has the cause of death been confirmed? That is, if you can give me that information.'

'The autopsy hasn't been done yet. The body's had to be flown to Guernsey for that, but there's little doubt about the fractured skull. It looks like a most unfortunate accident, but you'll understand we have to be sure. Of course we need to find out about next of kin and so on, and the American Embassy will have to be notified.'

'No end of headaches, in short. We'll leave you to it.'

'They'll miss him up at the church,' I said when PC Partridge had left.

'I suppose they will. Although . . .'

'Oh, you noticed that, too, did you?'

'I noticed that one of the women seemed less enthusiastic than the others about the man. If it is the same man.'

'C'mon! How many Americans named Abercrombie do you think there are on this island?'

'One less than yesterday, at any rate.' He stood up and stretched. 'Are you as ready for a nap as I am?'

FOUR

As the years have advanced, I've become more and more fond of afternoon naps. The trouble is, if you keep them short they're not terribly satisfying. And if you sleep as long as you want to, then getting to sleep at night becomes a problem. It's all very well if there's something you want to do that will keep you up late, but from what I'd seen, it didn't seem likely that there was much nightlife in Alderney. Unless one counted the bats and hedgehogs.

When we woke up it was mid-afternoon, and we decided to find the police station to check on what more, if anything, had been discovered about the man on the cliff. Someone in the shop next door told us where to find the station. It was only a few yards away, up a side street called Queen Elizabeth II Street (another royal visit, probably), but known to everyone, predictably, as 'QE2' Street.

'Victoria Street. QE2 Street,' I commented. 'For a place that isn't actually part of England they're sure devoted to the royal family.'

'I believe they're quite loyal to the Queen,' said Alan. 'It's their government that's independent, not necessarily the hearts of the people.'

We passed a small bookshop on the way to the station. I was tempted to stop, but first I wanted to hear what the police had to say.

The station turned out to be in part of a very imposing building. 'Courthouse?' I ventured.

'My dear, I don't know. It does say "Court Office", so you may be right.' He pointed out the sign I had missed, and I felt foolish.

The police station was indeed small, but quite official. The outer door was unlocked, but there was a reception desk behind glass with a microphone and speaker; very big city. No one was seated there, but when Alan cleared his throat, PC Partridge came into the room.

'Ah. Hello! I was coming to see you when I went off duty. Come in, won't you?' He gestured to a door at the end of the tiny entry lobby, and moved to let us in.

We sat in what I supposed was an interview or interrogation room, bare and functional, though nothing like as intimidating as the ones in city police stations. 'You'll have come about the poor American gentleman.'

We nodded.

'Well, you were quite right, on all counts. He did die of a fractured skull and he was in fact the Mr Abercrombie who'd been helping out at the parish church. We found nothing to indicate that his death was anything other than accidental. The autopsy isn't quite complete, but we've been told his injuries were entirely consistent with the rocks on which he fell. We are trying to learn anything we can about his family, if any, so they can be notified. His passport gave us his address, but so far we've been unable to find a phone number attached to that address.'

'His cell phone? I mean mobile?'

The constable smiled at my Americanism. 'He had apparently bought a new one when he arrived in England.'

'But – I thought Alderney wasn't England.'

'You're quite right. But Mr Abercrombie spent several weeks in England before he journeyed here, according to his passport. That is, he arrived at Gatwick Airport some three months ago. His passport isn't stamped for arrival here; as you know, visitors from England are not usually subject to customs or immigration formalities. But Mr Lewison steered me to one or two of the ladies who attend the Parish Church regularly, and they say the chap had come to Alderney about a month ago. One assumes that, since he apparently meant to stay in these parts, he found it more economical to buy a phone here rather than pay the charges for international calls.'

'So the only numbers stored in the phone were English and – what's the adjective for Alderney? – Alderman?'

He laughed. 'There isn't one, really. Just Alderney. And yes, only local phone numbers.'

'So – where was he staying?'

'A small holiday rental in town, near the High Street. And yes,

Mrs Martin, we have looked in his rooms for anything that might help us to find his next of kin, and were unsuccessful.'

I don't blush anymore, but if I did, I would have then. 'I'm sorry, Mr Partridge. I don't mean to interfere, or to suggest that you don't know your job. I'm just incorrigibly nosy.'

'And we're both relieved,' said Alan, taking over smoothly, 'that what appeared to be an accident was indeed that. Of course we're sorry about the poor chap, but I dealt with far too many murders *and* suicides in my career to want anything to do with another one.'

He gave me a look that meant 'keep still'. I obeyed.

We all stood. 'Thank you, constable, for giving us so much of your time. If we should happen to hear anything about Mr Abercrombie's American connections, we'll be sure to let you know.'

We were shown out politely, and I waited until we were a few steps away from the station before saying, 'You didn't want him to know about the murders I've investigated.'

'No. We're not going to get any further involved in this unfortunate incident, and I don't want him coming to you if he does have questions later. It's enough that you're American, like the victim. Let's not suggest that you're also a competent sleuth.'

'Alan.' I stopped walking and looked him straight in the eye. 'You don't think this "accident" was entirely accidental, do you?'

'I have no reason to think otherwise.'

'That's what the constable said. It sounds like the sort of things politicians say when they're trying to weasel. It means that neither of you is entirely convinced.'

'Let's go find a pint somewhere,' he said.

It was, we discovered, happy hour at the Georgian House, the restaurant/hotel just down the street from our B & B. We got our discounted pints and found a quiet corner, and after Alan had taken a healthy swig, he put his glass down and ran a hand down the back of his neck. 'I don't know what I think, and I don't like it. There's not a shred of a hint of a suggestion of evidence that Mr Abercrombie didn't simply tumble down that treacherous slope and break his head.'

'And yet,' I prompted.

'And yet, I'm not entirely happy about it. I don't know if you noticed anything about him.'

'As I said, I tried not to look.'

'Understandable. But I did look him over while we were waiting for the police. He was wearing excellent hiking boots, well worn. Ergo, he was an experienced walker. I didn't notice his stick, but I saw PC Partridge find it and pick it up as we were making our way back down to the road. It looked like a good sturdy one with a business-like spike on the end.'

'I didn't see that. It must have been one of the times when I was crawling down practically on my hands and knees. Not my finest hour.'

'I consider that you did very well. It's not the sort of terrain you're accustomed to. At any rate, here was a seasoned walker with appropriate equipment, and the path isn't as steep as all that. True, going up was far easier than going down, but then it always is. I simply cannot understand why he should have fallen so hard. If he slipped, he could have caught himself with the stick. Or he might have tumbled for a little way, but there's plenty of underbrush he could have caught hold of to slow his fall.'

'And he didn't?'

'I'm not an expert in such things, but I did look around and saw nothing crushed or uprooted. He seemed to have simply fallen headlong.'

'So you think he was pushed.'

'Dorothy, you know better than to make that sort of assumption! No, I don't think he was pushed. I'm just not entirely happy about how he came to fall.'

'And then there's . . .' I paused, not certain how to go on.

'And then there's what?'

'Oh, probably nothing. It's just that we both got the impression that the guy might not have been as universally beloved as he was painted.'

'So, you're saying, someone might have had reason to push him down the cliff.'

'Now who's making unwarranted assumptions!' I finished my beer. 'Are you going to have another?'

'Not unless you want one. I'd like to do a bit more walking before we go and find some dinner.'

'But not on the Zig-Zag.'

'Definitely not on the Zig-Zag.'

FIVE

We decided to walk around the town, taking a look at the residential part. There was actually a bit more to the town than we had thought at first. Victoria Street had nearly cornered the market on commercial establishments, though there were a few pubs and shops farther afield. The High Street, at right angles to Victoria Street, had one or two restaurants, as well as the pub and off-licence Alan had already found. There were a few more pubs scattered here and there, and a small but first-class supermarket. We saw houses of various vintages, including one with an impressive red archway that Alan thought might be very old, though heavily remodelled over the years.

By the time we found an impressive building that called itself the Island Hall, I was more than ready for my dinner. 'Do you know where we are?' I asked plaintively. I do not possess a bump of direction. I can read a map, but without one I'm helpless.

'More or less,' he said, smiling at me. 'I believe this intriguing little stair will take us back up to the High Street.'

'If you say so.' I wasn't prepared to climb too many more stairs, but this one was, as Alan said, intriguing. There were only a few steps, with a nice safe railing, and at the top was a small churchyard.

'But the church is over there somewhere, isn't it?' I pointed wildly.

'More like there.' Alan moved my arm. 'But the medieval one was here. See the tower? It's all that's left.'

'How do you know all that?'

'I picked up a leaflet in St Anne's. It has a brief mention of the earlier building. Now, love, if we go this way we'll be in the High Street, and then Victoria Street's up at the top, and Nellie Gray's is not far away.'

'I'm not dressed up.'

'You'll do nicely, I'm sure.'

Nellie Gray's turned out to be terrific. The décor was typic-
ally Indian, the personnel were friendly and the food was
outstanding. We were told that there had, some years before,
been a traditional English restaurant there called Nellie Gray's,
and when the Indian proprietors took it over they kept the
incongruous name, as well as the lovely portrait of the lady in
question.

We left well satisfied, and talked, as we walked back to our
room, of many things, not including the body on the Zig-Zag path.

It was after nine thirty when we arrived back at our B & B,
but the sky was still light. Though I've lived not far away for
several years now, I still haven't quite got used to the incredibly
early dawns and late dusks at midsummer in this land, every part
of which is north of every part of the lower forty-eight back
home. 'Alan, it's a beautiful evening,' I said on impulse. 'I don't
feel like going to bed. It feels like late afternoon. Let's walk
down to the harbour and work off some of that dinner.'

'We'll probably have to walk back up again,' he warned.
'I doubt we'd get a taxi at this hour. And you've already walked
quite a lot today.'

'That's all right. Something about the air here is rejuvenating.
And we slept late this morning. I'm good for another hour at
least.'

He tucked my arm through his. 'We'll take it at a stroll.'

We reached the bottom of Victoria Street, and I pointed
to the left. 'Why don't we go this way instead? It might not
be so steep.'

'Dorothy, I don't have the map with me. We wouldn't want
to get lost, with night coming on.'

'How lost can we get? The whole island is only about three
miles long. If we keep going down, we're bound to get to the
harbour eventually.'

'If we *can* keep going down. I suspect there will be some
uphill spots as well. However, nothing ventured, nothing gained.'
We headed off to the left. I opened my mouth to start a verse of
'The Happy Wanderer', but remembered in time that people might
be sleeping. It was getting late, even if the sky didn't look like
it. I'm afraid I tend to get carried away when I'm feeling good,
and my voice would never win any of those talent shows on TV.

I contented myself with a modest hum, and Alan hummed along, and there weren't any houses nearby anyway, so we weren't bothering anybody.

The road was very different from the one we had taken to the harbour before. That had been wide and residential. This one, after we passed a school and what might have been a hotel or resort or club of some sort, became very rural. We came to a place where the road veered off to right or left, with no signposts and no hint of which way we might want to go.

'Darling, I've no wish to damp your spirits, but it's going to be quite dark soon. I think we'd best be heading back.'

'I think you're right, much as I hate to admit it. But wait a minute. I want to see what this little lane leads to. It looks as though it should end at some special place.'

Moving ahead of Alan, I found that what it led to was a pocket garden. Nightfall was, as Alan said, not far away, so I couldn't see many details. Scents, of roses and other flowers I didn't know, perfumed the air. Crickets chirped. The scene was one of absolute peace and contentment.

Except that someone was sitting at the far corner of a large central flower bed. It had a low wall around it, and the figure was just visible in the diminishing light. It sat quite still, bowed in an attitude of utter despair. I heard one stifled sob.

I turned away as quietly as I could, took Alan's arm and headed with him back up the road.

'Should I have tried to help?' I asked Alan as we were getting ready for bed.

'My love, that's impossible to say without knowing more than we do. I didn't see the person at all. Was it a man or a woman?'

'I couldn't tell. It was getting darker by the minute. All I could see was a hunched-up shape; all I could hear was a sob. I felt I shouldn't intrude on such grief, but maybe . . .'

'You did what you thought was right at the time. If the person had wanted comfort, he or she wouldn't have gone so far off the beaten path. Stop fretting about it and come to bed.'

I crawled in beside him. 'It isn't just that. It's been . . . quite a day.'

'Better tomorrow.' He yawned and reached out his arm to draw me close. Just before I slipped over the edge into deep sleep, an idea tried to swim up into my consciousness, but I was too far gone to catch it.

The morning dawned (far too early) on another perfect day. We had another great breakfast, and I thought again about my waistline. Actually I no longer have a waistline, but I do believe there used to be one, years ago. At home I eat more or less sensibly, but when I'm travelling, it's harder to resist temptation. Oh, well. Alan and I would walk most of the day, and I'd work it off.

I told myself.

'Shall we go back to the information centre and see if there's something special we should be doing today?' Alan suggested as I finished brushing my teeth.

'What sort of special thing would be happening in a place this size? It's not exactly the crossroads of the world.'

'We might be surprised. A close-knit community makes its own entertainment, and it's often interesting to visitors as well. There were quite a number of notices posted at the centre, but I didn't bother to read them yesterday.'

'We might as well check, then. If there's nothing more interesting, we can always take another walk. Not along the cliffs.'

Alan gave me the sort of look that meant I didn't need to say that.

We stepped out of our front door and nearly collided with Constable Partridge. We exchanged apologies. Alan asked, 'Were you coming to see us?'

'No, sir, but I'm glad to run into you, all the same.' He grinned. 'In a manner of speaking, that is. I thought you'd both like to know that we have notified the American Embassy of Mr Abercrombie's death, and they are in touch with the police at his home city in Ohio. As soon as we know what family he had, we can contact them to find out what they wish done about his burial.'

'You're ready to release his body, then?' I asked in some surprise.

'There's no reason not to.'

That was the same sort of response he'd given earlier

about the circumstances of Mr Abercrombie's death. I found it equivocal and worth pursuing. 'You're fully satisfied, then, that the man died accidentally?'

'There were no witnesses, Mrs Martin. In an island this size, if anyone had seen the incident, they would have come forward. We may never know exactly what happened, but yes, we are prepared to release the body to whoever wants to claim it.' He nodded to Alan and me and went on his way.

'So that's that.' I sounded a little flat, which was how I felt.

'That's that,' said Alan, 'and we're not going to let Mr Abercrombie's unfortunate death ruin our holiday. We didn't know the man, Dorothy.'

'He was an American.'

'One of – what was it, at last count – three hundred million?'

'Something well over that by now, I expect. Okay, I take your point. I can't claim kinship with them all.'

'And wouldn't want to. The United States of America has its share of felons and racists and petty criminals and plain nasty people, just like any other country. Being American is no guarantee of good character.'

'But the people at the church liked him.'

'One of them didn't,' Alan reminded me. 'She had nothing good to say about him.'

'She had nothing to say, period. Maybe she was just in a bad mood that day.' I shook my head. 'I'm not being very consistent, am I? The fact is, I've got one of those uneasy feelings I can't quite pin down. The kind of feeling you get when someone is staring at you, and you can't see them doing it, but you know, somewhere at the back of your neck.'

Alan nodded understanding. 'And sometimes the feeling is justified, and often not. You know as well as I do, love, that the way to deal with that sort of thing is not to pursue it, but to forget about it.'

I nodded somewhat reluctantly. 'Like a name you can't quite remember, or a tune you can't name. Worrying over it makes it recede further. You're right, love. We'll forget about poor Mr Abercrombie unless he comes back to haunt us.'

'And meanwhile let's pop in here and see what they might have to augment our lunch.'

The bakery was full of mouth-watering aromas. Fortunately, we'd just eaten a large breakfast and weren't quite as susceptible as we might have been. Even so, we came away with two large pasties and two strawberry tarts. 'We'd better do a *lot* of walking today!' I muttered. Alan just grinned.

SIX

We stowed our purchases in our room and then went to the information centre. Alan picked up guides to several more walks while I looked over the notices pinned up here and there. This afternoon there was a guided walk around the town, concentrating on the history of the island. That sounded interesting, and not too strenuous, so we signed up for it.

'I don't imagine you'll want to try the Zig-Zag again, will you?' said the lady at the desk. This time it wasn't Sylvia, our acquaintance from church, but someone we'd never seen before. She smiled at our surprised looks. 'You *are* the couple who found poor Mr Abercrombie yesterday, aren't you? Word travels, you know. A tall, attractive man with an American wife who wears hats – not all that common a combination. And Sylvia Whiting is a friend of mine. My name's Eleanor.'

'Dorothy and Alan – but I guess you already know that. The small community here takes a little getting used to. Alan and I live in Sherebury, which isn't all that big, really. But the Cathedral and the university provide two more or less self-contained communities, separate from the rest of the population, and the town itself is somewhat spread out. News gets around, but not as fast as here.'

'Alderney is just like an English village forty or fifty years ago, with all the advantages and disadvantages that go with everybody knowing everybody else. There's always someone to help in a tight spot, but of course you can't get by with a thing.'

'St Mary Mead, in fact.' I was pleased when she laughed, recognizing the reference. 'Do you have a resident Miss Marple?' I went on.

She gave me a quizzical look. 'Perhaps. Now let's see what you might like to do this morning.'

'I thought perhaps this one,' said Alan, laying a brochure before her. 'It's short and not very strenuous.'

'Yes, and you'd enjoy it, but if you're going out with Robin this afternoon, you'll cover a lot of the same territory. I'd suggest this one instead.' She pulled a brochure from the rack. 'It's short and easy and offers some interesting little side paths you can take if you want.'

I looked dubiously at the cover, with the subtitle 'Southern Cliffs & Wildlife Bunker'. 'Um . . . cliffs?'

'Just the tops of them,' said Eleanor. 'No steep climbing. It isn't as beautiful now as in spring and autumn, but the view from the cliffs is spectacular.'

The visitor centre was getting busy, so we thanked Eleanor and left. 'We can do one of the others if you'd prefer, love,' said Alan once we were out in the street. 'They're all longer, though.'

'No, this will be fine. Just let me get my boots and my stick.'

The first part of the walk took us through familiar territory, but we soon found ourselves out of the town proper and heading toward open country. In fact, I pointed overhead. 'Alan, that's the plane we came in on. And it's headed in for a landing.'

'Yes, the airport is just over there.'

I looked over at the single runway, the small building that comprised the terminal, the miniature planes parked here and there. 'This whole island reminds me of one of those Christmas villages. You know, the ones people put under Christmas trees or on the mantle. Everything's there, but to scale. All that's missing is the little train running round and round.'

'There's one of those, too, though it doesn't go round and round. It's down near the harbour. We'll take the ride on Sunday, shall we?'

'It's a fairy tale. We've got into the pages of a book. Alan, I'm so glad you suggested coming here!' And then I thought about poor Mr Abercrombie.

Alan saw my face change. 'Live in the present, Dorothy. You can't do anything about yesterday, and it's nothing to do with us.'

'You're quite right.' I looked around. There were no houses nearby, and no other walkers. I grinned at Alan, took a deep breath and launched into 'The Happy Wanderer'. Alan joined me, and we marched along, getting the words wrong half the time, enjoying ourselves hugely.

We passed a standing stone that reminded me of the ancient ones in Orkney. 'What's that?' I asked Alan.

He consulted the brochure. 'It's called the Madonna Stone. It's been moved from a nearby field, where it was used for a cattle scratching post.'

I chuckled. 'Whatever that may be. I'm willing to bet it's ancient and mystical.'

'Could be.'

We followed the path down a hillside, not a very steep one, and then back up to the top of the cliffs. The view was indeed spectacular. The sun glinted off the waves far below and turned the beaches golden. 'I wonder what this is like in winter storms?' I mused.

'I've read about that somewhere. The waves are high enough to crash right across the breakwater, and in fact in 18-something a large part of the breakwater itself was destroyed by a storm. It isn't always idyllic.'

'Well, it is today, and we're not likely to be here in winter, so I guess I'll stop thinking about it.'

We had reached the spot where a path forked off to a structure called the Wildlife Bunker. It seemed an odd juxtaposition of terms. We walked over to see, Alan reading the brochure as we went.

'It was built by the Germans as a radio transmission station, but it's used now as a site for information about the island's wildlife, also a sort of museum of military history.'

It would also, I thought, probably provide a place to sit down out of the sun. The air was cool, but the sun was hot, and I thought I was getting a sunburn, even with my hat to protect me.

It was dark inside after the brilliant sunshine. As my eyes adjusted, I saw that we weren't alone. A woman looking at one of the displays seemed vaguely familiar.

'Good morning,' she said. 'We met at church yesterday.'

'Oh, yes. I'm afraid I've forgotten your name.'

'Alice Small. And I've forgotten yours, as well.'

'Dorothy and Alan.'

There was a little silence, the sort of awkward silence when no one can think of much to say. Then, abruptly, Alice said, 'I heard you singing a little while ago. You sounded happy.'

'Oh, dear, I didn't think anyone could hear us. We didn't intend
to disturb anyone.'

'You didn't disturb me in the least. I felt like joining you. I'm
happier today than I've been in a long time.' She said it defiantly,
and somehow not sounding happy at all.

Another awkward silence. A remark like that invites a question
like, 'Oh, why is that?', but we didn't know this woman at all
really, certainly not well enough for personal questions.

She answered what we hadn't asked. 'You'll be wondering
why I said that, and especially to strangers. Well, I'll tell you. I
don't mind telling you, of all people.'

That seemed to allow a question. 'Why us, in particular?'

'You found him. I don't know if you pushed him off the cliff
or not, and I don't care. The important thing is that he's dead!'

I remembered, then. This was the woman who had pointedly
refused to join in the paean of praise for Mr Abercrombie, the
one who had slipped away while everyone else was telling us
how wonderful he was.

I stood there with my mouth open. Alan came to my rescue.
'Alice, we didn't push him off the cliff. I don't think anyone
did. But it's obvious you feel strongly about him. You don't owe
us an explanation, but if you want to talk about it, we're happy
to listen.'

Alan said once that a policeman sometimes had to serve as a
sort of father confessor, and that unless the subject involved criminal
matters he was duty-bound to pass along, he had always found
himself as bound to secrecy as a priest in the confessional.

There were chairs. We sat down in them and Alice told her
story in a voice frighteningly devoid of emotion.

'I hated him, and I can't tell you how happy I am that he's
dead. I didn't push him off that cliff, but I could have. He killed
my sister.'

We waited. She had to tell this her own way.

'Aleta lived in America. We were twins; that's why our names
are so much alike. We hated it when we were kids. People were
always confusing us. We lived in a village in the Cotswolds,
and we looked exactly alike, and with almost the same name
. . . well, anyway. Our parents sent us to different schools,
because they saw that we needed to establish our own identities.

Then we both went to university, and it was there that we met our husbands. They weren't alike at all. My Robert was from Alderney, and he came back here to teach at the school. I came with him. He died at sea just after our son was born. He was a volunteer with the lifeboat service. That was over twenty years ago.'

She paused to regain her composure, and again Alan and I stayed silent.

'My sister, she married an American, and they moved to Ohio, a small town called Corinthia. He was – is – a computer technician, and she was a librarian. They never had children, but they were very happy until *he* came along.'

We didn't need to ask who she meant.

'He was the priest at their church. Aleta and Joe both thought a lot of him. He preached good sermons and the congregation grew, and all seemed to be well.'

'But,' I said.

'Yes. There began to be some rumblings. A few of the parishioners began to say that he wasn't honest. They thought he was actually stealing money from the church. Most people didn't believe it. Aleta didn't believe it. She went to talk to him about it, and . . .'

Alice was very still. It was too dark for me to see the tears I was sure were in her eyes.

'I don't know what happened. She would never talk about it, to me or to Joe. I think he threatened Joe in some way. A computer specialist is vulnerable to accusations of hacking or whatever. Joe says he doesn't know, either. But I think – well, if *that man* had claimed to know something damaging about Joe, and said he'd reveal it if she said anything more about church funds . . . anyway, Aleta became more and more depressed, and in the end, she . . .' Again she paused.

'He wouldn't even bury her. He said suicide was a sin, and he let her be buried from a funeral home, with no proper service.'

I had to swallow hard. This was appalling. I took Alan's hand and squeezed it hard.

'So when he turned up here, on this island I've loved for so long, this place of peace and refuge . . .'

'I can imagine,' I began.

'No, you can't. You can't begin to imagine how it felt to see him charming everyone here as he did back in America. I very nearly left the church. I couldn't bear to see what he was doing. I couldn't even tell anyone; they wouldn't have believed me. But I can tell you. You're visitors; you'll be gone soon. I just wanted you to know why I can't wait to see him buried, and I'm sorry it will be in consecrated ground. He doesn't deserve that.'

SEVEN

S he slipped out of the bunker before either Alan or I could think of any response to her terrible story, but not before we saw the tears start to course down her cheeks. My mouth was dry; I realized when I tried to stand up that I was trembling.

Alan took my arm without a word and led me back the way we had come. I had no heart to continue our walk, and neither, apparently, did Alan. We didn't speak. What was there to say?

We had passed, near the beginning of our walk, a pub called the Marais Hall. As we approached it now, Alan said, 'I think a restorative is in order. Come, love.'

'I think I'd rather just go back to the room.'

'Keep me company.'

It wasn't even eleven in the morning. I had no interest in anything alcoholic, but Alan ordered coffee with brandy, added sugar and told me to drink it down. He seldom gives orders. I drank.

'Better?' he said when I'd finished the cup. 'Want another?'

'No. I mean, yes, I do feel a little better, but no, I don't want another. Maybe just plain coffee, though?'

When he came back with it, he gave me a searching look. 'There's a little colour back in your face. You have no idea how pale you were.'

'I felt pale. I felt – Alan, what a perfectly dreadful thing!'

'Yes, love, but do keep your voice down. There aren't enough people in here to create privacy. I think we'd better look at the map and pretend to be planning our next little jaunt.'

'Why?' I did lower my voice, but I didn't see the point.

'You've forgotten the size of this community. Anything you say that is of any interest will be all over the island in about fifteen minutes. Now, we've still masses of time before we need to think about lunch. What if we walk down to the harbour, trying the way we were going when we got benighted?'

All I wanted to do was go to our room and lie down and try to empty my mind, but I had no resistance. I felt as though all my stiffening had been yanked out, leaving me like the Scarecrow without his straw. I nodded and followed him out the door.

Seen by brilliant daylight, the way we'd taken yesterday looked very different. We walked as quickly as the slope allowed; I don't know about Alan, but I was trying to leave a horror behind.

'Alan, stop,' I said after a long silence. 'Here's that little garden. I want to see it properly.'

There was a sign: *The Sapper Onions Peace Garden.* 'What does that mean?' I asked Alan.

'My dear, I've no idea. Odd name. It's a pretty little garden, isn't it?'

It was. There was no touch of the professional about it; rather it looked to be a labour of love. I noted the pictures of plants and animals worked into the low wall surrounding the central flower bed. 'Those look like children's work,' I said.

'I'd say so. Perhaps this is a project of the school.'

'Perhaps. It *is* a peaceful place. I can see why that poor man came here to be alone with his grief.'

'You've decided it was a man?'

I shrugged. 'No. Manner of speaking.'

The sun began to grow uncomfortably warm in that space enclosed by trees and bushes. I drew a deep breath. 'Let's get down to where there's a sea breeze.'

The road at that point seemed to lead far from where we wanted to go, so we chose a track leading through an area of underbrush and the occasional small tree. It wasn't hard going, but I was glad for my boots and stick. The place was alive with bees and butterflies, with crickets that hopped suddenly out of our way, with tiny wildflowers lavishing their perfume on the warm air. Almost without my noticing, I began to feel better.

We reached the bottom, coming out onto a road that skirted the sea, but the harbour was nowhere in sight. Alan did one of his magic tricks and decided we needed to turn to the right, and sure enough, a few minutes of walking brought us around a curve, and we could see the breakwater. 'I know it's early, love, but I could do with some lunch. How about you?'

'We've lots of food back in the room.'

'The room is back up at the top of the hill. We can have our pasties for supper.'

The mention of the hill was all it took. I was suddenly ravenous, and my knees were telling me they'd had enough. I let myself be persuaded. Another bit of a walk found us at a promising-looking fish-and-chip shop. Now, I can be as snobbish about food as the next person, but I've always loved well-cooked fish and chips, and these were excellent. Plainly the place had a good reputation; even though it was early, there were lots of customers – enough that we could enjoy a private conversation.

'Are you able to talk about it now?' asked Alan when I'd made my way through a generous meal.

'Yes. Sorry I went wobbly back there. I now know what a person means when they say they've had the stuffing knocked out. But I'm okay.'

'We have to decide what to do.'

Yes, we did. The dreadful story Alice had told us had removed the option of doing nothing, of pretending nothing was wrong. Now we knew there was at least one person who had an excellent reason to hate the late Mr Abercrombie. He was dead under circumstances that were at least questionable. And we had found his body. That squarely involved us.

'I don't believe in coincidence, you know,' I said with apparent irrelevance.

'I do know. Nor do I. You're saying there's a reason we found him.'

'Yes. We're meant to do something about it.'

'The police have come down on the side of accident. They're going to release his body when someone can be found to claim it.'

'But even they don't entirely believe it. Alan, do you think they'll get upset if we poke around? They're sure to know. Nobody can hide anything on this island.'

'It depends on what you mean by poking around. There's no reason we can't talk to people. We would, anyway, as visitors trying to learn about the place. And people talk to you. You have a way with you.'

He grinned at me and briefly touched my hand. 'Oh, Alan, we're both greasy! I'll need a good scrub before I can really touch anybody. But I do see what you mean. I like people, and they seem to like me. The trouble is, at home I'd know who to talk to. Here . . .?'

'Start with the people at the church. There's Morning Prayer again tomorrow. They were the ones who probably had the most contact with this chap.'

'They all seemed to think he walked on water.'

'And maybe they're the ones with the true picture. Let's see what sort of rounded picture we can get, and then if it seems as if there's more to look into, we can go from there.'

'You are a sensible and utterly delightful man, sir. I might just consider a closer acquaintance.'

'I would deem it a great privilege, madam. Would you wish me to engage a carriage for our journey back to the town?'

'No, but I wouldn't mind a hand to extract me from this chair.'

As we made our way slowly up Braye Road, I reflected again on my extraordinary good fortune in finding Alan at a time when I thought my life was over.

We got to our room with just time to wash hands and faces, and change from boots to shoes, before going back down to the Visitor Centre for our tour of the town.

The tour turned out to be just us and our guide, who was named Robin Whicker. A tall man with a deep voice and a crooked smile, he introduced himself as a retired school-master, which created an immediate bond. I told him I had taught for forty years. 'Indeed? In America, that would be, of course.'

'Yes, sixth grade, mostly, eleven-year-olds. In a public school in Indiana, which I'm sure you know is not what you mean by a public school.'

'Yes. You taught all subjects?'

'With varying degrees of success. I'm afraid I was hopeless at trying to teach the poor little things art; I haven't an artistic bone in my body. And thank heavens there was someone else to take them to gym. Physical education, that is. I'm no good at all at what you Brits call games.'

'Ah, well, we can't all be good at everything. And you, sir?'

'I was a civil servant.' He used his usual formula when he doesn't care to reveal exactly what he spent his life doing. I found his reticence interesting.

'Right,' said Robin. 'Now we'll start up Victoria Street, where some of the houses are actually quite interesting.'

I saw a row of houses, most of them now housing shops or businesses, painted in pastel colours, all looking quite similar. Robin seemed to have X-ray eyes. He pointed out that one building with what looked like a Georgian façade was actually Victorian, reflecting the more elegant older style, and that the 'cat slide' dormers on an earlier house suggested a previously thatched roof. He showed us where the original streets of the medieval settlement would have been, explained the origins of the French street names that still prevailed over so much of the island, pointed out the house where the renowned author T.H. White had lived (still called 'The White House') and confirmed Alan's guess that the house with the red archway was in fact medieval. His knowledge was broad, his enthusiasm contagious. When we fetched up back at the Visitor Centre, Alan asked Robin to join us for a cup of coffee, or tea, or a pint – his choice.

'That's very kind of you,' he said, with a charming smile. 'If you're happy with the Georgian House, it's near at hand and has all those things on offer.'

We sat in a corner on Windsor chairs that looked hard and unforgiving but were surprisingly comfortable. Alan opted for a pint; Robin and I chose tea and scones.

'You know such a lot about Alderney,' I said after I'd slaked my thirst with the excellent tea. 'Have you lived here all your life?'

'No, no. I taught for forty years at a public school – in our sense – in Dorset, and moved here only after my retirement. I'd holidayed here over the years, of course, and made friends. The community has been very generous in admitting me into their midst, though of course I'll always be an outlander. I've even begun to sing in the choir; I suspect they're happy to have me, as I'm the only bass.'

I began to hum the line from 'Seventy-Six Trombones': 'And I modestly took my place, as the one and only bass . . .'

Robin smiled. 'Exactly.'

Alan and I exchanged glances. I took a deep breath. 'So I suppose you know the man who fell down the cliff. Mr Abercrombie.'

'Ah.' Robin drained his teacup. 'Yes, I knew him slightly.'

We waited for more, some conventional expression of sorrow, at least. There was only silence.

Robin pushed back his chair and started to stand.

'We found him, you know,' I said quickly. 'We were doing the Zig-Zag walk and came across him. It was quite upsetting.'

'Yes, it must have been.' He stood. 'Now, this has been delightful, but I've things I need to do, so if you'll excuse me—'

'Please don't go,' said Alan quietly. 'We're trying to work our way through a rather devastating experience, and one way to do that is to learn more about Mr Abercrombie. My wife feels particularly involved with him, since he was also an American. Can you give us any impression of what sort of man he was?'

Robin looked at us searchingly. Funny, I hadn't noticed before how penetrating his eyes could be. He didn't sit down. 'I didn't know him well, so my impressions are worth little. You'd do better to talk to the church ladies, or perhaps his family, if they manage to find one.' He began to walk away.

'Robin, did you like him?'

He pretended not to hear me and walked out the door.

'Well, that was odd,' I said when we had gone back to our room. 'He was so pleasant, so courteous, until we started talking about Abercrombie.'

'It's fairly obvious he disliked the man,' said Alan, taking off his shoes. 'I wonder why he was unwilling to talk about him.'

'You don't suppose there's some awful story in his background, like poor Alice.'

'I don't see how their paths could have crossed. Abercrombie came to Alderney only a few weeks ago, and lived in America before that. Whicker spent almost his whole life in Dorset. There's rather a famous school there; I imagine that's where he taught. I think you're going to have to talk to a lot more people before you can get the picture you want of Abercrombie.' He lay down on the bed, ready for our afternoon nap. 'And I'll try not to interfere. I don't know if you noticed, but Whicker didn't believe my story about why we wanted to know more about him.'

'That was when he got that funny look on his face, wasn't it? No, we'll have to come up with something better. I can usually think up a good lie; I'll give it some thought.' I yawned. 'Later.'

My dreams were troubled, I think. I remembered nothing when I woke an hour or so later, but I felt a vague unease that had nothing to do with my pleasant surroundings. The sun still shone brightly, the room was just the right temperature, my dear husband was by my side. All was right with the world.

Except it wasn't.

Alan yawned and sat up.

'Did I have nightmares?' I asked him.

'If you did, you didn't cry out. I slept like a baby, which must mean you did, too.'

'Maybe. Something's bothering me.'

Alan gave me a 'no kidding!' look.

'I mean something specific, not just the general anxiety about the whole situation. I've missed something.'

'Another thing to erase from your mind until it comes back of its own accord.'

'Yes, but how can I *not* think about it, when it's occupying every corner of my mind?'

'Think about something else. I thought we could take a stroll over to the bookshop. We didn't bring very much to read, and we're bound to find books about the island there.'

'That's a good idea. I'd like to know more about Alderney, and reading some nice boring history might be just what I need.'

It didn't take me very long to discover that the history of Alderney is anything but boring. From the dim mists of prehistory right up through the Second World War, the island has had its troubles. Annie, the owner of the bookshop, showed us books about shipwrecks, one of them Elizabethan, about the strong fortifications built against the fears of French invasion, and a whole section dealing with the German occupation from 1940 to 1945. We bought reams of them.

'We'll have to ship these home,' said Alan with a groan. 'We can't carry all that weight on the Trislander.'

'I don't care. I want them all. There's so much good stuff here.'

Annie provided us with a couple of sturdy bags, and we hauled our loot back to the room, there to settle in for the evening with our pasties and our wine and lots of great reading material.

'Alan, did you know that the Alderney people evacuated when the Germans came? The people who lived on Jersey and Guernsey stayed, but almost everyone here was sent to England or Scotland.'

'Mmm. I've been reading about what happened to the island under the occupation.'

'Nothing very good, I imagine.' And we went back to our own books. After a time I found the story of the evacuation too painful and turned to a rousing adventure book about famous shipwrecks near the Channel Islands.

The books succeeded in freeing my mind from its preoccupation with Mr Abercrombie and his unfortunate demise, but they didn't help me dredge up the elusive thought I was seeking. Well, I'd remember, or I wouldn't. Meanwhile, nap or no nap, I was ready for a night's sleep.

EIGHT

I n the middle of breakfast it came to me. 'Eureka!' I said. Softly, so as not to startle the other guests.

'You've thought of it,' said Alan, who is used to me and not easily startled.

'Well, at least I've chased down what was bothering me yesterday, and I'm not sure it's worthy of all the mental energy I expended on it. It's only a tiny thing. But I'm wondering how Robin knows about Mr A.'s family.'

'Sorry, love. I've only had half a cup of coffee. Explain, please.'

'He made that comment about us talking to the man's family, "if they can find one", or something like that. Now, if his acquaintance with the man is as slight as he claims, how would he know that his family might not even exist? My pronouns are all mixed up, but you understand, don't you?'

'I think so. You're right, it's a very slight indication, but worth following up. Shall we seek out Robin and ask him?'

'I have the feeling he might not be terribly forthcoming. He's such a nice man, but he certainly clammed up there at the end. Maybe we'd do better to talk to people at the church who know Robin, as well as Mr A. We might get a feel for the kind of terms they were on.'

'Well, then, get your skates on, woman. Morning Prayer's in fifteen minutes.'

We arrived in good time and took our places in the choir stalls. There were a few more congregants than before; we took up two rows rather than just one. We noticed that Alice wasn't there. We were greeted, not with smiles and busy arrangements for our participation as before, but with nods and muted words. The young locum, Mr Lewison, read the service in funereal tones and had to pause during his prayer for the clergy to get his voice in order.

As soon as the service was over, the attendees left the church rapidly. Alan and I looked at each other with puzzled frowns.

'Have we suddenly turned into lepers?' I asked in a whisper. Alan shrugged. We walked out into the sunny churchyard.

They were all waiting for us. Oh, it wasn't quite that obvious. They stood in little groups of two or three, chatting, but when we came out they turned their attention to us. Mr Lewison cleared his throat in an embarrassed sort of way. 'We – er – wondered if you – that is—'

'We wanted to talk to you about Mr Abercrombie,' said Sylvia, 'and it didn't seem quite proper to do it in the church.'

'You see,' Mr Lewison went on, more confidently, 'we thought you might have heard some – er – rather odd comments about him, and we wanted to make sure you heard the real story.'

'But why? What does it matter what we think of him?' I wanted nothing more than to listen to people talk about him, but I thought it was peculiar, all the same.

'My dear woman, you've been talking to the police.' Sylvia sounded as if that explained everything.

Alan said, 'We have talked to the police because we had the misfortune to find Mr Abercrombie's body. Constable Partridge has been kind enough to keep us informed because he realized we had an interest in the matter. Come now! You know the constable far better than we do. You can talk to him any time, ask him anything you wish. He's one of you. We are outsiders.'

'Outsiders to Alderney, yes. Insiders with the police, though. And he's Methodist.' That was one of the other ladies, one whose name we didn't know.

Alan sighed. 'It's been a long time since I was an active policeman. But if there's something you want to tell us, I'm sure neither of us objects.'

'Then let's go for coffee, and we can sit and talk.' Sylvia was taking the lead again.

One or two of the ladies left us at that point, apparently satisfied that things were going as they had wished. The rest of us walked down to Jack's Brasserie at the bottom of Victoria Street and settled like locusts on the terrace.

When we all had our coffee, Mr Lewison cleared his throat. 'Perhaps the first thing we'd like you to know,' he said quietly, 'is that Mr Abercrombie had a few enemies here.'

'Not enemies,' said one of the ladies. 'Oh, I should introduce myself. My name is Rebecca, Rebecca Smith.' We nodded acknowledgment of the introduction. 'I do think that's too strong a word. Certainly there are – were – some people who didn't warm to him as the rest of us did. Most of them were English.'

I got the message. English people might be colder, more judgmental, than Alderney natives.

'You mustn't think there's any prejudice toward non-islanders,' said Mr Lewison quickly, sounding very priestly. 'I'm English myself, if it comes to that. It's just that people from outside don't always understand island ways. Mr Abercrombie certainly did. He realized that a small community relies heavily on volunteers, and he was always eager to volunteer where needed. A most generous man.'

'And that's what some people didn't like,' piped up another woman, a small, sweet-faced lady who looked like everybody's grandmother. 'They thought he was putting himself forward, making himself look better than anyone else. It wasn't like that at all! He simply saw things that needed doing and did them. He didn't expect thanks. He was a sweet, sweet man.' Her voice broke, and she fished in her purse for a tissue.

'Sweet, yes, but not smarmy,' said Sylvia. 'When plain-speaking was called for, he didn't mince words. You remember how he stepped in to organize the jumble sale accounts. We all love Lucille, but you know she's been past working with figures for years. It was time someone took hold of that, and I'm sure no one could have been more tactful about it than Bill.'

Ah. 'Mr Abercrombie' had become 'Bill'. Interesting. I refrained from looking at Alan. Sometimes a meaningful glance can be intercepted.

'Actually, Mr Abercrombie ended up running the sale, and very efficiently, too,' said Rebecca. 'Lucille was a bit hurt, I think, but she understood. She's nearly blind, bless her, and in the end she seemed grateful not to have to deal with it all.'

'It's a pity some of her friends misunderstood,' said Sylvia, somewhat belligerently. 'Their refusal to participate in the sale made the profits lower than usual, and that's certainly not what Lucille would have wished.'

'Are there others who – um – thought they had reason to resent some of Mr Abercrombie's actions?' I received several hostile looks and hastened into explanation. 'It's just that if someone seems to have disliked him, I want to try to understand why.'

Sylvia looked at me with narrowed eyes. 'I hope you're haven't decided his death wasn't accidental, after all.'

Uh-oh. This woman was a little too observant. Was she the Miss Marple of Alderney? Alan frowned and opened his mouth to speak, but Mr Lewison beat him to it.

'Oh, please don't misunderstand, Mrs Martin,' he said, sounding distressed. 'I'm sure Sylvia didn't mean to be critical.'

'We've heard of you, you know,' said the grandmotherly lady who hadn't introduced herself. 'Word does travel between southern England and the islands. You're a celebrated detective, aren't you?'

'Certainly not!' Alan and I spoke together. I gestured for him to continue. 'My wife has been fortunate enough to unravel a few problems. She has a keen mind and a healthy dose of common sense, and she's good at sizing up people. She is in no way a detective, nor does she go out of her way to look for trouble. I can assure you that we came to this island in search of a peaceful holiday, and that's what we intend to have.'

He didn't quite glare at the rest, but he came close.

'Of course, of course,' said Mr Lewison. 'Now, I wonder. Breakfast was some time ago, and I feel I could do justice to one of Jack's pastries. What about the rest of you? I favour a chocolate croissant, myself. My treat.'

I stifled the urge to giggle. A treat to placate the quarrelsome children. Not only that, but chocolate, the sure cure for a Dementor attack. Shades of Harry Potter!

It worked, too. The ladies all reacted the same way, first with half-hearted protests about their need to watch their weight, then with acquiescence and a 'just this once'. The conversation turned to general topics, and gradually the group broke up with murmured excuses about errands, chores, duties.

Sylvia was the last to leave. 'I hope I didn't offend you,' she said in a return to her normal friendly, efficient manner. 'I find it hard to keep still when I sense injustice, and of course you're right. There were other people who had a quite mistaken impression of Bill. I won't name names, but there was one man in particular who seemed to bristle whenever the two of them encountered one another. I must say I don't know why, unless – but no, surely not.'

I raised my eyebrows and cocked my head and looked as interrogative as I could, but she shook her head. 'No. It's too petty. For either Bill or – the other man. I must go. I can't say I have any appetite for lunch after our little indulgence, but my husband will be wanting some. Are you both still planning to take our walk this evening?'

For a moment I couldn't remember what she was talking about. 'Hedgehogs, darling,' Alan reminded me. 'And bats. It's Thursday.'

I refrained from shuddering at the idea of the bats. 'Oh, yes,' I said brightly. 'We're looking forward to it.'

I don't think I fooled anybody. Certainly not Alan.

We repaired to our room for a sandwich lunch and a conference. 'Well, I don't know that we accomplished much with that little exercise,' I said, swallowing a mouthful of cheese and chutney.

'Oh, I'm not so certain,' said Alan. 'Hand over some of those grapes, will you? We now know that Sylvia was half in love with Abercrombie.'

'Just because she calls him "Bill"?'

'And the fierce way she defended him, even when no defence seemed necessary. She's a courteous person, but she was damn near rude to you.'

'Yes, that was strange. And unexpected.'

'And the other thing was the money.'

'Money?'

'The jumble sale. Abercrombie took over and the takings were less than usual.'

'But that was because . . . oh.'

'You've got it. You haven't forgotten Alice's story? The problem with her sister started with Abercrombie being accused of embezzling funds from his parish in America.'

'Oh, good grief! And you think he was up to his old tricks here.'

'It's certainly a possibility. It would be a foolproof way to steal a few pounds; no one really checks on prices at that sort of event. And once he'd alienated some regular contributors and/ or buyers, he would have had a perfect opportunity.'

'But, Alan, think! A jumble sale never brings in big money. My church back in Indiana was over the moon one year when their annual sale netted over a thousand dollars. A percentage of that sort of profit, even a large percentage, is hardly enough for the risk.'

'What risk? Nothing could ever be proved one way or another. And you saw for yourself. He had many of the parishioners here, even the vicar, or this priest anyway, charmed. They refused to believe anything negative about the man.'

'Then you think the ones who hated him, like Alice and Robin, were right in their judgements, and the others were wrong.'

'At this point I don't think anything. All I'm saying is that there's room for reasonable doubt about his character.'

'And that means there's also room for reasonable doubt about the way he died. Alan, what I've been wondering about is why the man came here. It's a lovely place, but it's not the hub of the universe. And if he was up to something shady, I'd think this would be the last place he'd want to settle. He could get by with some shenanigans for a while, but not for long, with everyone knowing what everyone else does.'

'On the other hand,' said Alan, 'a remote island isn't a bad place to escape one's past. If his "shenanigans", as you put it, had begun to make things difficult for him in America, he might have thought it prudent to remove himself. England might not have proved far enough away, but if someone mentioned Alderney, it might have seemed ideal. And remember, there are no passport formalities to get here. Officially, so to speak, he never left England.'

'Making him hard to trace.' I yawned. 'You know, I'm really uneasy about this whole thing. Because we've met two people who might have had reason to give Abercrombie a good push, and the trouble is I like both of them a lot better than I'm beginning to like him.'

'I agree. But I don't see what we're to do about it at this point.'

I yawned. 'Oh, well. Nothing right now, I guess. When in doubt, sleep on it. It's nap time, especially since we're going to be up late tonight chasing bats. I just hope they don't start chasing us.'

NINE

When we woke up, we went for a nice walk up and down Victoria Street. I did a little shopping, buying some really attractive tops that I didn't in the least need, and a gorgeous Aran-type turtleneck that would be very useful indeed come winter. Then we wandered down to the harbour to investigate a little more fully what was there.

It was plain that most of the establishments were meant to serve the maritime crowd. There were showers and a small launderette for the benefit of people just off their boats. I took note of that in case I needed to use it later. There were lots of small places to eat casual food or pick up groceries. On the other hand, a shop called London House sold high-end electronics and was doing a thriving business. It seemed an unlikely spot for such a business, but I was reminded that many places I consider to be picturesque and unspoiled are in fact very much a part of the twenty-first century, with all its wonders – and troubles. We walked into the store, and one glance told me I'd find nothing of interest here.

Alan had other ideas. He was looking, in a half-hearted sort of way, for a new computer. It's appalling how fast these things go out of date, and his was beginning to run more and more slowly. He was dragging his feet because he didn't want to learn how to use a new one, and I could certainly sympathize. The older I get, the harder it seems to be to adjust to new technology. I was still just barely competent with the cell phone I'd bought some months before, the one I'd bought only because my simple old one had been smashed to bits in a fall down some extremely unyielding marble steps.

'Alan, you wouldn't want to buy a computer here,' I said in a low tone. 'You'd have to ship it home; it's way too heavy for the Trislander.'

'I'm just comparing prices,' he said. 'Some of these are real bargains.'

A salesperson came up just then. 'I imagine you're surprised to find such a good selection here, but computers are very important in Alderney. If you have any questions, I'll be happy to help,' he went on with the warm smile I'd come to expect from island people. 'Are you off a yacht, or staying in the town?'

'Town,' I said. 'We've been here since Monday, and we're loving it. But we're just browsing.'

'You're American, aren't you? Or Canadian?'

'American, but I've lived in England for quite a while now.'

'Ah.' He gave us a closer look. 'You wouldn't be the couple who found the chap on the hill, would you?'

I think Alan and I sighed together. There was no escaping it, not on a small island. 'As a matter of fact we are,' I said. 'It wasn't a very pleasant experience.'

'No, no, I'm sure it wasn't. It was bad enough just hearing about it. He was a likeable chap, and a good customer, as well.'

'Really,' I said. 'Now that does surprise me. Although I don't know why it should. A retired clergyman is just as entitled as anyone else to enjoy the latest gadgets, I suppose.'

'Ah, well, not too many of the clergy, retired or otherwise, can afford the very latest in audio equipment. And a brand-new laptop as well. He had an iPad on order, and my best TV. I've had to cancel those orders now. Yes, he'll be sadly missed.'

Another customer claimed his attention, and he left Alan and me to a feast of speculation. 'He was splashing a lot of money around,' I said as we walked out the door.

'And on very conspicuous purchases.' Alan frowned. 'It's almost too much of a good thing.'

'What do you mean?'

'If he came to this remote place to run away from his misdeeds in America, as we've been speculating, wouldn't he have tried to keep a low profile? Concentrate on helping in the church, doing good works?'

'He did all that.'

'But he also went out and bought some very expensive electronics, toys obviously meant for himself. As you pointed out, it would have cost a great deal to ship them somewhere else. And it was rumoured that he was planning to buy a house. It seems he meant to turn it into a palace. That doesn't reconcile very well with our idea that he had come here to hide.'

'Oh, dear. You're right. It doesn't. Do you suppose we're all wrong about him? He really was a nice man, generous with his time, greatly loved in his church?'

'One thing we know: he was a complex man. There are too many different opinions about him. And I very much fear that if we're to come to any intelligent conclusions, we're going to have to sample a few more opinions. Come along, love. It's nearly happy hour at the Georgian House, and I'm in need of a pint.'

We had our pints, and then we had a leisurely dinner at the Thai restaurant one street over, and then we came back to our room and read some more about Alderney until it was time to assemble at the Wildlife Trust office for our evening walk.

It was still quite light out. The sun only just set, but we had brought flashlights. Plainly before we were home again it would be dark, and we had no idea where we'd be walking. Quite a crowd had chosen to go on the walk, and I was amazed at the interest in bats, of all things.

Our guide on the walk was a French girl with an accent that was charming, if a little hard to understand. She explained that she was finishing her degree work in France and was in Alderney to do some research into the island's wildlife. She stressed that her English was not perfect ('A whole lot better than my French,'I whispered to Alan) and begged us to ask if there was something we didn't understand.

'We will look first for bats.' She explained the species we expected to find, and I was extremely relieved that they did not include the huge fruit bats I had seen in a zoo back in Indiana. She handed us little black boxes and explained their use. 'Bats use echolocation to find their way in the dark,' she said. 'They make very high-pitched sounds, too high for human ears to hear. These devices turn those sounds into clicks. If you hear the box clicking, it means there are bats nearby. Slow clicks tell you the bats are flying slowly, looking about for food. Very fast clicks mean the bats are flying fast, fast, catching insects.' She showed us how to turn them on and wave them around, pointing in different directions to 'hear' bats.

I was too proud to cling to Alan's arm, but I stuck very close by him as we ventured out into the twilight. We headed first for the churchyard. Of course, I thought. There's a belfry. The saying isn't just a cliché. I once visited a church in northern Indiana that did in fact have bats in its belfry. And on that occasion, also down in the church. I shuddered at the memory and moved a little closer to Alan.

We found no bats in the churchyard. 'It is perhaps too early for them, or too open,' said our guide. 'We will go to a place that is more wild, more trees and bushes.'

After a little while I began to enjoy our walk through the lowering twilight. No one in the group was inclined to talk much; there was an intimacy to our quest that I found pleasant. Now and then someone's little black box would emit a rapid series of clicks and we would all look around to try to spot the bat.

It wasn't until we got into a woodsy area, with trees and undergrowth all around, that we actually saw bats. Then it seemed they were everywhere, crossing our path, swooping purposefully to catch food. The area was damp, and I began to wish I had brought some mosquito repellent, until the guide answered someone else's question on the subject. 'A bat can eat as many as five thousand mosquitoes in a night,' she said. 'That is what they are doing right now, eating the mosquitoes that would rather be eating you. They are very useful animals!'

I had to agree about that. Mosquitoes love me, and yet I hadn't had a single bite. Well, hooray for bats!

Then our French guide turned the excursion over to Suzi, the hedgehog expert. She explained that the blonde hedgehogs were not native to Alderney. Legend had it that someone had bought a pair at Harrods, years ago, and brought them to the island, where they adapted beautifully to their new environment, obeying the biblical injunction to be fruitful and multiply. They had no natural enemies and were thus not wary, but could actually be approached and picked up. 'And you don't have to worry about doing that, because their quills aren't especially spiny, they have soft fur on their undersides and they have no fleas!'

We trudged over a large portion of the island, farming areas, cliff tops, woods. We shone our flashlights into hedges. We turned down tiny lanes and came back again.

We saw not one hedgehog of any colour.

'You know,' I said to another member of the party, 'I've never seen a hedgehog. We don't have them in America, and for some reason they don't seem to like my part of England, either. All I know about them is from Beatrix Potter: Mrs Tiggy-Winkle.'

'And you know,' said the woman, without a trace of a smile, 'they really aren't very good at doing laundry.'

We ended up in the garden of Suzi's house. She explained that she regularly put food out for the hedgehogs, but it appeared that this evening her husband had forgotten to do it. No hedgehogs.

'I'm so sorry,' she said to the group. 'They're wild animals, of course, and not entirely predictable, but . . .'

'Another time,' said one of the party. The trouble was, for some, perhaps most, of the group there might not be another time. Alderney is hard enough to reach that a visit might be a once-in-a-lifetime event.

I was mildly disappointed, but we would probably still be here next Thursday. At least the evening had given us a break from the vexing problem of the dead American. And all the walking we'd done that day had tired my body. I hope my brain would consent to shut down for the night, too, and let me sleep.

'Nightmares, darling?' asked Alan in the morning, as he was shaving.

'Why, did I disturb you?'

'Not much, but you were a trifle restless.'

'I don't remember anything except waking once with a vague sense of discomfort. Of course that could have been just because I needed to go to the bathroom. Whatever it was, it was gone when I went back to sleep.'

'Probably bats. Though I thought you did very well with them last night.'

'They'll never be my favourite animals, but I admit my opinion of them went up when they kept the mosquitoes away. I was sorry about the hedgehogs, though.'

'Someone said the golf course is a good place to look for them. Perhaps tonight we'll head that way and see if we can spot one.'

'If we can find the place in the dark. You know, I never realized how much light there was at night in Sherebury until we came here, with almost no lights at all away from the town.'

'And this is midsummer, with a fair amount of sky-light even in the middle of the night. Think what it must be like in the dead of winter.'

I shivered. 'With winds strong enough to destroy the break-water. Thank you, but I'll stay away in winter. Hand me that sweater, would you? It's chilly this morning. And oh, Alan, look at the fog.'

He had pulled the curtains open. 'It'll burn off. See, the sun is trying to break through. Did you have any particular plans for the day?'

'If the fog hangs around, I might just stay in and read. Some of those books we got are fascinating, and there are some good ones in the lounge, too.'

'You know, even if the fog does dissipate, and I'm reasonably sure it will, it might not be a bad idea to take it easy today. We've been keeping up a fairly brisk pace, and this is supposed to be a holiday. I hate to admit it, but I'm not as young as I was.'

'Whereas I, of course, get younger every day. It's just my muscles and bones that don't seem to know that. Let's not make any plans, just go with the flow.'

With the weekend approaching, some of the guests we'd begun to know a little were leaving and others coming in. I wondered, as I ate my simple breakfast of yogurt and fruit (chosen in guilty atonement for all the rich food I'd been eating), if it was possible that a murderer stood in the chatting group waiting for the taxi to the airport. We'd never actually talked to the other guests except to exchange greetings when we passed in the hall, small talk about the weather, that sort of thing. What if one of them . . .

There were no Americans among them. I wasn't sure what difference that might make.

And it was not, I emphatically reminded myself, any business of mine anyway. Mr Abercrombie had not been murdered. He had met with an unfortunate accident. The fact that a number of people on the island had hated him was neither here nor there. Those innocent tourists could leave whenever they liked.

I looked up and saw a half-smile on Alan's face. 'Oh, hush!' I said crossly, and asked for another cup of coffee. He hadn't said a word, but sometimes it can be very annoying to have one's mind read so consistently.

The fog had gone by the time we finished eating, and the sun was shining for all it was worth. We made a pot of tea and took it and our books out into the lovely little garden behind the B & B. The sun warmed the small walled space so much that I didn't need my sweater, though we sat in the shade of a large fuchsia bush. This, I thought, was more like it. This was a holiday. Sitting in a garden, doing nothing, listening to the hum of bees and the liquid song of a blackbird, so unlike the harsh cries of blackbirds back in Indiana.

That mellow mood lasted for about ten minutes. I picked up a book, read a few paragraphs, put it aside. Picked up another one. Didn't get past the cover illustration.

I stood up. 'Alan, I can't stand it.'

'I didn't imagine you would,' he said, never looking up from his book. 'Did you bring a notebook?'

'No, I took everything out of my purse that I could, because of the weight restrictions.'

'You'd better go buy one. And a pen or two.' He looked up then.

'You look exactly like the cat that swallowed the canary!'

'Yes, dear. Do you want me to come with you?'

'No, I need a little time to get over being transparent.'

He chuckled and returned to the book.

TEN

I love my husband dearly. I do. There are times, though, when I wish he understood me a little less obviously. A woman likes to think she has a *little* aura of mystery, even when she's nearing the end of her seventh decade.

It didn't take me long to find a notebook. There was a kind of general store just a few steps from our B & B. It sold almost everything, from shampoo to dog food to greeting cards to – aha! – notebooks. I had to buy a packet of ten of them, but no matter. I'd ship them back home along with our books, and I'd certainly use them. I didn't need pens. I had at least three in my purse; I carry several because I'm forever losing them.

I had stopped being irritated by the time I got back to the little garden. It was too beautiful a day to cherish a snit. 'All right, love, I'm properly equipped now. All ready to make lists. Where shall we start?'

Alan had evidently been giving the matter some thought. 'Suppose we list everyone we've talked to about Abercrombie, and what they think of him.'

'Or what they told us they think of him,' I amended.

'Indeed. There might be a difference. Very well. I think the first name ought to be Constable Partridge.'

'But he's a Methodist. He didn't really know the man. At least, he didn't tell us anything about him except the basic facts.'

'Didn't he?'

'Oh. You mean his unspoken belief that there was more to Mr A.'s death than met the eye. You don't think we're wrong about that, do you? I mean, wrong about what the good constable believes.'

'He's a good policeman, Dorothy. He doesn't know us, doesn't know anything about us except what we told him. By now I'm sure he's done his homework and knows my credentials check out. He also knows the difference between evidence and speculation. *And* he has a very small force here. He can't afford to go chasing after faint possibilities.'

'Okay, but that doesn't really answer my question.'

'I think he has recognized in us a couple of unofficial deputies. He has let us see what he thinks without ever speaking a word that could be held against him. So yes, I think he believes there's reason for doubt about the way Abercrombie died.'

I wrote that down: *Partridge, has doubts.* 'And there's something else, too. I'll bet he knows more about the man than he let on, even if he doesn't attend St Anne's. How could he help it? It's a small island, and the guy was making himself conspicuous. A finger in every pie at the church, spending money like mad, talking about buying a house – of course he'd be well known.'

'I'd wondered about that myself. But it never hurts to pretend ignorance.'

I grinned. 'Playing your cards close to your chest, we'd say in America. In some circles.'

'But not the ones you moved in, I'm sure. Who's next? Robin?'

'No, I'd say definitely Alice. We know the most about her.'

Alan nodded, sighing. 'I'd far sooner not have heard any of that story. Not only is it horrific, but it leads one to suspicions of Alice I don't want to entertain.'

'Neither do I, but we can't just ignore the story, can we?' I made a note. 'Then there's Robin. He's sort of like the good constable, in a way. He's told us quite a lot, but not in words.'

'He's a reserved sort of chap. I don't think he likes speaking ill of anyone. And then, as he's not a native islander, he might feel a bit – what shall I say? – diffident, about making judgements.'

'Abercrombie wasn't an islander, either. Worse, he wasn't even English. And I say there's no doubt Robin didn't like him. I wish we knew why. I think that's something we're going to have to find out.' I made another note.

'So we come to the church contingent.'

'But we can't lump them all together,' I objected. 'Yes, they're all on Abercrombie's side, but there are nuances. I'm willing to bet that if we could talk to them separately, we might hear some slightly different stories. Sylvia's a strong-willed woman, and I think most of the others wouldn't dare disagree with her. I'd like to see if I couldn't get that grandmother-type off by herself. She never told us her name, but she thought I was a detective. I think she'd talk my head off if I let her.'

'She's very much in the Saint William camp.'

'I know, but she could be useful all the same. For one thing, she might have a clue about why Robin didn't like the man. All of them might, for that matter. Help me remember their names, Alan.'

'Sylvia Whiting.' He counted them off on his fingers as I wrote them down. 'Rebecca Smith. Three who didn't give us their names. The priest, Mr Lewison. And then there's "Lucille", who took umbrage when Abercrombie stole her jumble sale job.'

'Yes, I imagine we'll have to find her, too. How? How are we going to find any of them? We can hardly call on Mr Lewison and ask for their addresses.'

'I have two suggestions. No, three.' Alan started counting on his fingers again. 'The first is Victoria Street. I'm sure you remember the old saying that if you sat in Paris at the Café de la Paix long enough, everyone you knew would pass by. The world has changed too much for that to be true now, if it ever was, but certainly everyone in Alderney traverses Victoria Street. All we'd have to do is look as if we're shopping and walk slowly, and I'm sure we'll become involved in conversations.'

'We?'

'Separately. We can cast the net further that way.'

'Okay, I'll buy that one. And your other two suggestions?'

'The first is Jack's. It seems to be a popular spot for the church-goers. If we go there for morning coffee, for lunch, for tea, we ought to run across a fair sampling of the people we want. And the other, a long shot, is the Georgian House. It seems more of a haunt for the imbibers of alcohol, but I wouldn't be surprised to find Robin there, and perhaps some of the others as well.'

I could find nothing wrong with any of his ideas, except – 'I do hope Jack's and the Georgian House have good loos. If we're going to be practically living there, I'll need them.'

It was nearly lunchtime, and although I would have been happy to eat in our room, I saw the wisdom of Alan's plan. 'Jack's?' I stood.

'It's a bit early yet. Let's stroll Victoria Street for a few minutes. We might find someone we could ask to join us.'

'Okay. You go up and I'll go down. Let's meet at Jack's in – what? – half an hour, with or without other members of the party.'

It was a beautiful day for a stroll, if I hadn't been preoccupied. I prefer a somewhat brisk walking pace, but a stroll was all I could manage at midday in Alderney. Busy shoppers were everywhere. The post office van was making its leisurely way up the street, stopping at every address, squeezing past the scaffolding at the construction site. The driver had pulled in his side mirrors, but even so pedestrians had to wait for him to get by, or huddle in shop entrances, and of course no car could get past. Everyone seemed to accept the inconvenience with great good humour.

One little knot of women, chatting on a corner, backed away from the van without noticing that I was behind them. I was pushed into the doorway of the fishmonger's and barely avoided stepping on the toes of someone coming out.

We offered mutual apologies. 'It's rather a crush, isn't it?' said the woman, and then took a closer look at me. 'Why, it's Mrs Martin, isn't it? I'm not sure I ever introduced myself. Martha Duckett. We met at the church.'

The grandmother. This was a piece of luck! 'Of course I remember you. How wonderful that you remember my name. I'm hopeless with names, myself. And I'm so glad I ran into you. Sorry it was literally so, though! I'm just going down to meet Alan at Jack's for a bite of lunch. Could I persuade you to join us? We do enjoy having company for a meal.'

'Oh, I really should go home. I've my lunch here.' She held up a small parcel wrapped in white paper.

'Oh, do come. I'm sure Mr McAllister would be happy to put your fish back on ice for you, and you can have it for supper.'

I held my breath. Of everyone we'd met so far, she was the one I most wanted to talk to. I'd been sure that she wanted to talk to us, too . . .

'Well . . . it *is* lonely eating alone . . .'

'Splendid.'

'I'll just pop back in the shop and explain to Mr McAllister. I'll come down in a tick.'

'Oh, I don't mind waiting.' I was not about to let her go, now that she was hooked. I was pleased to see that there was a queue in the shop; it would take a few minutes for her to get to the counter to return her fish, and that would give Alan more time to get to Jack's. I hoped he would be alone. Another person might make Martha less willing to open up.

My luck held. Martha and I met Alan – alone – just as he was going into the brasserie. 'Look who I persuaded to have lunch with us, love!' I introduced her, and Alan played up beautifully.

'This is a real pleasure,' he said in his warmest manner. 'We were hoping to get to know you better. Shall we sit inside or out?'

'Oh, outside, don't you think? It's such a fine day, it would be a pity to waste it.'

We settled ourselves at one of the sunny tables, and while I was trying to work out whether this was the sort of place where one ordered at the bar, a waitress appeared with two menus, which she handed to Alan and me.

'I'll have a pint of bitter to start,' said Alan. 'Dorothy? Mrs Duckett?'

'Oh, please, it's Miss, but do call me Martha. I'd like a half, please.'

'Me, too,' I said. 'By the way, Martha, this is our treat. No, we insist. Everyone on this island has been so kind to us; this is a small chance to repay. Now, what's good to eat?'

Martha was obviously well-known here and needed no menu. 'Oh, everything's good. I do like their Caesar salads, but my very favourite is the crab sandwich. It's the best I've ever eaten.'

'Done,' said Alan and I with one voice. Our beer arrived in a few moments, and Alan proposed a toast. 'To friends, old and new.'

We chatted while waiting for our food. Our impressions of Alderney, the beautiful weather – the small talk one uses to fill time. When we got our sandwiches, they looked so good we dived right in and couldn't say much for a few minutes.

Martha was the first to push away her plate, with her sandwich only half finished. 'I'll take the rest home,' she said. 'It's so good, but they give one such a lot to eat here.' She was such a small lady, it surprised me that she'd been able to put away as much as she did.

She dabbed at her lips with her napkin, then looked around the patio. It had filled up with customers. No one was paying the slightest attention to us, but when she began to speak, it was very quietly.

'I hope you won't mind, but I did want to talk to you about Mr Abercrombie. I could see that you were confused by what other people had to say about him. I was so happy to bump into you in the shop, because I didn't know where you were staying, and I wanted to see you.' She paused for a sip of her beer, which she had scarcely touched. 'You see, he was such a dear man that I just cannot bear to think you might take away a wrong impression of him.'

'He does seem to have inspired strong feelings, one way or the other,' I said cautiously.

'And that's why some people started imagining things that weren't true.' She leaned over her plate in earnest pleading. I moved it out of the way just before the bow on her blouse touched the mayonnaise. She didn't notice.

'Jealousy is a dreadful thing, Mrs Martin,' she went on. 'It can turn the nicest people into monsters. Ladies, and some men, too, who have been stalwart workers at the church for years, well, some of them took offense at how Mr Abercrombie won people's hearts, and how well he did the little tasks he took on.'

'I'm not quite sure what you mean,' I said. 'What could have given them reason to be jealous?' I knew perfectly well what she meant, but I was hoping she would be more specific.

'Well, take one of the men, for example. I won't name him, but he's been a great help, even though he hasn't lived on the island all that long. He sings in the choir, very reliable, never misses a practice or a Sunday service, and as the vicar is the only other bass, that's been most welcome.'

Aha! I didn't dare look at Alan.

'Rob— this man seemed to get on quite well with Mr Abercrombie when he first came. I think they lunched together once or twice. Robin likes Americans. But then something happened, and the two men became very cool with one another. Why, Robin would walk right past Mr Abercrombie without a word, as if he didn't even see him. It was most embarrassing. I can only think it had to do with the new choir folders.'

'Choir folders?' said Alan with a questioning frown.

'Yes, you see the old ones are getting terribly shabby. Our choir isn't professional, of course, like the big cathedral choirs, but still we like to see them well turned-out. I don't sing in the choir anymore – I'm far too old, my dear – but I hated to see them having to use those old folders on Sunday morning. Music actually fell out more than once, and it was quite distracting when it sailed across the chancel. So Mr Abercrombie noticed, of course, and volunteered to help pay for new ones, lovely leather ones. We're a small parish, and as you can imagine, we have very little money to spare.'

'And the other man objected?' Alan carefully didn't use his name, but he sounded incredulous. I thought about what Sylvia had said about something that was 'too petty, for either man', and wondered.

'Oh, he said he thought it was an unnecessary expense, when the church, and the community, had so many other needs. I think he just wished he had thought of it first. But most of the choir, and most of the congregation, agreed with Mr Abercrombie, so he went to a great deal of trouble to find out the cost of new ones, and showed everyone in the choir several styles to choose from. They're blue leather, with a gold edging, and they'll have the name of the church stamped in gold on the front. He said he'd take contributions from anyone who cared to give, but he would make up the difference himself. He ordered them a few weeks ago, and we were so looking forward to having them for our festival in July. Now with him gone, I don't know what will happen to the order.'

'I imagine it was paid in advance, so it will arrive in time,' I soothed. 'This would be the festival of Saint Anne? When is that, exactly?'

'The Sunday closest to July 26. It isn't as glorious as it was in the old days. We're not very High Church now. But we still celebrate, and the new folders will mark the occasion, and serve as a memorial to a man very dear to our hearts, even though he was here for such a short time.'

ELEVEN

'A re you thinking what I'm thinking?' I asked Alan as we trudged back to our room.

'Probably. That dear sweet woman rather missed the point about the folder issue, didn't she?'

'Alan, did you follow the Watergate scandal at all? Nixon and the burglars and all that?'

'Vaguely.' He gave me an odd look.

'No, my mind isn't wandering. This really is to the point. You probably remember that there was a mysterious informant they called Deep Throat, who gave Bob Woodward lots of information. One of the things this guy said was "Follow the money".'

Alan smiled. 'Ah. Indeed. Here we have another little situation where Abercrombie could have made off with a bit of cash.'

'And all in the name of charity, which makes it even more infuriating. Alan, what would you like to bet that those folders were never ordered?'

He spread his hands. 'I'm not a gambling man, Dorothy, and in any case I would never bet on a sure thing. It isn't sporting.'

'We're taking sides again. You know, it's entirely possible that the man really was as delightful as some people thought.'

'Anything's possible. But you haven't forgotten Alice, have you?'

'No, as hard as I've tried, I haven't forgotten her horror story. But look, Alan.' I stopped dead in the middle of the sidewalk, causing people to detour around me with the usual courtesy and lack of impatience I'd come to expect here. They apologized for almost running into me.

Alan pulled me into a doorway. 'What's on your mind, love? And you'd best keep your voice down.'

'I don't understand what all this penny-ante stuff is all about. Alice implied that the man had stolen big-time from his church in Illinois. All we've heard about here is nickel-and-dime stuff. What was he up to?'

'Let's walk.' He led the way, not back to our room, but up
Victoria Street to QE2 Street. We walked past Annie's bookshop
to the police station, and Alan gestured me in, having said not
a word in the meantime.

'What?' I whispered.

'I have an idea,' he replied.

Constable Partridge was in. Alan and I were admitted to
the little interview room and invited to sit down. 'I have only
one quick question,' said Alan, still standing. 'Gambling. Where
can I find more information?'

Mr Partridge didn't seem at all startled at the question. 'The
Gambling Control Commission offices are just up the street.
They'll be happy to tell you anything you need to know.'

As we turned to go, I thought the constable wore a satisfied
expression.

'What was that all about?' I demanded as soon as we were
outside. 'What do you mean, gambling? You said just now that
you're not a gambling man, and I know that's true.'

He glanced up and down the street and then turned toward
Victoria Street. 'It's nap time. Let's go to our room and I'll tell
you a little bedtime story.'

I was seething with curiosity by the time we were safely in
our room with the door firmly shut.

'We might have some tea,' he suggested. 'This may take a
little while.'

So I brewed a pot, and we sat at the tiny table, and Alan talked.

'Once upon a time,' he began in approved bedtime story
fashion, 'there was an American man with expensive tastes and
not a great deal of money to gratify them. He had a decent job,
and the salary was sufficient to support him in modest comfort,
but he wanted much more. He began to see chances to slip
a little more into his pocket than he was entitled to. He was a
trusted employee; he was in fact the boss at his place of business.
And he was a charming, plausible fellow. Most people believed
what he told them.'

Alan finished his tea and poured himself another cup. 'As his
peculations grew and grew, it was inevitable that they would be
discovered. By the time they were, he had piled up rather a
nice little nest egg, enough to take him out of the country just

before the authorities were called in. He had heard of a small island in the English Channel where gambling was not only entirely legal, but entirely respectable. He thought if he could get there with his nest egg and add a bit to it, he'd be in a very nice position to accumulate the wealth he had desired all his life.'

'Alan, he wasn't a stupid man! He would surely have realized that gambling is a good way to end up in the poorhouse.'

'Ah, but he didn't intend to be a gambler. He was going to set himself up in business.'

'What, a casino? Here?' I could not wrap my mind around that idea. Casinos belong in glitzy places, not tranquil islands.

'Not a casino. A computer. Electronic gambling.'

I abandoned my tea and made a pot of coffee. My brain needed stimulation. 'Alan, I don't have the slightest idea what you're talking about.'

'That's because you're not a gambler, either. But you play card games online.'

'FreeCell, yes.'

'And you know that some online games are played against other players.'

'I suppose. I've never played those.'

'All right, then. I don't know the details of the operation myself, but I presume that one can play such games as poker, or blackjack, or any card game online – for money. One would presumably have to pay to join the game, and make wagers, just as in a casino, except that it would all be done from one's own computer. And computers, according to the man at the shop, are very important in Alderney.'

I mulled that over. 'How would you pay, though, or collect your money if you won?'

'Credit cards, probably. Or you could set up an account that would be debited. I'll need to find all that out. The point is that, as with any gambling, the "house" always wins in the long run. So if one set oneself up to run such an operation, one could quite legally make enormous sums of money.'

'But . . . but . . . there must be regulations. And taxes, and all that. I mean, they wouldn't let just anybody set up a cyber-casino, would they?'

'I'm sure not. I intend to find out. But wouldn't it be a sweet little operation for a man who, we suspect, had very little in the way of conscience? Not only lucrative, but legal.'

'But it isn't *right*!'

'That depends upon one's view of gambling. Our man's view may well be flexible. After all, he stole from unsuspecting parishioners to get the seed money. And remember all that expensive electronic equipment he was buying? Perhaps it wasn't just for entertainment.'

'Somebody should do something!' I raged.

'Simmer down, darling. Don't forget that this is just a fairy tale I'm spinning. It's a possibility, certainly, but probably no more than that. Although it would explain why he came to Alderney.'

'If that man was planning something like that, then I hope someone did push him down that hill! I wish I'd done it myself!'

'No, you don't. You would have liked to give him a piece of your mind, I've no doubt, but you know you can't even smack the dog when he's been naughty, much less use violence to a human being.'

'I'm not so sure he was a human being,' I grumbled, but Alan was right, of course.

I jumped up suddenly and reached for my purse, pulling out my phone. 'Alan, I want to call Jane.'

'To check on the animals? You know they're fine. She spoils them.'

'Well, it was the mention of Watson that made me think of it, but it's not just that. I want to hear her voice. She's so sane and sensible and just plain good. She'll be an antidote to all this poison.'

Jane Langland is one of the saints of the earth. She doesn't look like it. I've never been able to decide whether she looks more like Winston Churchill or one of her many bulldogs, not that there's a great difference. Her gruff manner hides the kindest heart imaginable. She's a retired schoolmistress, who has been my next-door neighbour ever since I moved to England years ago, and is a dear friend, pet-sitter and source of information about everything under the sun. I badly needed a dose of Jane.

She answered the phone promptly. 'Hello, Dorothy. Thought you might be calling about now. Missing your miserable little toads?'

'I am, badly. How are they all?'

'Fat and lazy. Cats sleep all the time they're not eating. Not even interested in chasing the birds.'

'They never catch them, anyway. Thank goodness. And Watson?'

'Oh, *Watson*.' Her voice had softened. She enjoyed the cats, and was always good to them, but dogs were the great love of her life, and she pampered our mutt just as much as her own highly pedigreed pets. 'Missing you, of course, but being good. Needn't worry.'

'I know. I just – oh, Jane, I just wanted to talk to you. Something awful has happened here.'

'Man on the cliff.'

'Jane! How on earth . . .? It can't have made the news. A man falls down a hill and hits his head – it's not the most riveting news.'

'Been keeping an eye out for Alderney news. Friend used to live there; saw this in a Guernsey paper; told me.'

Of course. If Jane had relayed news from a friend in Kathmandu or Kamchatka, I wouldn't have been surprised. 'I should have known. You have your spies everywhere.'

'Suppose you were the ones who found him.'

'Now I'm sure your friend didn't tell you that!'

'No. Know you two. Good at finding trouble. Accident, was it?'

I hesitated just a fraction too long, and heard her chuckle.

'Thought not. Know a little about the man.'

I sighed. 'Why does that not surprise me? Just a second, Jane, I'm going to put you on speaker phone, so Alan can hear, too. Wait a minute, he may have to do this for me.'

When Alan had pushed a button or two, I said, 'Okay. Shoot.'

'Don't know much. Student went to America, some uni in Ohio. Wrote back about a local priest. Saint on earth, apparently. Too good to be true, boy thought. Left without much ado. Fishy.'

I'm used to Jane's style, and translated without much difficulty. One of her former pupils had gone to America, heard about Mr Abercrombie and mistrusted him, especially when the priest flew the coop.

'We're hearing some things, too, Jane, that have made us

wonder, but it still seems as if the guy just fell down that hill. It's awfully steep.'

'Jane, there's another thing,' Alan put in. 'What do you know about gambling in Alderney?'

'Big business. Huge business. Big source of income for the island. All on the up-and-up. Why?'

'It's too complicated to get into, Jane. We just wondered, that's all.'

'Hmm.' Jane was given 'furiously to think', as Hercule Poirot used to say.

Alan signalled me with his eyebrows, so I said, 'We have to sign off now, Jane. Thanks for the info, and for looking after our menagerie. We'll let you know if anything exciting happens.'

'Better,' she said, and we rang off.

'She'll be exploring connections between Abercrombie and Alderney gambling before we finish our nap,' I said, putting the phone away.

'I hope so. It'll save us some legwork. If that woman had lived in America, the FBI and the CIA would have been battling to obtain her services.'

'They're not half so efficient,' I said, yawning. 'The tea and coffee don't seem to have done much. But wake me in an hour. I want to try to find Alice. She might know how much Abercrombie was supposed to have stolen. I can't imagine that it's cheap to set up a gambling operation.'

It was an hour and a half before I came back to full consciousness. Alan and I had both been doing too much intensive thinking, and we fell into a heavy sleep. I actually woke first (all that tea and coffee), and felt logy and unrefreshed, even after I'd splashed cold water on my face.

'All right,' I said to Alan when he was awake and functioning, 'where shall we try to find Alice?'

'Do you have any idea where she lives? Or works?'

'Not a clue.'

'Then our only contact is the church. Where, late on a Friday afternoon, there's not likely to be anyone around.'

But we were lucky. A middle-aged woman was working with

flowers at the font, an apron tied around her sturdy waist. 'There's a christening tomorrow,' she explained. 'Can I help you at all?'

'We're trying to find Alice Small, and we don't know where she lives,' said Alan. 'We met her at Morning Prayer, and we'd like to – er – invite her to tea.'

'She's not at home. I know because she had said she'd help me with the flowers today, so when she didn't turn up, I phoned her. No answer. I can't imagine where she's gone. It's not like her to be irresponsible, but she has been acting a bit odd lately.'

'Oh, what a pity,' I said. 'I wonder – do you think it would be all right if you gave me her phone number? We could try later.'

'Oh, well, if you met at church, I suppose it wouldn't matter.' She pulled out her own phone, found the number and read it off to me while I entered it in mine. 'You're that couple who found Mr Abercrombie, aren't you?'

We were becoming used to this. 'Yes,' said Alan, 'and please accept our condolences. It appears that this congregation will miss him very much.'

'Hmph. That's as may be. He was a charmer, but there was something about him . . . however. If you do manage to talk to Alice, you might remind her about the flowers. There'll still be plenty to do tomorrow morning.'

'Well, there's another one in the negative column,' said Alan as we walked back to our room.

'Or at least not one of the walked-on-water crowd. Alan, what are you going to do about following up on your gambling idea?'

'First, I'm going to find a computer somewhere and see what I can find there. If I still have questions I'm going to the Commission in the morning. Meanwhile, it's too late for tea and far too early for dinner. Why don't you come with me to the library? They're sure to have at least one computer for public use, and I'm sure you can find something of interest while I surf.'

'I didn't even know there was a library. Lead the way, great explorer.'

It wasn't far away. Nothing is very far away from anything else in Alderney. It was small, as one might expect, but new and clean and well-stocked. An assistant showed Alan the somewhat antiquated computer he could use, and helped him to log on.

I was pleased to find the mysteries of some of my favourite American authors on the shelves, and took one down at random to while away a few minutes. Of course I knew I couldn't check it out, but if I couldn't stand not to finish it, Annie could always order it for me.

Alan was taking a long time. He must be finding something of interest. I got tired of my book – not as good as I'd hoped – and went outside to get some fresh air and try to call Alice Small. I got no response, not even voicemail. Oh, well, maybe she was one of those people who hate voicemail. I went back in the library and wandered about, went outside again to place the call, went back in. I finally sat down next to my husband, who was still absorbed in his research.

The assistant approached. 'I'm sorry, sir, but we're closing in a few minutes. Perhaps if you could finish up what you're doing? I can print a few pages out for you, if you like.'

He sat up and stretched. 'No, that won't be necessary, thank you. You've been a great help.'

'So did you find what you needed?' I asked when we were out in the sunshine and I'd tried Alice again.

'There's a lot of information on the Net. Too much, indeed. I may stop at the Commission offices tomorrow for help in sorting it all out. But I learned several things that seem to knock my theory into a cocked hat. For one thing, a licence to operate an e-gambling operation out of Alderney costs a great deal of money. If I read it correctly, the cheapest licence, for the first year only, is over £17,000. After that it doubles, at least. That's just for the licence. Then one must prove one has adequate funds to operate, that is, to pay out on bets. There are all sorts of forms and requirements, and frankly I was getting a headache trying to make my way through it all.'

'Hmm. It does sound daunting. I'm not sure our get-rich-quick priest would want to get involved in that.'

'No. And I thought it was such a good idea. Have you managed to reach Alice?'

'No, and I've tried over and over again. It just rings and rings, no voicemail, even. I thought modern phones always responded in one way or another.'

'Perhaps it isn't a modern phone. I suppose there are still a few old-fashioned ones around. Still, given her state of mind, it's a bit worrisome, don't you think?'

'I do, actually. I'd like to make sure she's all right, but I have no idea where she lives, or works, or anything. Do you suppose the Visitor Centre is still open? Someone there might have some ideas.'

'It's well past their official closing time, but we could try.'

It was closed, but someone was just leaving the Wildlife Trust office next door. We hurried.

'Sorry, we're just closing, but was there something you needed?' The man looked tired, but he was still pleasant. Of course he was. This was Alderney.

'We're sorry to bother you,' I said, 'and actually we were hoping to talk to someone next door. I'm trying to find the address of a lady I met at church, and I don't know where to begin.'

'You've tried the church?'

'We did, earlier. Someone gave us her phone number, but she doesn't answer.'

'What's the lady's name?'

'Alice Small.'

'Oh, Alice! Yes, of course. Actually she lives quite close to me – I'm Philip Cooper, by the way – and I'm going home. If you'd like to come with me, I can show you.' He sized us up in a quick glance. 'It's not too far, but I'm afraid I didn't bring my car.'

'We're spryer than we may look,' said Alan with a smile, 'and we like to walk.'

It was, indeed, not far, and all downhill, to the bottom of Victoria Street and then just a short walk down Braye Road.

Our guide showed us her front gate, and then paused. 'That's odd,' he said. 'She always leaves her door just a little ajar, so the cat can get in and out. Perhaps the wind blew it shut.'

'There's not been any wind today to speak of,' said Alan, suddenly sounding very much like a policeman. He walked up to the tightly shut door and rapped sharply. The only response was a frantic mewing from somewhere within.

'Why, she's shut even the windows! And her car's here.'

The uneasiness I'd been feeling turned to real fear. Alan hammered on the door again, and called out. Only the cat responded.

Alan tried the door. It was locked.

'She never locks her door!' said Philip. 'Nobody in Alderney ever locks a door!'

Alan turned, looking grim. 'Dorothy,' he ordered, 'check for an open window somewhere. We need to know what's happening.'

'Now, wait a minute,' said Philip in alarm. 'I admit this is peculiar, but there must be some reasonable explanation. I really can't let you—'

'I am a policeman,' said Alan. 'I have no authority here in Alderney, but my wife and I have reason to be worried about Ms Small's emotional balance. You may notify the police if you wish, but I intend to enter this house and make sure that all is well.'

I found a window that was slightly ajar. It was upstairs, over-looking the roof over the back stoop. There was a sturdy trellis.

'Dorothy, you weigh less than I do. Do you think you could climb up?'

'No. My knees won't do it.' I turned to Philip, who was looking more and more upset. He was middle-aged, but a small man who looked fit and active. 'I know you don't know who we are, and have no reason to trust us. But my name is Dorothy Martin and this is my husband, Alan Nesbitt, and we had a conversation with Alice a day or two ago that disturbed us a good deal. I do urge you, as her friend and neighbour, to get into her house and see why she's shut herself in and isn't answering her door – or her telephone.'

The cat yowled again. That must have decided him. He scowled, but he climbed up the trellis nimbly enough, pushed the window open and disappeared inside.

It was only a minute or two before his head and shoulders reappeared at the window. 'She isn't here. And the cat's bowls are empty. She would never have left without providing for him. Something's wrong. I'm coming down.'

TWELVE

'Philip,' I asked as he stood outside once more, 'if Alice somehow ran into trouble, wouldn't she have called you?'

'She doesn't have a mobile. She couldn't phone anyone. We need to do something!'

Alan wasted no time, but pulled out his phone and called 999. 'Constable Partridge? Ah, good. Alan Nesbitt here. We have a possible emergency. I'm at—' he turned to Philip – 'where am I?'

'Seventeen Braye Road.'

Alan repeated it. 'The resident appears to have left the house in rather peculiar circumstances. Can you come, or send someone? Good.' He clicked the phone off. 'Good man,' he said. 'No unnecessary questions, and he'll save the necessary ones till he gets here. I could have used a few like him back in Belleshire.'

I watched the light dawn in Philip's eyes. 'You're the ones – did you find Mr Abercrombie?'

'We did,' I replied, 'and, in a way, that's why we're so worried about Ms Small.'

'Mrs. She prefers Mrs, even though she's a widow. And I hope you don't think she had anything to do with that man's death.'

'No, we don't. As far as anyone knows, Mr Abercrombie's death was accidental. He fell down a steep hill, hit his head on a rock and died of severe brain injuries. Why do you ask?'

'Oh. Well.' Philip shifted from one foot to the other and looked anywhere but at us. 'No reason, really. I mean – you said . . .' He came to a stop and looked unhappy.

Neither Alan nor I said anything. We just looked at him and waited.

He couldn't stand a silence any more than most people. 'Oh, it's just that – well, she didn't care much for Mr Abercrombie, and she's been acting odd since he died, and I wondered if – that is, whether – but she's a truly fine person, she would never . . .'

I took pity on him. 'Mr Cooper, nobody thinks Alice had anything to do with Abercrombie's death. We knew about her feelings toward him, and we also knew she was very unhappy. That's one reason we wanted to see her.'

'One reason. What was the other?' He was beginning to sound belligerent.

I was trying to decide whether to tell him the truth, and try to find out if he knew anything about Robin's attitudes, when a police car rolled up and Constable Partridge got out.

He went straight to the person who had the best right to be here. 'Phil, what's wrong here?'

'It's Alice. She's gone. And the house was locked up tight as a drum, with poor Sammy not able to get out, and not a bite of food nor a drop of water left for him. Her car's here, but she isn't. Something's happened!'

He turned to us. 'And how is it that you are involved?'

It could have been an accusation, but it sounded like a simple question, and Alan answered it that way. 'We wanted to talk to Alice, perhaps invite her to tea, and she wasn't answering her phone. Mr Cooper offered to show us the way to her house, and when we got here we couldn't get a response to our knock. We became somewhat alarmed, so I'm afraid we broke into her house and found the situation he described.'

'I was the one who went in,' said Phil. 'No one else could climb the trellis. I didn't really want to, but they insisted – and I'm glad they did. What are we going to do, Derek?'

The man was near tears. I can be slow on the uptake, but I saw in his eyes what I should have seen before. This man was, if not in love with Alice Small, at least very, very fond of her.

Poor guy! I was very much afraid something awful had happened to the woman, and even if it hadn't, she was so sunk in her grief, and her hatred of Abercrombie, that I doubted she had emotional space for other feelings.

The constable was responding to Phil's question. 'First, we make a thorough search of the house. There may be some indication of where she's gone, and why. I'll ask Mr Nesbitt to join me in that search. He was a very senior police officer in England, and he won't have lost his skill. Mrs Martin, perhaps you could talk to Phil, see if he can call up any ideas that might help.'

And keep him out of our way, was the silent message. I nodded my understanding.

When they had gone inside, Phil and I looked at each other. 'I'd rather go in and help them look. She's my friend. I might spot something out of the ordinary. I think I should help look.'

'Phil, they're trained policemen. They know what to look for. I'm sure they'll ask you about anything that seems odd. Meanwhile, perhaps we could find someplace to sit? I hate to admit it, but I'm feeling a little rocky.'

It was the truth. Every now and then I feel my age, and this was one of the times. I was also feeling more than a little guilty. Alan and I had known that Alice was in great distress, and had done nothing about it. True, she had lots of friends on the island who could have stepped in. But they didn't know her story. She said she had told no one but us. We should have followed up, and we hadn't.

Phil broke into my thoughts. 'We could go to my house. It's just over there.' He pointed. 'We could have some tea, or something stronger if you prefer.'

'Thank you. I'll just tell Alan.'

I called into the house, told the men where we'd be and left with Phil.

His house was small, but brightly painted and spotless. 'Do you mind sitting in the kitchen?' he asked.

'I live in my kitchen at home. I don't mind at all.'

We both decided tea was just what we needed, and while he went about making it, he asked, 'Why did you really want to talk to Alice? Was it true, what your husband told Derek?'

'Yes, in part. We had a very curious conversation with Alice a few days ago, as Alan said. She said she hated Abercrombie, and was glad he was dead, but she didn't act happy. We got to worrying about that and decided to talk to her. But that wasn't the only reason. Oh, thank you,' I said as he began to pour my cup of tea. 'Yes, milk and sugar, please.'

I took a sip of tea. It was too hot to drink. 'I said there was another reason,' I continued. 'Alan and I have taken an interest in Mr Abercrombie, since we were the ones to find him, and we've found something rather odd. So many people, at the church especially, seem to have loved him. But there are a few besides

Alice whose opinions are quite different. We thought Alice might have some insights into that.'

'Why?'

'Because we thought perhaps other people who felt as she did might have talked to her about—'

'No. Why do you care? You never knew him. You only found him dead. That's a shock, I can see. But why do you care what kind of person he was?'

I paused for thought. 'I've heard that in some Asian cultures,' I said after a moment, 'if someone saves a person's life, he or she becomes responsible for that person forever. There's a connection that can't be severed. Alan and I are discovering that to be true in this case as well. We didn't save his life, we found his body, but in some way we can't quite explain, we have a connection with William Abercrombie. He may not have had much in the way of family – at least the police haven't been able to trace anyone yet – but we have become something like family to him. It's important to us to get to know him. And if that sounds peculiar, well it feels peculiar to us, too.'

None of what I had said was untrue. I had more or less been making it up as I went along, because I didn't want to say we were looking into a possible murder. But as I said it aloud, I realized it was true. Some kind of bond had been forged between us and the late Mr Abercrombie, and we had some sort of responsibility to him.

Phil's reaction was a snort, or what would have been a snort if he hadn't been a courteous man. 'Yes, it does sound peculiar, and I have to say I don't envy you a connection with that man. If you're looking for someone to tell you why some people didn't like him, you've come to the right place.'

My tea had cooled. Too much. I drank some of it anyway and settled back. 'I'd be interested in anything you want to tell me.'

'I don't know why Alice hated him. She wouldn't tell me. But I was there the first time he walked in the church door. She was clearing away after Morning Prayer, and I was waiting to take her for coffee. He was wearing his collar, and he came up and smiled at her and said something, I forget what. She smiled back. Then he said his name and put out his hand, and I never saw such a look on anyone's face. I thought for a minute she was going to be sick. She didn't say a word, just looked at him and turned around and left the church. I went after her, but she had her car there, and got in, and drove away. I tried to phone her, but she wouldn't answer.

'The next time I saw her I tried to talk to talk to her about it, but she refused to say a word, and she'd changed. We'd been good friends, but it seemed she didn't want anything to do with me anymore. She was like that with everybody, I noticed. Cold and distant. And she'd always done volunteer work at the church, but she wouldn't stay in the building if he was there.'

'How did he react to that?'

'And that's the oddest thing of all. You'd think a clergyman, of all people, would try to talk to her, find out what was wrong, mend fences. He did nothing. He acted as if she weren't there.'

'Hmm.'

'He was always at the church, it seemed. Helping with this, doing that, suggesting the other. A finger in every pie. Most of the ladies thought he was wonderful.'

'Was he good-looking?'

'I thought you'd seen him.'

I shuddered. 'He'd just fallen down a hill and hit his head on rocks. He was . . . not a pleasant sight.'

'No. Well, he wasn't handsome, but he was pleasant-looking. Saintly, I heard one of the women say. The men in the church weren't quite so impressed. I don't know what they all thought, but there was one man who obviously despised him. I think you've met him. Robin Whicker?'

'Yes, Alan and I like him very much. We had noticed that he seemed not to think highly of Abercrombie, though he didn't talk about him to us. Do you know why?'

'He doesn't discuss his feelings readily. I think he had some idea that the man was hiding something, that he wasn't as much of a paragon as he tried to appear. I know no more than that.'

I sighed. 'I see. It seems people either loved him or hated him. That's odd, if you think about it. Was no one neutral?'

He shrugged. 'Most people, I suppose, even in the church. There are the volunteers who do everything, the ones who come to services every Sunday and sing in the choir and run the jumble sale and all the rest.'

I nodded. I suspect all churches are the same, all over the world.

'And then there's the rest of the congregation,' he went on, 'the ones who come to services on occasion, and go home and feel they've done their Christian duty for another week or month. I doubt they cared about Abercrombie one way or another.'

'What about the townspeople, the ones who don't go to church, or go to the Methodist or the Catholic church?'

'The shopkeepers loved him. He spent bags of money. Most of the island knew who he was, of course.'

Of course. Everyone knew who we were, and we'd been there less than a week.

'To most of them, I suppose he was just another American tourist.'

'Tourist? I had heard he planned to stay here, perhaps buy a house and live here.'

'Perhaps. He said a lot of things.' Phil picked up his teacup, sipped, set it down again with a grimace. 'You've asked me your questions,' he said. 'Now I have one for you? Why are you so interested in who loved him and who hated him?'

'I told you, we wanted somehow to get to know the man—'

'I know what you said. Now I'll tell you what I think. I think you believe the man was pushed down that hill, and you're trying to work out who might have done it. And I'll tell you one more thing. I didn't push him, and Alice didn't, and if someone else did, I hope he's never caught.'

THIRTEEN

I t was a good thing Alan and the constable showed up just then, because I had no idea what to say to Phil.

He lost interest in me, of course, the minute he saw the men. He stood up so abruptly he knocked over his chair. 'Did you find anything? Do you have any idea where she is?'

Constable Partridge put a hand on Phil's shoulder. 'We found nothing. Which is not necessarily a bad thing. There was no evidence of a struggle, nothing to indicate that she was taken away forcibly.'

'She wouldn't have left Sammy with no food!'

'I agree. Incidentally, there was plenty of food for him in the larder. Mr Nesbitt gave him food and water, and he's now blissfully sleeping it off. But it does seem as if Alice left voluntarily. We found her handbag, with her car keys inside, and no sign that anything had been removed. I called the library. She didn't come to work this morning.'

'Then she's been hurt! An accident—'

'We would have known immediately about a road accident. Now, Phil, I know you're upset, but what I want you to do is think carefully about where she might have gone. We know she was upset in her mind. Was there a place she liked to go to think, to be peaceful?'

He righted his chair and collapsed into it. 'The church, usually. But not of course recently. That bastard had ruined it for her. She liked to walk the cliffs.'

'We saw her in the – what do they call it? The Wildlife Bunker. Could she have gone there?' I suggested.

'Why wouldn't she have come back?' said Phil.

The constable cleared his throat. 'Phil, did she ever talk about exploring the tunnels?'

'Tunnels?' I asked.

'Oh, God, not the tunnels!' Phil turned as nearly white as I've seen a human being look.

I glanced from my husband to Phil to the constable, trying to understand.

'Part of the German fortifications,' said the constable. 'Some are safe to enter. Some . . . are not.'

I felt the blood drain from my own face. One of my deepest horrors is of caves and tunnels. My claustrophobia isn't nearly as bad as some people's, but the very idea of an enclosed underground space is enough to make me weak in the knees. Even reading about it in a book . . . and now we might be faced with the possibility of someone lost in one of those places.

'Are they . . . deep?' I forced myself to ask.

'Not so very,' replied Partridge. 'The danger is that they are unstable. The timbers holding them up rotted long ago, and there have been collapses . . .'

I swallowed hard. 'Then we'd better start looking for her, hadn't we?'

Constable Partridge phoned the police station to organize a search. Phil started frantically phoning his friends. Alan and I stood by, wondering what we could do to help.

'One thing you will not do, Dorothy,' he said in a low, but firm, voice. 'You will not go into those tunnels.'

'But I feel so helpless! There's poor Alice, maybe trapped—'

'I do not often issue orders, my dear. You know that. But this is an order. You can't help by going inside. You can serve coffee for the searchers, you can provide snacks, you can aid in any way you like, *except* in the actual search.'

I said nothing.

'If for no other reason, look at it this way. If you were to freeze with panic in a tunnel, you would have to be rescued. That would take searchers away from the reason they're there. You don't want that.'

'In short, I'd be more of a nuisance than a help.' I suppose I sounded bitter. I was.

'In short, yes. And you know that without my telling you.'

'Right. And just how am I supposed to make this feast? You're forgetting I have no kitchen just now.'

'You don't have to cook anything. The moment the word goes out, I'll wager every household on the island will move into action. This won't be the first time something of the sort has happened. Just stay available to help in any way you can.'

I fought against the common sense in what he was proposing. Finally I sighed. 'Oh, you're right, as usual. I do get so tired of you always being right.'

He ignored that as the cry of a petulant child, which is exactly what it was. I hate feeling that I'm not in control. 'I wish we'd never found the dratted man! I wish we'd never come to this dratted island!'

And that, too, was sheer petulance, and it wasn't helping. I pulled myself together. 'Sorry, love,' I muttered. 'I'll behave. Where do you want me to go?'

'With me, as soon as Derek has the search organized. Then we'll see.'

It didn't take them long to get things rolling. As Alan had predicted, a search was a well-rehearsed part of island life. Everyone knew his or her role in the effort, and stepped into it without much fuss.

Both Alan and I were kept well away from the tunnels.

'With all due respect, sir,' said Derek, 'you don't know this island as we do. There are all sorts of hazards once one leaves the established walking routes. I would like you, and your wife if she wishes, to go to the Wildlife Bunker. Alice went there once; she might go again. I'll have someone drive you as far as the road goes; that will save some time.'

Alan accepted his marching orders without a word, which made me ashamed of my little fit of pique. *Get a grip, Dorothy*, I admonished myself. *This isn't about your feelings. It's about a woman who's in deep distress, and is missing.*

None of us wanted to even think about the other possibility.

We didn't pause to admire scenery or wildlife on our way to the bunker. We walked as fast as we safely could, and talked not at all. Alan held my hand when the path was wide enough to walk two abreast.

We broke into a near-run as we approached the bunker and heard voices, though we couldn't make out words. We must have startled the two people there as we rushed in, breathless.

They were tourists. After only a few days on Alderney, I could spot them. They had been looking at the exhibits and exclaiming over them, but when we entered they stopped and looked at us blankly.

Alan recovered his breath before I did. 'Good afternoon,' he said quietly. 'We're sorry to disturb you, but we're looking for a friend who may have come this way. Have you seen anyone else here?'

The woman looked helplessly at the man. '*Pardon*,' he said. 'French.' He pointed to himself and then to the woman. 'No English.'

'*Ah, je vous demande pardon, monsieur. Nous cherchons une amie. Avez-vous vu une femme ici, une femme Anglaise de peut-être cinquante ans?*'

I was filled with admiration. My high-school French had deserted me years ago, and I could no more have inquired about a fifty-year-old English friend than I could have flown out of the bunker. I thought I was doing well to understand most of what he said.

I couldn't understand a word of what the couple said in reply, but from the gestures and head-shakings, I gathered the answer was no. Alan thanked them politely, and we stepped out of the bunker.

'You got that?' he asked.

'Not the words. They talk so fast! But I could understand "*non*". What shall we try now?'

'We report back, and do whatever Derek wants us to do.'

'You're a lot better about following orders than I am.'

'Years spent in an organization run along quasi-military lines will do that to a person.' He pulled out his phone and made his call. I could make little of his end of the conversation and waited till he punched off, looking despondent. 'There's very little we can do without transport,' he said. 'Nearly all the places that need to be searched are reached on foot, but from a nearby road. It would take us too long to walk to them, even if we were sure of where we were going.'

'This is so *frustrating*!'

'I agree. Derek said he'd call if he thought of something, but I doubt he will. He's busy dealing with people who *can* help.'

'Well, then, we might as well get ourselves back up to civilization. At least then if someone does turn up with a car, we can climb right in.'

'You're right. But wait one moment.' He went back into the bunker and spoke a few words to the French couple. I understood only '*neuf, neuf, neuf*', but that put me more or less in the picture.

'You told them to call Derek if they saw any signs of her,' I said when he came out.

'Indeed. You're coming along, my dear.'

'I do still remember how to count in French, at least up to ten.' We were silent the rest of the way back up to the road.

We walked all the way back to our room. 'Are you hungry?' asked Alan.

'No.'

He nodded and sat heavily in the more comfortable of the room's two chairs. I stretched out on the bed, but I wasn't sleepy, either. The silence stretched out.

Of all the things a human being is called to do in a crisis, waiting is the worst. Actions, even if they're difficult or painful or dangerous, occupy one's mind. Waiting simply expands the fear till it fills one's heart and soul.

I stood up. 'Alan, I have to do something.'

He stood, too. 'Right. What?'

'First we're going to go over to the church and say a prayer for Alice, and ask for guidance.'

'Sounds good to me. But first let's eat something. I'm not hungry, either, but our bodies know it's dinner time, and we're both aware of blood sugar levels and the way our minds work, or don't.' He rummaged in the drawer where we kept our few supplies. 'There's a bit of cheese left, and a few biscuits, and some grapes. Not really a meal, but it'll help.'

It all tasted rather like sawdust, but I saw the wisdom in Alan's words. Yes, we needed some fuel.

That took only a few minutes. Then I put on my hiking boots and grabbed every map and guide book we had, also flashlights. Alan carried both our sticks. We might find nothing to do with them, but at least we were prepared. Just before we went out the door, I reached for my jacket, and handed Alan his. Who knew how long we might be out there? The day had been warm, but nights could get quite chilly.

I suppose we had expected to find the church dark and quiet, late on a Friday afternoon. It was dark, but not quite quiet. A little group of women talked in low tones in a corner. A few more, and a handful of men, including Mr Lewison, the locum, knelt in the pews. We weren't the only ones seeking the help of God.

We didn't speak to any of them, but left quietly after we'd done what we came to do. I looked at the flowers in the church-yard, remembered the bats and had an idea. 'Nature,' I said.

'Mmm?'

'She likes nature. I'm sure it was the nature part of the bunker she sought, not the war memorabilia. And Phil said she liked to walk. I think she would have looked for a place where she could find the peace that nature can provide. But I don't know the island well enough to know which place she might seek out.'

'Nor do I. Let's see what you have there.'

We studied the brochures. 'This looks like a good bet,' said Alan pointing out something called the Longis Nature Reserve, 'but it's too far away to walk.'

'Then let's find a car. I wonder if Mr Lewison would drive us.'

'We can but ask.'

He was coming out of the church as we turned to go back in. Alan approached him and explained what we wanted to do.

'But of course! I'm deeply disturbed about Mrs Small. I have tried to sound her out about what's been bothering her, but she wouldn't talk to me. I very strongly feel that we must waste no time in finding her. My car's just here.'

Clouds had moved in, and the dusk was deepening to that deceptive time when there seems still to be plenty of light, but everything appears in shades of grey. We drove up the High Street at a speed that seemed reckless to me, but I am still uneasy on the narrow roads one finds on this side of the Atlantic. In another way I was happy about the speed, however. I felt as the priest did; we needed to find Alice as soon as possible.

We arrived at a place called, our driver said, 'The Nunnery'.

'A convent?'

'No. Never was, so far as I know. I don't know how it got the name. It's extremely old, originally a Roman fort. Even back then they were worried about invasion. Now from here I'm afraid we'll have to walk. Have you torches?'

We produced them.

'Then I propose we follow the trail as described in your brochure. Please do be careful. There will certainly be rabbit holes. Alderney is overrun with rabbits.'

Our progress was slow. The landmarks indicated in the brochure were probably easy to find in broad daylight. In the half-light of a long dusk, we had a hard time. However, I assumed it didn't really matter if we strayed off the track. Alice might be anywhere, off the trail or on. It was a large, remote area, and to me, at this hour, infinitely menacing.

We stumbled on. I was glad we'd brought our sticks and worn stout boots. We were silent, but the evening wasn't. Crickets sounded on all sides, and here and there a late bird. I was bitten by a mosquito, then another. Well, at any rate we wouldn't encounter bats.

The evening grew darker. I clung to Alan's arm. We didn't speak. We shone our flashlights this way and that, looking for hazards, for any sign that a woman had been here before us. Nothing.

The crickets paused for a moment, and I heard something else. A frog, perhaps? The brochure said there was a pond near here somewhere. I just hoped I saw it before I fell in.

The sound came again. A bit high-pitched for a frog, unless they were different here.

Alan put out a hand. 'Stop.'

We stopped and listened, and heard the sound again. This time there was no doubt. 'Is someone there? Help!'

FOURTEEN

S he was lying so near the pond that I went cold at the thought of what might have happened, had she been a step or two closer. She was exhausted, and cold. Her skin was cut in several places by the rough underbrush into which she'd fallen, and even in the dim light I could see dozens of mosquito bites. But she was alive.

I covered her with all our jackets while Alan called Derek and we waited for rescue. 'It was a rabbit hole, I think,' she said, through chattering teeth. 'I wasn't looking where I was going, and suddenly I just came crashing down. I think I've broken my ankle. It hurts quite a lot if I try to move it.'

'You poor dear! How long have you been here?'

'I came out for a walk early in the morning, about six, I suppose.' She tried to change her position and drew in a hissing breath.

'If you can, try not to move until the ambulance gets here. They'll know how to make you more comfortable without damaging anything. I do wish we had brought some hot coffee, or tea.'

She was shivering strongly. 'As long as I can shiver, I'm all right. I don't know much about first aid, but I do know that.'

'So you went for a walk,' I prompted. One of the few things I thought *I* remembered about first aid is that it's often better to keep the victim awake and talking. 'Your neighbour, Mr . . . what's his name, Alan?'

'Cooper. Phil Cooper.'

'Yes. Well, he thought it was odd that you'd gone off with the windows and doors closed. He said you usually left something open for the cat.'

'Yes, well . . . Sammy has been very naughty lately, killing birds and staying out all night. I didn't want him to go out until I was there to keep an eye on him.' She made another impatient movement, and cried out.

I was greatly relieved to hear the sound of the approaching ambulance.

'It's a clean break,' said the doctor. Alan and I, along with Mr Lewison and Phil Cooper, had been waiting at the little hospital for a report. 'But lying outside for all those hours didn't help any. She was close to hypothermia. If she hadn't been found when she was . . . but she *was* found, and she'll be fine. Of course she had to be flown to Guernsey to have the bone set and the cast put on. She'll be back here tomorrow, and I'll want to keep her here for a day or two until I'm sure she has recovered from the exposure, and we're able to regulate her pain. She's not going to be doing any serious walking for quite some time, I'm afraid.'

'I wanted to see her,' said Phil, sounding bereft.

'She wouldn't have known you were there. She's being given morphine and won't wake up for a while. Best thing for her right now.'

'I still wanted to see her.'

'He's got it bad,' I murmured to Alan.

'Mmm. How old do you think they are?'

'Fifties? She's a widow. We don't know about his background.' I turned to Phil. 'Now look, friend. You're worn out, and so are we, and I don't know about you, but I'm starving. Will there be a restaurant still open anywhere?'

'Braye Beach Hotel, perhaps, but I'm not hungry.'

'Then come with us and have a drink. And I think we need a taxi. I'm not sure I can walk another step.'

The restaurant at the hotel was still open, and the menu was inviting. By the time Phil had downed a stiff whisky, he had recovered his appetite, as I had hoped he would. Once we had a lovely dinner of fresh seafood in front of us, he had relaxed enough to talk.

'I don't understand about the cat,' he said, buttering a piece of crusty bread. 'He's never killed a bird, that I've seen. Mice, yes, and voles, but not birds. And he's neutered, not interested in chasing after the ladies. She's never shut him in before.'

'That's interesting.'

'And another thing. She's never gone out walking so early

before. We – she usually walks after she gets home from the library, or in the afternoons when she isn't working.'

'You walk together?' I asked casually.

'Well, yes, as a matter of fact.' He sounded like one of my long-ago school children, ready to add, 'You wanna make somethin' of it?'

'How nice.' Good grief. I sounded like a nanny. 'Alan and I love to walk together. It's one of our favourite things.'

'And even when she went walking alone, she always, always told someone where she was going. It can be dangerous—' He broke off suddenly. I was sure he was thinking, not only of Alice, but of Abercrombie tumbling down that steep hill.

I wasn't sure how, or whether, to broach the subject that was on my mind, but Alan was less timid.

'I'm sure this isn't something you want to think about, Phil, and I'm sorry to bring it up, but you know that Alice was not her usual self these past few days. Do you think that her depression could have led her to thoughts of self-destruction?'

'No! No, she would never do that! No, I'm certain she's never thought of such a thing!'

I looked at Alan. Too much denial. He'd worried about it, for sure.

'I ask only because of her unusual behaviour,' Alan went on. 'She went for a walk at an unaccustomed time, without telling you or, apparently, anyone else. She locked her cat inside, when she normally left him a way to get out. She didn't take her car or any money or identification. All this suggests to me that she may have planned not to return.'

'I – she – oh, I don't know!'

It was, I thought, a good thing we were in a public place, or Phil might have broken down completely, and he would have hated that. The people of Alderney may not be English, but the stiff-upper-lip tradition prevails, nevertheless. He spoke quietly, but there was pain in his voice.

'A month ago I'd have said I knew Alice better than anyone else on this island. We . . . enjoyed each other's company. Then it all changed, and the past few days, since he died, she wouldn't talk to me at all. I don't know what's going on in her head. Certainly she's not mourning that man; she detested him.'

'The death of someone you hate can create really complicated feelings,' I said. 'Guilt, among other things, especially for a Christian. Why wasn't I nicer to him while he was alive, why didn't I forgive him – that sort of thing. Even fear that somehow one's hatred contributed to the person's death. Not very sensible or productive, but we can't manufacture our feelings as we choose.'

'If she would only have talked to me!'

'Perhaps she'll talk to you now,' I said. 'She's had a terrible experience today. Sometimes that can change a person.'

And that was my five-cent psychology for the evening. We were all nearly falling asleep, so Alan paid our bill and the hotel people summoned us a taxi to take us to our well-earned beds.

Just before Alan turned out the light, he said, 'Why do you really think Alice went out for that solitary walk?'

'The same as what you think. She intended to kill herself.'

'Does that mean she was involved in Abercrombie's death?'

'I have no idea. 'Night, love.'

Alice was flown back to Alderney Saturday morning, and we went to visit her as soon as they would let us. She was sitting up, looking uncomfortable. The scratches on her face and arms were unsightly but didn't look dangerous. What did rouse my sympathy were the mosquito bites on every visible area of skin. I started to feel itchy myself.

'My dear woman, are they doing something about those bites? Calamine or something?'

'They've given me antihistamines. They don't help much. It isn't just mosquitoes; there were fleas, too. I slept last night. I was so tired, and drugged, but it's bad now I'm awake.'

'Not a romantic sort of suffering, but miserable all the same. And how is your ankle?'

'Painful.'

'The morphine doesn't help?'

'I refused it. I don't want—'

Don't want to become addicted? Don't want relief from the pain? I changed the subject. 'When are they going to let you go home? And who will take care of you once you're there?'

'I can manage.'

'Alice, I broke my leg once, several years ago. I was amazed at how much I couldn't do. Even getting dressed was a challenge. I absolutely could not have coped without Alan. Your cast isn't as cumbersome as mine was, but it's bad enough. You'll be on crutches. That will limit what you can do with your hands. Even feeding Sammy will be tricky, because you'll need to bend over, and it's so easy to lose your balance and fall. Trust me: you'll need help. Who among your friends might be able to stay with you for a few days?'

She was silent.

'There's always Phil,' I said, and waited for her response.

'He will want to help,' she said, 'but . . .'

'Yes. Well, give it some thought. I'll go now, but I'll be back. Is there anything I can get for you?'

'No. There's nothing I want. Thank you.' There was so much pain in her voice I bled for her.

As we left, we met Mr Lewison coming in. He was carrying a small wooden box.

'Oh, you're bringing her Communion. Wonderful!'

'How is she?'

'In great distress. There's the pain, and the terrible itching from mosquito and flea bites, but it's more than that. I do believe that she intended suicide, and is sorry that she didn't succeed. Last night the physical pain drove those thoughts out of her head, and she wanted to be found, but now . . .'

'Oh, dear. That's bad. Will she talk to me, do you think?'

'You can only try. And there's one other thing. She's going to need home care once they release her.'

'I've thought of that. It can be arranged. I don't know the resources here very well, but one of the ladies at the church has the information at her fingertips. I don't know if you've seen the charity shop in Victoria Street?'

'Yes, and we plan to check it out soon. I love charity shops.'

'The woman who runs that also runs a good many programs for the aged and infirm, including a home care service. I've learned that she's an amazing woman, full of energy and compassion. She'll work it out.'

I was once again full of admiration for the way the good

people of Alderney stepped up to meet the present need, whatever
it was.

He sketched a salute and moved on, and Alan and I left the
hospital. 'I love islands,' I said.

'The spirit of fierce independence, allied with fierce benevolence
– if that isn't a contradiction of terms.'

'It is,' I said with a nod, 'but it fits, all the same. They take
care of their own.'

'One more reason why Abercrombie didn't fit in.'

'And never would have. Alan, I'm convinced that the
only benevolence Abercrombie ever exercised was directed
toward Abercrombie. Whatever possessed the man to become
a priest?'

Alan shrugged. 'You have to keep on remembering, Dorothy,
that we're dealing with hearsay, and there is as much evidence
on the positive as on the negative side. None of it would stand
up for a moment in court.'

'Alice's evidence would. She knows for certain what he did
to her sister.'

'She knows what her sister told her. I say again, it wouldn't
hold on the witness stand.'

'Well, I believe it!"

'So do I. Simmer down, love. What I'm trying to say, badly,
I'm sure, is that we can *know* almost nothing about this man.
What we choose to believe is our own business, but I'm trying
to remember that everyone is a mixture of good and bad. Isn't
it possible that Abercrombie entered holy orders for honour-
able motives and then became corrupted by the power he found
he could wield? He was a handsome man, we're told. He was
apparently unmarried, since no family has yet been traced. He
had great charm. Is it any wonder that the ladies in his congre-
gations fell under his spell? Is it any wonder that he was
unable to resist the temptation to use his popularity to cover
his actions?'

'Priests are supposed to fight temptation,' I said stubbornly.

'My dear, we're all supposed to fight temptation. Perhaps you
can always do that. I can't.'

'Oh, for heaven's sake, *you* should have become a priest!'

'I chose another way to try to fight the evils of the world.'

He said it lightly, but I realized he meant it, and was suddenly ashamed of myself. What had I ever done to deserve this wonderful man in my life?

'All right. You win. I'll try hard not to paint Abercrombie in unrelieved black. And you've reminded me – we set out to learn all we could about the man and decide whether his death really was an accident. We keep getting side-tracked. What should we do next?'

Alan looked at his watch. 'It's nearly lunch time. Why don't we try Jack's? We might be able to join a conversation, or eavesdrop on one.'

'That sounds good. I'd rather eavesdrop, if it works that way. Maybe we can sit near some people who don't know who we are.'

'On Alderney?' Alan grinned. 'Best of British luck.'

We got lucky. Jack's was crowded, as usual, but there was a small table for two tucked away in a corner, where we were in a good position to hear what was going on without being seen. And a group of ladies from the church was seated quite close to us, talking nineteen to the dozen.

'Well, you may say what you like,' said one, 'but he hasn't been seen in church since it happened, and if that isn't guilty conscience showing, I don't know what it is.'

'Now, Nora,' said another (we didn't recognize any of them), 'we don't know that he's guilty of anything.'

'We know you always think the best of everyone,' chimed in a third, 'but in this case Nora may be right. He always comes to the Friday Eucharist, always—'

'Except that week when he had the flu.'

'—and that was only because he didn't want to pass it along to anyone else,' said the voice I recognized as Nora's. 'He's been absolutely faithful. And he didn't come to choir practice, either. Rebecca was very upset! That's why I say something is very wrong.'

'Perhaps he's ill,' said the peacemaker. 'Has anyone called on him?'

'Twice!' said Nora triumphantly. 'He wouldn't answer the door. And Catherine, don't say he wasn't home. I saw the curtain twitch.'

Tell us his name, I urged silently.

'I still think we should give him the benefit of the doubt.' Catherine wasn't giving up without a struggle.

'Of course. But no matter what you think, it's odd, isn't it? He made no secret of his dislike for poor Mr Abercrombie, wouldn't even speak to him. Now the dear man's dead, and Harold's disappeared from church. I call it peculiar, to say the least.'

Harold. Harold. *Last name, please?*

But there our luck failed us. The waitress bringing an order to the table next to ours somehow managed to drop a large glass of beer, which shattered, spewing froth everywhere, and making a good deal of noise. All conversation stopped for an instant, all heads turned toward the commotion, and in the sudden quiet I heard a shushing sound from the St Anne's table.

'Over there . . . asking a lot of questions . . . accident . . .'

I made a rueful face, gave Alan a shrug and sat back to wait for my hamburger.

FIFTEEN

'Harold,' I said when we had eaten and were on our way back to our room for a nap. 'How many Harolds will there be on the parish rolls?'

'Could be several. It's a popular name.'

'How are we going to find out?'

'Ask someone.'

Alan can sometimes point out the obvious in a most irritating way. 'No kidding. But who? Not Mr Lewison. He could give us a list of Harolds, if there really are several, but he won't know the parishioners well enough to identity this particular Harold. And I doubt if any of the pro-Abercrombie crowd will talk to us anymore. I heard a distinct clank of closing ranks back there at Jack's, and I thought it was strange. I would have thought they'd want to bring his murderer to book, if there is a murderer out there somewhere.'

'Ah, but to do that they'd have to admit that their paragon had done something to make someone want to murder him. And that would force them to admit that their own attitudes about the man might be wrong. No, you're right. They won't talk. But we know two people who might.'

'Phil!' I said.

'And Robin.'

'Robin wouldn't talk to us before. He dried up like the desert in summer.'

'That was before Alice was injured. That may change things.'

'You don't think he's in love with her, too?'

'No, I don't. I think he's a man who will guard his tongue until he finds it necessary and productive to speak. A suicide attempt might meet those conditions. Let's sleep on it, shall we?'

We slept longer than we usually did in the afternoon. Last night had been short, and the past few days stressful. The room was almost too warm when I finally opened my eyes to see the afternoon sun streaming in. I looked at the bedside clock.

'Good grief, Alan, it's after four. We've slept the day away.'

'We needed the rest. I do hate to remind you, but we're not—'

'Getting any younger. I know, I know. I think we need to go see Phil.'

'I have another idea. It's tea time. Let's pop over to the Georgian House and see if perchance Robin is there. If not, we can have a quick cup of tea ourselves and then search out Phil.'

'I'm not in the least hungry. But I am thirsty, and they do good tea. And Robin likes the place. He might just be there. You're on.'

There was no one in the bar when we walked in, but the barman, seeing us look around, said, 'You might want to have your pint, or your tea, in the garden. Fine afternoon.'

'What a good idea,' said Alan. 'Through here?'

There were several people eating and drinking in the garden, and sure enough, there at a table by himself, was Robin with what was left of a pint in front of him.

I was uncertain about barging in on him, but he looked up, gave us his sardonic smile and gestured. We obediently came and sat down.

'The game is afoot?' he asked by way of greeting.

'Yes, if you're willing to assist, Watson,' said Alan. 'Tea and scones, please,' he said to the waitress. 'For three?' he asked Robin, who nodded.

'In what way do you want me to assist?' he asked quietly when the waitress was out of hearing. 'You'll have learned that I'm not, shall we say, heartbroken at the man's death.'

'Yes,' I said. 'Nor are we, as you may have surmised. We've heard conflicting stories about him, wildly conflicting, I may say, but I'm afraid we're inclined to believe the negative ones.'

'With a grain of salt,' Alan added.

'No one,' said Robin, 'is wholly evil. Hitler, they say, truly loved his dog.'

The implication shocked me. 'You're saying . . . you're comparing—'

'Let me tell you a story. It is hearsay; I was not there. Accept it or not as you wish. An American man, a widower who attended the church where Abercrombie was rector, has a daughter, only the one. A couple of years ago she was expecting her first child, the man's first grandchild. She developed serious complications and was airlifted to a hospital in a much bigger city some distance away. The man phoned his rector in the middle of the night to ask if he would come to the hospital with him and pray for his daughter, who was at grave risk, and administer what is sometimes, erroneously, called the Last Rites.

'Abercrombie had turned on his answering machine. The man left an urgent message. He did not receive a return call. He went to the hospital alone. His daughter survived, barely. The baby did not. She will never be able to have another, and her husband, who badly wanted children, has left her.'

Robin cleared his throat. 'That man is the dearest friend of a member of the Parish Church here. They met at a conference in London, some years ago, something to do with computers – well, that doesn't matter. What does matter is that they are like brothers. The parishioner here sings in the choir. We have become good friends, close enough that he told me the story.'

Our tea arrived. I poured out with a shaking hand, too upset to speak.

'You may be interested to know,' Robin added when we had sipped some scalding tea, 'that Abercrombie never sent condolences, never referred to the matter at all until the man accosted him about it. He said he never listened to his phone messages; he got so many crank calls he'd begun to ignore them all. He apparently told the woman's father that he couldn't have done anything anyway, he wasn't a doctor, the baby would have died with or without his presence, so what was the fuss all about?'

I was hard put not to cry. A childless woman myself, I could not listen to such a story without a visceral reaction to the heart-break of it all. Alan, who has children and grandchildren, recovered his equanimity before I did – but he had to clear his throat before he could speak.

'Why did you decide to tell us this story?' he asked. 'You were unwilling earlier to explain, or even admit, your dislike of the man.'

'Alice Small could have died. It's quite possible she meant to die. That man – whom, incidentally, I did not dislike, but hated to the core of my being – has caused enough tragedy. If I can prevent more, I believe it my duty to do so.'

'Then are you willing to give us the name of the man at St Anne's?'

'I will give it to you with the understanding that, if you discover that he was responsible for Abercrombie's death, I will deny everything I told you and will, if he is arrested for murder, use all of my resources – and they are not inconsiderable – to set him free.'

'Robin,' I said, around the lump in my throat, 'do you know Alice's story?'

'The bones of it, yes. She did not tell me, but my friend had heard it from his friend, who had known Alice's sister from his church. Alice told you?'

'Yes. I think because we're strangers, foreigners. We'll leave soon and she'll never see us again. And because she had to tell somebody. The poison was eating at her like acid.'

'Yes. Hatred does that. My friend's name is Harold Guillot.' He pronounced it the French way, *ghi-yo*. 'One of the old Alderney families; French background. Mr Lewison may be able to tell you where he lives. I will not. A foolish scruple, perhaps, but there you are.'

'Would you tell us where he works?'

'He is retired.' Robin stood. 'I won't wish you well in your quest, but I think I'm relieved to have told you. It washes my hands of any responsibility in the matter. Just call me Pilate.'

We had gone back to the room. I lay on the bed, staring at the ceiling, watching the play of light as the evening slowly, slowly faded toward night. Alan sat in the chair pretending to read.

'I want to go home,' I said after an eternity of silence. 'Now. Tomorrow. As soon as we can get a flight.'

'Do you?'

'Yes. I don't want to know what happened to Mr William Bloody Abercrombie. I hope someone *did* push him down that hill.'

'You've said that before. You know you don't really hope that, not in your heart and soul.'

'He was a monster! A murderer himself, if there's any meaning to the word. Murderers are put to death.'

'In America, perhaps. Not here, not anymore. Two wrongs

don't make a right, if you'll excuse the cliché.' He came over and lay down on the bed beside me. 'You're tired, love, exhausted with other people's troubles. They're terrible troubles, and you've never learned to pass by on the other side. You try to shoulder everyone's woes. You're not Atlas. It's not your job.'

The tears were beginning to come. 'Somebody has to care. I can't just ignore somebody's pain.'

'No. But when it eats you alive, leaves you with no resources, leaves you wanting to give up, your compassion doesn't help you or anyone else.'

'I . . . it's too much, Alan! If I hear one more story about what that man did to someone, I'll . . . fall apart, I think. I want to go home and forget I ever heard of this island.'

'The trouble is, you would never forget.'

I lay letting the tears flow, holding Alan's hand.

After a while I felt the discomfort of wet hair, dampened by tears flowing unchecked. My pillow was wet, too, and my nose . . . I sat up. 'I need a tissue.'

Alan was ready with a handful.

'I must look awful.'

'I've seen you looking better, for a fact.'

That pulled me together as no sympathy would have. I muttered something and got up to splash cold water on my face. I didn't look in the mirror. Puffy red eyes and a red nose aren't a pretty sight.

'You think we ought to stay,' I said, coming back and collapsing onto the bed again.

'I'm not going to make that decision. If you want to go, I'll call Aurigny tonight and book a flight.'

'Who's Aurigny?' I blew my nose again.

'The airline that flies here. Also the old French name of the island.'

'Oh. I forgot.'

He patted my hand, got up and rummaged in the drawer where we kept our food supplies. He held aloft a bottle of wine. 'I'm not usually in favour of curing one's troubles with alcohol, but in this case, I think a little wine might be a comfort. Yes?'

'All right. I don't care.'

'Dorothy.'

I looked up listlessly.

'I love you and I think you're a marvellous person, no matter what you decide to do. Now have some wine and snap out of it.'

The room was growing dim. It was really late. I'd had nothing to eat since lunch, having lost my appetite with Robin's horror story. I wasn't hungry, but if I was going to drink wine, I'd better have something to eat. 'Do we still have any cheese or anything?'

'Not a crumb. There's a pizza place in the High Street, just at the top of Victoria Street, or we could have Chinese takeaway, or Indian, or Thai. Anything sound appealing?'

'Not really. You choose. I suppose we have to eat something.'

'All right.' He took out his phone. 'How about some nice vindaloo?'

'No! You know I can't stand that hot stuff. I changed my mind about you choosing. Get Chinese. You know what I like.'

He phoned in an order and then took off to pick up the food. It would probably be ready by the time he walked up the street. I used the time while he was gone to shower and change into night things. I wanted to look a little less forlorn when he came back.

It's amazing what a shower can do for one's spirits. Somehow, along with the grime of the day, some of the day's worries washed away. I came out feeling much better, cleansed in mind as well as body. I dried my hair and brushed it into some sort of order, put on my nightgown and poured wine just as Alan came in.

'I got a pizza, too, and stopped in at Nellie Gray's, as well.'

'Heavens! We'll never be able to eat all that.'

'They're good about letting us keep stuff in the fridge downstairs. I thought comfort food was in order.'

'I'm sorry I was such a wimp. I don't usually fall apart like that.'

'I know you don't. No apology needed. Now would you rather start with Mongolian beef, lamb korma or pepperoni pizza?'

'I'll have a little of each. I'm going to have the most awful heartburn.'

He put a loaded plate in front of me on the bed and handed me a glass of wine, and sat down on the other side with his own meal, dangerously rocking mine. 'If we manage to eat this without getting cheese and soy sauce all over the bedding, it'll be a miracle,' I said.

'*Mph*,' he said with his mouth full.

I found I was hungry, after all, and we made respectable inroads on our peculiar supper, and finished the wine. I helped Alan tidy away and opened the window wide to help dispel the strong smell of garlic.

As Alan turned out the light, ready to crawl into bed, I said, 'Don't make any phone calls. We're staying to see this through.'

He ruffled my hair and kissed my cheek, and we were both asleep in minutes.

SIXTEEN

Sunday dawned clear and cool, another beautiful day. I woke early. Alan was still snoring away, so I made a cup of tea as quietly as I could, left Alan a note and went down to the garden.

The chairs were wet with dew, but I had put on heavy jeans, so it didn't matter. By the time they soaked through, I'd be ready to come in anyway.

There is a special feeling about Sunday morning. It isn't just the absence of the usual bustle and noise of everyday life. There's a sense of peace, a hush as if the ordinary has been banished for a brief moment. At home, where the Cathedral's bells peal out before every service, the hush is somehow enhanced by their clamour, rather than disturbed.

Here in the garden, with the dew-diamonds sparkling from every leaf, every petal, it might have been the morning of the world, Eden before the serpent.

I had not forgotten the shadow that lay over us. How could I? The stories of the anguish caused by one wicked man would haunt me for the rest of my life. Here in this peace, though, it was possible to believe that there was justice, if not in this world, then in the next, and that in the end all manner of thing would be well.

I closed my eyes, basking in the warmth of the sun and the serenity of my thoughts, when Alan spoke.

'Sleeping in the sun?'

'No, actually just thinking about Julian of Norwich.'

'"And all shall be well, and all shall be well . . ." Not a bad antidote to yesterday's angst.'

'In this place, on a Sunday morning, I can believe it. Later, of course . . .'

'Yes. So let's enjoy it while we can.'

He had brought a fresh pot of tea and his own cup. We sat in amiable silence and drank our tea.

We began to hear activity from the kitchen. Voices, the clatter of pans. Alan looked at his watch. 'I was going to ask if you wanted to go to church at eight or ten thirty, but the question is now moot.'

'What time is it?'

'Eight forty-two.'

'Well, then, I'd better get out of these sopping wet jeans and into Sunday go-to-meetin' clothes.'

'You can take the woman out of America, but you can't take the Yank out—'

'Yank, indeed! That's pure southern lingo, I'll have you know. My mama was from a tiny little town near the Indiana/Kentucky/Illinois border, and she talked southern all her life. She'd've been mighty insulted to be called a Yank.' I had tried to put on my best Hoosier accent, but it didn't come off. I've spent too long in England to remember how folks talk back home. The thought made me sad for a moment, but only for a moment. The Sunday peace was still upon me.

When we went down to breakfast I was sure I couldn't eat anything much after last night's late, wildly assorted supper, but the smells were irresistible. 'The works, please!' I said to the waitress. 'Except no beans.'

She laughed. 'Americans never want beans. I can't think why.'

The English have this very odd habit of eating beans with breakfast, to go along with the bacon and sausages and eggs and mushrooms and all. I guess it's an acquired taste. I don't plan to acquire it.

We had finished eating and I was on my second cup of coffee when the bells began to ring. St Anne's, I had read, had a very fine ring of twelve bells, and twenty ringers to do them justice. I didn't know enough about change ringing to know what 'method' they were using, hearing only a delightful cacophony, what Dorothy L. Sayers called 'the one loud noise that is made to the glory of God.'

'Let's go a bit early,' I said to Alan. 'I'd like to have some quiet time before the service begins.'

'Quiet?' replied Alan, cocking his head, the better to catch the strident tones of the bells.

'In a manner of speaking.'

The bells grew louder the closer we got to the church, but inside the sound was somewhat muted. The congregation, however, was buzzing a bit. At home, worshippers entered in silence and conversed, if at all, in hushed whispers before the service began. Here, people greeted each other and inquired after family and other concerns. It was quite a lot like a family reunion. Here and there signs of sorrow were evident, but I realized that what Phil had said was very true. Most people didn't care much about what had happened to William Abercrombie.

How terribly sad.

We found a place near the back, hoping we weren't taking someone else's usual pew, and knelt a moment to try to pray, though the conversation around us made it a little difficult. The choir lined up, Mr Lewison said a prayer, and the service began.

With slight variations, it was the service we enjoyed every Sunday at Sherebury Cathedral. Some of the responses were slightly different. The choir, which I noticed was led by Rebecca Smith, was a good one for a small church, but of course it wasn't the fine cathedral choir we were used to. But we were comforted by the familiar words, the familiar hymns, the deeply satisfying mystery of the Eucharist.

I thought for a moment about some friends who came to church with me, back in Indiana, years ago. They were Baptists, unfamiliar with a liturgical service. I couldn't remember now what special occasion had led me to invite them to my church, but they came, and were, I think, mystified by the way we did things. 'All that kneeling and standing and all,' they said afterwards. 'And such a measly little sermon. Do you really do that same thing every single Sunday?'

'Well, the Bible readings change every week, and some of the prayers. But yes, it's basically the same thing every Sunday.'

They were too polite to say that they found it boring beyond belief, but I could see it in their eyes. I couldn't find the words to tell them how soothing and reassuring I found the liturgy, how I looked forward to those same beloved words and actions every Sunday. To each his own.

The final hymn was one I particularly loved, 'I heard the voice of Jesus say,' set to a lovely tune by the great English composer of church music, Thomas Tallis. In its quotation of

Jesus' invitation to rest in Him, I found comfort not only for me, but, I hoped, for the soul of William Abercrombie. If even he could find rest, surely I could.

Leaving the church in that exalted frame of mind, I was in no way prepared for what Mr Lewison told us after the service.

We had partaken of the refreshments after the service, had chatted briefly with a few of the parishioners and had stopped to shake hands with the priest on our way out. He asked us to stay behind for a moment, so we tarried in the churchyard, reading some of the interesting names on the stones. 'A lot of French influence,' I commented.

'As one would expect,' said Alan. 'We're a mere eight miles from France, and of course the whole island was Norman property for centuries.'

I'm not good about the intricacies of property traded back and forth between England and France at the whim of various monarchs over the millennia. I kept still.

Mr Lewison hurried out of the church as soon as his duties were completed and he could get away from the last lingering churchgoer. 'I have something rather disturbing to tell you,' he said. 'Perhaps we could find a private place to talk. I'm staying at the vicarage, but it's a bit of a walk, and I didn't bring my car.'

'We're at the Belle Isle, just across the street,' I said. 'Why don't we go there? No one will be in the lounge at this hour.'

So we settled down in the lounge and looked at the priest inquiringly.

He seemed ill at ease. 'This is embarrassing. I hardly know how to begin.'

'I'm sorry we have no sherry or anything to offer you. We can make tea, though. Would you care for some?' I hoped he would say no. I'd had enough caffeine to keep me flying for hours. Three cups of tea, two of coffee . . . I was also needing the bathroom soon.

'No, thank you. I must say this and get it over.'

Now I was ill at ease. What on earth?

'I had a conversation last night with Constable Partridge.' He took a deep breath. 'He plans to talk to you, also, but he thought I should know first. He has had word from America about Mr Abercrombie.'

My nerves tightened. Alan reached across the couch and touched my hand.

'Partridge was able to speak with Abercrombie's diocesan bishop in Ohio. He learned that the man had no living family at all, so we could do as we wished with funeral arrangements. He also learned . . . this is distressing. I'm sorry.'

Beads of perspiration appeared on the priest's forehead, though it was not warm in the room.

'It seems that Mr Abercrombie would have been severely disciplined, probably excommunicated, even defrocked, had he stayed in his diocese. He was accused of having stolen more than one hundred thousand dollars from the coffers of his parish. If the crime was proven, he would of course have faced severe civil penalties as well.'

'A hundred thousand dollars!' I couldn't keep my voice down. 'We had no idea . . .' Too late, I shut my mouth.

'What my wife is saying, Mr Lewison, is that we had some inkling of this sort of thing, learned from various people. The scale of it, however, is staggering.'

'You knew? But why did you not tell me? These parishioners are my flock only temporarily, but this news will be devastating to them. Further, I must make a decision now about his burial. If this is true, I would have scruples about burying him in consecrated ground. I should have known as soon as possible.'

'We were told a story in confidence, Father.' I used the title out of habit. 'We didn't feel at liberty to pass it on. Now I suppose it would be better to tell you the whole thing.'

I told him Alice's story as simply as I could, shorn of all but the essential facts. At some point in my narrative, Alan slipped out of the room.

'And I'd better tell you what else we've heard. It doesn't make good hearing, but it has a bearing on your burial decision, among other things.' I looked around for Alan, but he hadn't returned. 'It concerns, indirectly, another of the parishioners, Harold Guillot.'

'I don't believe I know him. But tell me, please.'

I tried to leave my emotions out of it, but I couldn't. I was near tears by the time I finished the story. 'If it were my deci-sion, Father – which thank God it is not – I wouldn't bury the man within ten miles of consecrated ground. But you have to remember that both stories are hearsay. It's remotely possible that they're not true.'

'The report from his bishop is certainly true. There's been an audit. The diocesan lawyers were preparing a case when he disappeared.'

The man sounded near tears himself. Where, I thought desperately, was Alan? I need some support in this thing.

He walked into the room at that moment, carrying a large paper bag. 'I had a feeling we required sustenance,' he said, taking a bottle, some glasses and a small box out of the bag. 'Sherry. I hope you like Amontillado, Mr Lewison. And digestives. Sorry about the plastic glasses. At least they're approximately the right size and shape.'

SEVENTEEN

The wine and biscuits helped restore a more normal atmosphere in the room.

'Thank you,' said the priest after downing half a glass. 'I was distraught. I am still, for that matter, but your hospitality has helped. Mr Nesbitt, as a policeman, what do you think I should do? Should any of this appalling history go to the police?'

'Since they know about the American charges, and since nothing can be done about the matter, with the accused lying dead, I see no reason to fill in any of the details. To the police, that is. You must decide for yourself what to tell the vicar of this parish, and the bishop.'

'The bishop, yes. The decision about burial must be left to him. It's a weighty matter, refusing Christian burial. And what I'm to tell the dear ladies of the parish I do not know. They adored the man! And I confess I was completely taken in by him myself. His manner was above reproach, and he was a genuine help in so many ways. I blame myself very much.' He was actually wringing his hands.

'But plainly the vicar thought the same, or he would not have allowed the man to continue in his activities,' said Alan.

'And at least,' I added, 'since he'd not yet passed the various screenings, he was not allowed to act as a priest. You can be grateful for that, at any rate. You don't have to worry about any possibly invalid sacraments.'

'No. You're right. We must be grateful at least for that small blessing.' He put his glass down. 'I must go and offer what comfort I can to poor Mrs Small. I don't know what I shall tell her, but I trust I will be guided.'

'Let us know how she's doing, will you?'

'Certainly. Mr Nesbitt. Mrs Martin.' He gave the slightest of bows and hurried off.

'*Well!*' I kicked my shoes off. 'That was a stunner, all right. Even though we knew most of it. Having it confirmed officially . . .'

'And the amount of money! That's – what – sixty thousand pounds or so?'

'More than that, at the present rate. The last time I looked, that would amount to about sixty-five thousand. Major money. How on earth did he manage to sift off that much from a parish budget?'

'Large, wealthy parish, would be my guess. And criminally inadequate oversight!'

'Indeed. And Alice Small's sister gets a sniff of it, and dies for her pains. I am reminded of something Lord Peter once said about an ingenious and diabolical criminal: "My religious beliefs are a little ill-defined, but I hope something really beastly happens to him in the next world."'

'Of course, if we were all to get our just deserts . . .' said Alan.

'Oh, you're right, of course. And I'm not to judge. Take it as read. All the same, I really can't work up a lot of enthusiasm for tracking down his murderer. If there is one.'

'Nevertheless, I think we need to talk to Mr Guillot, if we can find him.'

'Do we have to do it today, though? It's Sunday, and somehow . . .'

'I understand. No, I don't imagine one day will make much difference. Why don't we go and find ourselves a proper Sunday lunch, and then go down to the harbour and ride the train?'

'Ride it to where?'

'Nowhere in particular. That's part of the fun. Come, let's see who serves Sunday lunch.'

We stopped and asked someone on the street and were told that Le Pesked, despite their French-sounding name, did an excellent roast beef and Yorkshire pudding, and as it was almost next door, we decided to try it. 'I wonder what a "pesked" is?' I mused. Alan didn't know.

We weren't sorry about our choice. We discovered that our stomachs were set to somewhat different clocks than most of Alderney; we were the only customers in the place when we walked in. But the staff was friendly, the service was fast and the food delicious. It was indeed traditionally English, but with a subtle French flair.

We never did find out what 'pesked' meant, though the

sign implied that it was some sort of fish. Alderney French, perhaps.

I was ready for a nap, but the train left at two thirty, and we had to get out of our church clothes and then get down to the harbour to catch it, so we ambled, full of food, down Braye Road to the station, and Alan told me about the train.

'It was originally built to carry materials from the quarry down where they were building the breakwater. That was in the middle of the eighteenth century. Over the years its function and location have changed somewhat, but its main use for most of its career was hauling stone. Now it's simply an excursion train for tourists, and runs only in summer except for Easter and Christmas, when they have special runs, mostly for children, with eggs at Easter and presents at Christmas.'

'Where do you *get* all this stuff?'

'From the source of all wisdom, O best beloved. The Internet.'

'You don't have a computer here.'

'I looked up a good deal before we left home. I like to plan ahead.'

'But where does it *go*? The island isn't that big.'

He took his map out of his pocket, unfolded it and showed me the route that was laid out. 'I'm told the lighthouse is well worth a visit, if we want to stick around and come back on the second run.'

'Why not? We can pretend we're on vacation.'

The train was driven by Suzi, the hedgehog lady. I'd grown accustomed to the many roles played by Alderney people and was only mildly surprised. I *was* surprised, and amused, to see that the train cars (all two of them) were from the London Underground, complete with the maps above the windows. 'Look,' I said, pointing. 'We're headed for King's Cross.'

'Long journey,' said Alan. 'Especially since we're leaving from Swiss Cottage, which isn't on the same line.'

He pointed out the sign posted above the door to the tiny station. I giggled. 'I was wrong when I said we were in a Christmas village. No. We've gone Through the Looking Glass to the place where everything is backwards and upside down.'

We started with much important blowing of whistles and

clanging of bells, and headed out, past a few houses and then into open country. We crossed a road or two, again with whistles; at one crossing, a man and his dog waited patiently for us to pass, and waved as we went by. The wildflowers were spectacular.

The quarry, when we came to it, was as ugly as most quarries. Long disused machinery sat rusting, a blot on the landscape. 'Someone ought to clean that up,' I whispered to Alan. 'A disgrace to Alderney.'

'Costs money, love. And it wouldn't be easy, given the terrain and the remote location. Look in the other direction.'

I looked and saw the sea, glittering in the sun, and smiled. 'All in one's point of view, isn't it?'

It was a brief journey. We pulled into the station at the north end of the line and saw the lighthouse just over the hill. Alan asked Suzi about the schedule and was assured that we had plenty of time to go and see it. 'We'll signal ten minutes before we're ready to leave. And we'll wait for you if you're not here. There's no rush.'

That seemed to be the philosophy on Alderney. No rush.

The path to the lighthouse was a little harder going than I had anticipated, and I wished I'd worn boots instead of slippery sneakers. But with the occasional help of Alan's arm I made it unscathed, and there it was, gleaming white with a broad black band.

'I never realized a lighthouse was so big. They don't look huge in pictures.'

'Ah,' said Alan. It's one of his favourite non-reply replies, usually meaning he found my comment too inane for a reasonable rejoinder. Well, he was perhaps right about that. This time.

There was a small admission fee to tour the place, and when we had paid we joined the small crowd gathered around our guide.

Robin!

Why didn't that surprise me? He was an authority on local history, and the lighthouse was historic. I wondered if we'd have any chance to talk to him privately.

He greeted us with the same impersonal smile he bestowed on everyone and launched into the story of the structure.

It seemed the lighthouse had an active life, with a light keeper, of a little over eighty years, during most of which the light was fuelled by kerosene (he called it 'paraffin'). The enormous rotating lens magnified the light's power, so that it could be seen for many miles out to sea, and the fog horn had amazing range and power as well. Sadly (to my mind), the light was altered for electric power in the seventies sometime, and was now decommissioned altogether, replaced by two LED lights on the outside of the tower. The light keeper was long gone, and though the giant horn remained on the tower, it no longer sounded. The whole thing was now controlled electronically from somewhere in England.

'There is *no* romance left,' I muttered as Robin explained that modern navigational aids made powerful lights and foghorns unnecessary.

But the impressive lens was still there, if disused, and the views from various levels of the tower were terrific. The climb to the very top, up a steep ladder with handholds in the steps, was a bit scary, but I managed it and felt triumphant.

'Well,' I said as we got back to the bottom and were ready to head back to the train, 'now I've seen a lighthouse. It wasn't on my bucket list, but it would have been had I known they were so interesting. Now, where's Robin?'

'We haven't a lot of time to get back to the train, Dorothy. And it's rather a long walk back to the harbour on a hot day.'

'No rush,' I said airily, inwardly smiling at Alan's description. A 'hot day' in southern Indiana meant temperatures and humidity levels both in the nineties. A temperature in the sixties with a fresh sea breeze was not 'hot' to me, though I admitted the sun was a bit warm. 'Ah, there he is.'

Robin was chatting to a pair of elderly ladies, pointing to various parts of the house surrounding the tower. I moved up beside them and tried to catch his eye. He steadfastly ignored me. They talked on and on.

I heard the whistle of the train. Alan came up beside me and touched my arm. 'We must get back, Dorothy.'

'They won't leave without us. Suzi said so.'

The two ladies left, reluctantly, and Robin turned to go, still ignoring us.

'Robin, wait.' He turned, and the look he gave me wasn't encouraging.

'Have you heard the news?' I asked.

'About what?' He sounded forbidding.

'The Americans have told our police that Abercrombie was on the verge of being arrested for theft.'

'The least of his sins, I'd have thought.'

'But don't you care that the story has been confirmed officially? It made us feel – I don't know – vindicated, somehow.'

'I was never in doubt about any of the stories. Nothing that man did would surprise me. Unless he was found to have been altruistic and compassionate.'

The whistle sounded again, several toots.

'But will you tell Harold, please?'

'Why? It makes no difference. The man is beyond the reach of human justice and is now incapable of making restitution for any of his many crimes against humanity. You'd better go.'

We went, at a speed that surprised even me. Suzi, from the window of the little engine, gave us a look as we bounded onto the platform. We hurled ourselves through the doors just as they were closing.

EIGHTEEN

'I thought he'd be interested, at least.' I was feeling put out.

'My dear woman, he put his thoughts quite succinctly. What difference does it make now? All the damage is done, and the one who did it has been placed past all human retribution. The only matter that now concerns Robin is whether his friend Harold had a hand in putting him there.'

'Oh. I hadn't thought of it that way.' I hit myself on the forehead. 'Stupid, stupid.'

We'd gone back to our B & B, had our naps and were back to our problem.

'We need to talk to the chap,' said Alan. 'More sherry?'

'No, I've had quite enough, thank you. I wouldn't mind another couple of biscuits, though. How are we going to find him, to talk to him?'

'Robin suggested Mr Lewison.'

'He doesn't know him. He told me so, just before you came back this morning.'

'He'll be on the parish rolls.'

'They'll be kept in the church somewhere, probably under lock and key. I suppose there's always the phone book. There must be one downstairs somewhere.'

'I'll look.' He put down his empty glass and left the room, to return after only a couple of minutes. 'No listing for Guillot. He may use a mobile only; so many people do these days.'

'Drat. I don't want to disturb Mr Lewison today. He has enough to deal with. That poor man didn't know what he was getting into when he took this temporary job!'

Alan ran a hand down the back of his head. He was thinking. 'I wonder,' he said. 'I don't want this to drag on too long. I have an uneasy feeling . . . Do you suppose we could find Martha Duckett? She would know where Guillot lives, and she'd be indignant about his attitudes, so she might tell us.'

'That's a great idea, Alan. And I'll bet she's the old-fashioned type who still has a landline. I'll go down with you to look her up.'

Martha was in the phone book. She was at home. Yes, she said disapprovingly, she knew where Mr Guillot lived. (She pronounced his name 'ghillet', to rhyme with skillet, another sign of her dislike, I thought.) No, she didn't have his phone number. Why would she want to call him? No, she didn't have the address, but she could tell us where his house was.

'Here, I'll let you speak to Alan. He's much better at directions than I am.'

He repeated them after her, and I began to write them down. They sounded complicated enough that I wished we had a better map, ours being sketchy in the extreme.

'White with blue shutters and a red door. Right. Thank you so much.'

'Sounds like we'll need to leave a trail of breadcrumbs,' I said when he'd rung off. 'We should have bought an OS map.'

'They're not always of much help in town. You jotted it all down?'

'As soon as she had you turning off the High Street into something I couldn't spell. I suppose it must be French, like so much around here.'

'And not even pronounced like proper French, but in the local patois.'

'I wrote it down phonetically, as best I could.'

'Ah, well. We can but try. How lost can we get on an island this size?'

'We keep saying that, but I have my doubts. If it had sounded easy, I'd have been willing to start out right away, but it isn't easy and I'm not up to a hunt at this point. I'm hungry. Do you suppose the Thai place is open on Sundays? The food was really good.'

'If not, we could always fall back on the takeaway we stashed in the fridge last night.'

'It would be pretty awful cold, and I've never asked if we could use the microwave.'

'Then let's go to Nellie Gray's. I know it's open on Sunday; the sign says so. And it's in the right direction; we can go from there on our search for Harold.'

'You know what I'd really like to do? I'd like to sit down in our own kitchen in my bathrobe for leftover meatloaf and some brownies.'

Alan gave me a look.

'All right, that's my grumble for the evening. Let me put on some decent pants and shoes, and we'll go do Indian.'

We had a light meal, which was very good, as I'd come to expect. I really do like Indian food; I was just being contrary, and besides, we'd had some last night. No matter. Onward and upward.

Literally. We toiled on up Victoria Street, turned left into the High Street, and then tried to follow Martha's directions.

Most of my transcriptions were wildly off, but we persevered with the help of the landmarks she had mentioned, finding ourselves eventually in something called La Brecque Philippe. 'What do you suppose it means?' I asked.

'Haven't the faintest. This would be old Norman French evolved into Alderney French, and I learned only the standard modern language. Look for a white house with blue shutters and a red door. Martha didn't know the number, but said it was quite a long way up the street.'

Like almost all Alderney streets, this one was on a slope. The grade wasn't too bad, but I was tired, and not looking forward to the conversation we hoped to have.

There were plenty of white houses, several with blue shutters, several with red doors. We finally came to one with both.

Evening was beginning, as the poets like to say, to lower. 'Getting home is going to be fun,' I said. 'We should have brought a flashlight.'

'I remember the way,' said Alan. 'Most of it,' he amended, which didn't make me feel a bit better. He went to the door, picked up the brass knocker and let it fall, once, twice, three times.

Somewhere in a neighbour's garden a dog barked. A blackbird trilled in a tree several yards away.

He knocked again, hammering hard.

Nothing.

'He's obviously not home,' I said, perhaps more relieved than disappointed. 'We'll have to try again tomorrow.'

'I wish we had his phone number.'

'Me, too. Maybe if we see Robin again we can ask him for it. We can tell him we already know where he lives.'

'If this is indeed the right house.'

'Oh, dear. Yes, there's that. Well, tomorrow we can maybe get at the parish rolls and find out his phone number and his proper address, and make sure.' I couldn't help sighing, and Alan took my hand.

'I'm sorry, love. This is turning out to be a wretched holiday for you.'

'A bit like the curate's egg, perhaps. "Parts of it are excellent, m'lord",' I quoted, and we both laughed. 'Anyway, it's not your fault. We just seem to fall into these things. I sometimes remind myself of a cartoon character from my childhood. There was a strip with a guy named Joe something – a name with no vowels in it at all. If you tried to pronounce it, it sounded like a sneeze. Anyway, he walked around with a little black cloud over his head all the time, spreading disaster wherever he went. I look up now and then to see if there's a little black cloud there.'

Alan peered, and shook his head. 'All I see is a rainbow, my dear.'

After which delightful comment he took my arm, and we walked contentedly back to our room.

We woke early Monday to a truly disgusting day. A weather front had moved in overnight, with cold winds and fitful rain. I was sorely tempted not to get up at all, but I could smell breakfast being prepared, and my stomach decided it needed sustenance. So I dragged myself out, dressed in clothes that would dry quickly if I was forced to go outside, and we got to the breakfast room just as they opened up.

'I think I want porridge, please. And coffee.' It was that kind of a day. At home I would have called it oatmeal and made it with raisins and possibly apples, but this wasn't home. I was deeply suspicious of other people's porridge, but it was worth a try. Alan opted for the same, and shook his head when I spooned coffee sugar in liberally. Defiantly, I asked the waitress for some butter, and put quite a lot of that in, too.

It actually wasn't bad. Not like home, but smooth, hot, tasty. 'All right, I don't care if you think the way I like oatmeal is

weird. It's the way I grew up with, so there. And I feel much
better about the weather with some comfort food inside me.
Now what on earth are we going to do today? It's the kind of
rain that penetrates any defences. And darn it, I was going to
go down to the harbour and do a little laundry.'

The waitress, who was clearing away our dishes, stopped and
said, 'You can give me your laundry if you like, madam. I can
do it here when we've finished with the linens.'

I had dimly realized that she was not only waitress, but cook
– and now it appeared that she was laundress, as well. And a
real sweetheart. 'Why, bless your heart! It'll just be one load –
underwear and one outfit that I got really muddy the first day
we were here. Are you sure it won't be too much trouble?'

'No trouble at all. You don't want to be walking all the way
down to the harbour on a day like this!'

A gust of wind flung rain against the front window. It hit
like a handful of pebbles. No, indeed, I didn't want to step foot
outside my cosy den.

'Oh, and I meant to ask, we put some leftover takeaway in
the fridge. Would anyone mind if I popped it into the microwave?
I promise I'll clean up any mess I might make.'

'There's one in the lounge that's meant for guests, for just
that sort of thing. Have you not seen it? Here, I'll show you.'

So that settled lunch. We had no table wine left, but tea would
do in a pinch.

I went up to get my laundry, gave it to the girl with my
profound thanks, and settled down in the lounge with Alan and
the morning papers.

After we'd worked our way through *The Times* and the
Telegraph, I went upstairs and brought down a selection of the
books we'd bought at Annie's. The wind blew. The rain continued.

At about ten I could stand it no longer. I was reading the same
page of my book over and over, and absorbing none of it. I tossed
it aside and stood up. 'This is ridiculous! We ought to be doing
something.'

Alan laid his book down. 'I agree. I've thought about hiring
a car. I wonder if they'd deliver one here.'

'You can ask.' My lethargy was gone. The thought of being
able to go anywhere we liked, quickly, was intoxicating. I had

never realized how much a car meant until we didn't have one. 'Honestly, I love to walk, but it's very limiting, isn't it?'

'Especially on a day that makes one think about building an ark. I know I saw some advertisements for car hire somewhere.'

'There should be phone numbers in here.' I picked up the glossy Alderney guide book from the coffee table, and leafed through. 'Here you are. You do have brilliant ideas occasionally, my dear!'

We were given a street map of Alderney with the car, much more detailed than the one in the tourist guide. It also, thank heaven, had the one-way streets clearly marked. We hadn't paid a lot of attention while we were walking; now we realized that in a car we'd need to make a round-about approach to Harold Guillot's house. 'If,' Alan reminded me, 'that is his house. I think our first stop needs to be the church, to look him up.'

'And if that fails, I've had a thought. Surely the police would have contact information for everyone on the island.'

'Mmm. Probably. But my dear, do we really want to go to the police and tell them we're looking for Harold Guillot, who had an excellent reason for hating Abercrombie?'

'Oh. I suppose not. St Anne's first, then.'

But there was no one at St Anne's, and no indication of where the parish directory might be. 'It was really stupid of us not to get Mr Lewison's phone number,' I said. 'And I have no idea where the vicarage is. Now what?'

Alan had been thinking while I'd been fulminating. 'I'd say there's a good chance he's visiting Alice. We need to do that, in any case, and if he's not there, the hospital will almost certainly have his phone number.'

'Alan, something about foul weather seems to set your synapses synapsing. That's the second brilliant idea you've had today. My brain, on the other hand, seems to be about the same consistency as that oatmeal I had for breakfast.'

'You're a fair-weather sort of person,' he said. 'All that hot Indiana sunshine when you were young, perhaps. You blossom on a fine day.'

'I certainly droop on a miserable one. However. Yes, let's head to the hospital, if you think you can find it.'

NINETEEN

I had not noticed on our previous visits to the hospital how small it was. The building was modern, the staff pleasant and efficient, but there seemed to be very few rooms. We stopped at the nurses' station to ask a few questions.

'No, Mr Lewison was here earlier, but he's left. Yes, certainly I have the number of his mobile.' She gave it to us. 'And I'm sorry, but visitors aren't allowed before eleven. Clergy, of course, can visit at any time.'

'I wonder,' I said, 'where the rest of the rooms might be.'

She laughed. 'You're American, aren't you? I imagine you're accustomed to huge hospitals with hundreds of beds. We have twenty-two, fourteen of them in the continuing care wing.'

'So – um – eight beds for the ill or injured?'

'That's right.'

'You must be a healthy bunch here in Alderney!'

She laughed again. 'Anyone with a complicated problem goes to Guernsey. We deal mostly with emergencies, post-op patients and the occasional baby that comes too soon to make it to Guernsey. But yes, on the whole we are a healthy lot. Some would say too strong-willed and independent to get sick.'

'Well, then, good luck to you! And would you tell Alice that Mr Nesbitt and Mrs Martin came to visit, and we'll try to get back later today?'

'I will.' She went briskly on her way as a call bell sounded.

I phoned Mr Lewison, who looked up Guillot's address and phone number in the parish directory, which was in fact kept at the vicarage. He didn't ask why we wanted them, and I, for one, was thankful. As it was, I felt we were betraying Robin's confidence – but he hadn't said we weren't to visit the man, or even talk about him to anyone.

'Is this the number of the house we saw last night?' I asked Alan. 'I can't remember.'

'Yes, I remember seeing it on the door. Thirty-seven. It's a long street.'

We got there, eventually. The heavy rain reduced visibility and made the cobbled streets slippery, but Alan drove slowly and carefully, and finally stopped in front of Guillot's door. 'There's no place to park,' he said. He didn't sound as irritated about it as I would have. A village in this part of the world often has 'no place to park', as cars are a very recent innovation in the long history of civilization here. 'I'll stay with the car, if you wouldn't mind knocking on the door. I'm afraid you'll get very wet.'

'I have an umbrella.'

Even so, I did get very wet, and to no avail. There was no answer to my knock, and no light showing inside on such a dark day.

I brought a good deal of water into the car with me. 'It's a good thing the seats are leather,' I said, trying to arrange my raincoat to shed the least possible amount. 'Nobody's home.'

'So I saw. So the next step is the phone.'

Several rings. Voicemail. I left a brief message and punched off. 'Well, that's that. Shall we try the hospital again, or is it still too early?'

'Still a little too early. And before I forget, I'm running out of cash. Let's find a cash point somewhere.'

There were several banks in Victoria Street, one very close to our B & B. 'Alan, don't even try to park. Let me out and I'll run to the bank while you drive around. I'll wait at Belle Isle.'

'"Run" being the operative word. I think you're right, love.'

He dropped me off just in front of the bank. There was an ATM on the front wall, and I tried to shield myself with my umbrella while punching in my PIN and completing the trans-action. A sudden gust of wind caught the umbrella and turned it inside out, and in the process of trying to close it and put my money away, I dropped a twenty-pound note, which went flying.

A woman just coming up to the door stepped on it just as it was about to head for France, and bent over to pick it up and hand it to me. 'A trifle soggy,' she said with a smile, 'but still negotiable, I think. Here, you'd best come in out of the rain to deal with that brolly. Isn't this weather frightful?'

She held the door open for me. We stood and dripped in the foyer.

I had known her the moment I saw her, and when she took off her plastic rain hat and shook it, and wiped the rain off her glasses, she recognized me, too.

'Why, Mrs Martin!'

'And you're Rebecca Smith. I'm glad to run into you. I've been wanting to say how much I enjoyed the anthem on Sunday.'

'Yes, that's a beautiful setting of the Twenty-Third Psalm, isn't it? I've loved it ever since I heard it on *The Vicar of Dibley*. But one of our tenors was missing, which spoiled it a bit. One needs a good tenor section for that piece.'

'Oh, yes, I believe someone mentioned him. Mr Guillot, wasn't it?'

She gave me a sharp look. 'What have you heard about him?'

Uh-oh. She was in the Saint William camp. I'd better be careful. 'I overheard someone say that he was a regular churchgoer and a member of the choir.'

'And did someone tell you he was one of the principal forces in the group that disliked poor Mr Abercrombie?'

'Well, as a matter of fact—'

Someone walked in the door just then.

'Oh, dear, we can't stand here blocking traffic. I'll let you finish your banking.'

'I work here. And I'd better get on with it.' She pushed open the door leading to the bank proper.

I followed her. 'Actually, if you have a moment, I wondered if you have any idea where Mr Guillot might be. I'm anxious to talk to him, and he doesn't seem to be home.'

'I have no idea where he's got to, nor when he'll be back. He has never before missed choir practice, much less a Sunday service. I'm quite anxious about him; if you find him ask him to call me.' She lowered her voice. 'And you can tell him, too, that I don't believe a word of all those rumours that are going around about Mr Abercrombie and his supposed crimes back in America. I wouldn't be a bit surprised if Harold hadn't started them himself. He's probably gone off-island to avoid the backlash!'

There was no point in telling her that the 'rumours' came straight from American authorities. She'd find out soon enough, and it would upset her greatly, poor dear. I went back out in the rain and did my best imitation of a sprint across the street to wait in the doorway of Belle Isle for Alan to come round again. It occurred to me that the name was another example of Alderney French; if I remembered correctly, the 'real' French would be spelled Île.

Alan arrived, and as I got in the car, dripping still more rain on the seat, he said, 'Do you want to change into dry clothes before we visit Alice?'

'No. I'd just get wet again. Might as well wait until we're settled for a while.' I told him about my encounter with Rebecca. 'She's now definitely wary of me. I doubt she'll talk to us again about anything important.'

'Making enemies left and right, aren't we? For speaking the truth.'

'That's been known to happen.'

Alice was looking a good deal better. They had managed to find something to deal with her mosquito and flea bites; the lumps were down and she looked as though she had slept. She greeted us with a half-smile. 'Thank you for coming. You're my only visitors, except for Phil.'

'Well, Mr Lewison . . .'

'Yes, but he's clergy; it's part of his job. No one else from church, no neighbours . . . I'm sorry. I didn't mean to moan.'

'Your son?'

'He lives in New Zealand. He phoned and asked if he should come; I told him it wasn't as bad as all that and to save his money.'

'Wise decision, I think. Does he have a good job there?'

'It's with a start-up tech company. He's confident they'll grow, but at the moment he's struggling. I'm thinking of moving out to be with him.'

She sounded listless; her voice was grey.

'I think Phil would be unhappy about that,' I ventured.

'Phil wants me to marry him. I thought I might, before That Man came to Alderney. Now . . . there's nothing left of me to give anyone. Everything was eaten up in my hatred of him.'

'Have you talked to Mr Lewison about that?'

'No. What's the point? Everyone at the parish church thought he was a marvel. No one would believe me.'

I hesitated, looking over at Alan, who was sitting silently on the other side of the bed. He gave the slightest of nods. 'Alice, there are a few things you need to know. First, we told Mr Lewison about your experience. He didn't mention it to you?'

She sat up, looking less grey. In fact, she looked very angry. 'How dare you! I told you that in confidence!'

'I know that. We told him only after he told us something that I want to pass along to you. Mr Abercrombie's thefts at his American church have been discovered, and he would have been arrested if he had not left before he was discovered. Nothing has been proven, and now he is dead the case will be dropped, but I thought you'd want to know. Everyone in Alderney will soon know the truth.'

She sat back, stunned. 'Too late,' she whispered finally. 'Too late for Aleta.'

'But not too late for her memory. Or for you.' I leaned forward and touched her hand. 'Alice, she died, but you're still alive. You have a son who loves you and a good man who wants to marry you. You have a life ahead of you. You can let yourself be consumed by hatred of a man who is now in the hands of perfect justice, or you can let go of it. I don't say forgive him. That may come eventually, but for now you need to stop letting him control your life. He never did deserve that kind of power, and he certainly doesn't now.'

She had turned her face to the wall. I clasped her hand firmly, then let go, and we left.

'Any good?' I asked as we got back into the car.

'Time will tell. She needed to hear all that, but whether she'll do anything about it . . .' He shrugged. 'I want a thumping good lunch. Let's go and change clothes and then find one.'

The rain was slacking off, which was a good thing, because Alan had to park quite a long way from Belle Isle.

'We're going to have to walk to wherever we eat,' I said when we were changing. I put on the lovely clean clothes that our wonderful helper had washed, dried, folded and put neatly on our bed. 'Are you sure you don't want to eat leftovers right here?'

'Quite sure.'

'Then let's try Gloria's. It's close, and they might not be booked up, as it's early.'

We were lucky. We got the last table and had a lovely meal of tapas, portions generous enough that we could take some back to add to our eclectic collection of leftovers.

When we had finished, we went outside to find that the rain had stopped and a watery sunshine was trying to brighten the day. I pulled out my phone as we walked back to our room and tried Guillot again. Voicemail.

'You know,' I said, 'I'm beginning to get a little uneasy about this man. I mean – Alice hated Abercrombie and she disappeared, possibly intending suicide. Harold hated Abercrombie and he seems to have disappeared. I'm sensing a pattern here, and I don't like it at all.'

'Nor do I, but I don't know what we can do about it, unless we talk to the police. And what could we tell them? The man's gone away? It's a free country, and he has no employer to whom he's beholden.'

'Yes, but – we were concerned about Alice, and we were right. She was in trouble. Why aren't we as concerned about Harold Guillot? Just because we don't know him? That doesn't seem right. Besides, he might very well know something about Abercrombie's death. Either way, he ought to be found.'

Alan is not given to sighs. He sighed now. 'You know, I was hoping, now that the weather has cleared, to forget about our troubles for a time and go out this afternoon on the bird-watching boat to see the puffins. We've never seen puffins together, and I thought you'd enjoy it.'

'I don't believe in puffins. For one thing, they're just too silly-looking to be real, but it's not just that. Frank and I, over the years, went to a lot of places where puffins were supposed to be found. It was always like the White Queen's jam. Puffins last month, or puffins next month, never puffins this month. They're invented for the tourist trade.'

'I assure you, there are puffins on a nearby island right now, in the hundreds.'

'I'd love to have you prove that to me, but . . .'

'I know. You can't leave the Abercrombie thing alone.

You want to find Guillot. Are you thinking of going to the police, then?'

'Not yet. I want to talk to Robin,' I said stubbornly.

'He won't tell you where to find Guillot. He said so.'

'I know, but if he knows where his friend is, I can stop worrying.'

'You won't stop worrying about the possibility that he might have killed Abercrombie.'

'No, but one thing at a time. First, let's find Robin.'

'First you catch your hare,' Alan muttered.

'I cannot imagine,' I said irritably, 'why we haven't been getting people's phone numbers. It's ridiculous to have to wander around town hoping to run into someone.'

'They'll have his number at the Visitor Centre, I imagine, as he's a volunteer. Or next door at the Wildlife Trust. We can try them. And while we're at it, I'm going to book us on that boat for tomorrow. This *is* meant to be a holiday, after all.'

'I'm not very good at holidays, am I? The Cotswolds, Wales, Orkney . . .'

'It's not you. It's that little black cloud. Come on, old dear, put on your hat to dispel the cloud and let's go in search of Robin.'

We got Robin's phone number with no difficulty, and while we were at it, Sylvia's. 'And tomorrow at Morning Prayer we can pick up a few others,' I said. 'Welcome to the wonderful world of the twenty-first century!'

I stepped outside the office to make the call, and I was surprised when Robin answered his mobile. I had begun to think mine would connect only to voicemail. 'Yes?' he said in that tone one uses when the caller ID shows an unknown number.

'Robin, don't hang up. It's Dorothy Martin.'

'Yes?' Same tone of voice. Perhaps even a little cooler.

'Alan and I have been trying to talk to Harold Guillot. He isn't at home and he doesn't answer his phone, and we're worried about him. I know you won't help us locate him, but do you know where he is?'

Long pause. Then: 'Yes.' Nothing more.

'And he's all right?'

'Yes.'

'Then we'll stop worrying. Thank you, Robin.'

He had already hung up. I realized his end of the conversation had consisted entirely of the one word.

Alan joined me outside and I reported. 'So that's all we can do for now. He's somewhere safe, I suppose. It was hard to get any nuances. One word doesn't leave much room for interpretation.'

'So that being that, we're going to see puffins. There was room on today's boat, and we've just time to get down to the harbour. I'm going for the car.'

TWENTY

I looked at the not-very-big boat that was to take us to see puffins, and worried for a moment. The waves in the harbour were almost non-existent, but beyond the breakwater they looked more formidable. Then I remembered that I had some candied ginger in my purse, and hurriedly chewed a couple of pieces. There! I was ready for anything.

It took a few minutes of cruising and half listening to the guide's comments before I could rid my mind of its big concern. We still didn't know for sure whether Abercrombie had been pushed to his death. And if he had, who was responsible? Not Alice. Not Robin. Harold?

Where had Harold gone? And *why* had he gone, if not to escape prosecution? We really, really needed to talk to him.

Or maybe we needed to tell the police everything we knew and let them take it from here. Except it was all hearsay and speculation about possible motives. There wasn't the shadow of a hint of evidence, one way or the other.

'. . . eleven species of breeding birds on Burhou Island, the most popular of which is the puffin. We're coming up to it soon on your right, ladies and gentlemen. And there, just there, is a puffin out fishing.'

It disappeared, of course, before I could spot it with the binoculars that were thoughtfully provided on board. But it wasn't long before we were close enough to the island to see dozens of the birds, scores of them, in the water and on land. I was converted. I now believe in puffins! And they are adorable. I don't see how they can walk or swim properly, with those outsize beaks, but the beaks are useful for catching fish; I saw one bird carrying at least four small fish caught at one dive.

They're such comical creatures that it wasn't long before everyone on the boat was laughing. Puffin therapy! Just what I needed. I smiled at Alan and ducked as the boat hit a high wave and we got splashed with spray.

Our next destination was the island called Les Etacs (more peculiar French), where there were thousands of gannets. I'd never even heard of gannets, and I didn't find them as immediately appealing as puffins, but they were certainly impressive – big white birds with yellow heads and amazing wingspans. Unlike the puffins, which hunted fish from the surface of the water and bobbed like ducks when they found them, the gannets soared high, riding the thermals until they spotted their prey, when they dove like a screaming rocket, hitting the water at incredible speed. Up to sixty miles an hour, the guide said, with special skull structures designed to absorb the impact.

They were beautiful, but for me a trifle frightening in such high concentration. What if one of them made a mistake and decided we were fish? Ouch. And the rock was white with their droppings, which was unattractive; the pilot of the boat was careful to stay upwind of the guano.

Give me puffins every time.

I was tiring and glad the tour was over as we neared the harbour. Another boat was at our landing place, so we had to disembark via a ladder set into the side of the pier, something of an adventure for an old lady with two artificial knees.

'That was good, and I'm glad we went, even though we missed our afternoon nap,' I said as we made our way back to the car. 'It cleared some of the cobwebs out. Now I think I know what our next step should be.'

Alan didn't need to ask, our next step in what?

'We talk to people. Or rather, we let people talk to us. We don't seek them out. We just sit somewhere having a meal, or a drink, and they'll come. Bet on it?'

'No bet. After a week in Alderney I know you're right. By now everyone knows us and knows we're the ones who're asking questions about Abercrombie's death.' He looked at his watch. 'We're too late for Jack's, but just in time for happy hour at the Georgian House. Let's do it.'

I was beginning to recognize some of the regulars at happy hour. The same group of three or four sat always at the table nearest the bar. The same couple of elderly men sat, separately, in the back corner. And there was Robin in his usual place with an untouched pint in front of him. We nodded to him but didn't join him, choosing instead a prominent table near the door.

'White wine,' I told Alan. 'Small. I need a clear head for this.'

It might have been a full minute after he brought my wine and his pint back to the table that a woman asked if she could join us. She looked vaguely familiar. 'We met at church the other day,' she said. 'I was doing the flowers. Pat Vickers. And you're Mr and Mrs Nesbitt.'

I let it pass. 'Oh, yes, now I remember you.' I remembered, too, that she had been ambivalent, at best, about Abercrombie. I raised my glass in salute.

'I understand you've been spreading some rumours about our late parish helper.'

With her I felt no need to tiptoe. I nodded to Alan, who said, 'I'm afraid they're more than rumours. The information came from his American bishop. He was days away from a criminal charge when he left. His church is missing a great deal of money, and apparently there's ample evidence that he embezzled it.'

'Nothing they can do about it now,' she said after a thoughtful sip of her wine.

'No. Fortunately or unfortunately.'

'Fortunately for him, I'd say.' She shook her head. 'I don't imagine they'll ever get the money back.'

'It won't be easy. I'm told he's been spending quite freely.'

'Well, I for one am not altogether surprised. I thought from the start he was a bit too good to be true. When someone sets about to act saintly, it's almost always a sign that the other thing is lurking about somewhere.'

'And yet,' I put in, 'so many people at the church loved him.'

Pat shrugged. 'I'm a teacher, have been for years. History, at the school here. One learns a good deal about character.'

'One does. I was a teacher myself, eleven-year-olds. It wasn't long before I could spot a troublemaker when I first laid eyes on him. Or her, though at that age most of the worst brats were the boys.'

'I teach all ages. It's a small school. And you know, it's remarkable how little they change from babyhood to age fourteen. Not all of them, but most.'

'I imagine the problem children become even more so at adolescence.'

She shook her head ruefully. 'Frightful! Raging hormones . . . I actually feel sorry for them, you know. It's a terrible time in one's life. Everything changes so fast, and you don't know whether you want the familiar security of childhood back, or the freedom of adulthood, and you don't understand your own emotions . . . terrible time.'

'You know,' I said, 'I've never quite understood the Faust legend. Myself, I wouldn't want my lost youth back at any price. If the devil offered it to me, I'd throw it back in his face.'

We both laughed. 'Of course, we're women,' said Pat. 'It might be a little different for those cursed with the Y chromosome.'

Alan looked a little taken aback, and I thought it was time to change the subject. 'But you were saying, about Mr Abercrombie . . .?'

'Yes.' She looked around the room and said in a lowered voice, 'The word is that you both think he was murdered.'

'Oh, dear.' I looked at Alan for help.

'That's not true, Ms Vickers, and I hope you'll help quell that rumour. It is true that we think there might be the bare possibility that his death was not entirely accidental.'

She looked amused. 'A good many of my older pupils have become adept, when an essay must be of a given length, in using twice as many words as necessary to make a statement. I've learned to translate. To me, it sounds like you've just said you think he was murdered.'

'There's a difference, I assure you. We have some doubts, yes. But there is absolutely no evidence to support a charge of murder against anyone. You have probably heard that I am a retired policeman, and believe me, I do know what I'm talking about.'

'Evidence is one thing. Belief is another.'

This was getting into dangerous territory. I turned the argument back on her. 'And what do *you* think, Pat? Did he fall, or was he pushed?'

'Me? I think he probably fell. But I know of several people who would have liked to push him.'

'Such as?'

'Oh, no, you're not going to trap me into saying. I've not yet had enough wine to be indiscreet!'

Alan took that as a hint and got up to buy her another, as Robin came to our table. 'Still at it, Mrs Martin? Still trying to convict someone of an act that should win him a medal? If such an act was committed, which is plainly open to doubt. I'd have thought better of you, Pat, than to encourage such rubbish.'

'Stop bullying me, Robin. I'll say what I like, thank you very much. I was no friend of Abercrombie's, and neither were you.'

Her voice was rising, and heads were turning our way. This could turn into a row. I stood. Alan brought Pat her glass of wine and took my arm. 'Good evening, everyone.'

We got out before things got ugly.

'Whew!'

'Yes. I don't know that we learned anything from that except that we're treading on sensitive ground. Tonight, my dear, is definitely a night to stay in our cave and eat leftovers.'

I had nightmares that night, brought on partly by an incompatible mixture of cuisines and partly by anxiety. I didn't remember details in the morning, only a sense of disquiet and lack of rest, which, along with the weather, led to an attack of grumpiness.

'Rain! We don't *need* any more rain. We can't do anything, we can't go anywhere – drat!'

'We have a car,' Alan reminded me patiently. 'We can go anywhere we need to go. Here – I made coffee.'

Alan thinks any of my moods can be cured by an appropriate beverage. Coffee, tea, wine . . . and the infuriating thing is, he's usually right. I sat up in bed and sipped the coffee sullenly, but I began to feel better, almost unwillingly.

'Had a bad night, love? You were very restless.'

'Oh, I suppose I did. I'm sorry if I kept you awake. Was I talking in my sleep?'

'The odd groan now and again. Nothing serious. And you didn't keep me awake. I went back to sleep straightaway. What was it about?'

'I don't know. I woke up with a sense of panic, but I don't know why. I have a vague feeling it might have been one of those awful dreams of being chased and not able to run. Or maybe I was the one doing the chasing. Anyway, it was unpleasant. Sorry to take it out on you.'

'That, my dear, is one of the things a spouse is for. Let's go down to breakfast and talk about interesting things we can do in the rain.'

When I was a child I loved to walk in the rain, but some pleasures fade with age. I don't like cold, wet feet or glasses so obscured with rain that I can't see, or treacherous wet cobblestones. Of course, we did have a car. But what was there to do indoors on this island?

We talked about it over breakfast. 'I don't want to sit around and wait for people to come and talk to us again,' I said with determination. 'We're making enemies left and right.'

'Or pro and con, one might say. The pro-Abercrombie faction thinks we're demeaning his memory, and the antis think we're looking for his murderer, whom they don't especially want found. Not that they'd put it that way.'

'No. But it's true. Alan, I'm out of ideas, short of turning the whole mess over to the police.'

'Who have already marked it "case closed". Or rather, never opened. I think we need to let it rest for a while and wait for inspiration to strike.'

'I'm not feeling very inspired. This weather shuts down my brain cells.'

'So let's wake them up. I'm told the museum is quite good, and would give those brain cells of yours some exercise. And when we tire of that, we can go around the corner to the library. There's a display there that you missed before, and I think you'll like it.'

It sounded like a rather dreary way to spend a dreary day, but the alternatives were limited. I finished my coffee and acquiesced. 'But Morning Prayer first.'

'We may be royally snubbed.'

'Doesn't matter.' I badly needed a dose of serenity, and the lovely words of the Book of Common Prayer always soothed my soul.

We timed our arrival at the parish church so that there was little time to talk to anyone, and left promptly at the conclusion of the blessing, earning some disapproving looks in the process.

But as I'd said, it didn't really matter. We had walked to the church, it being just across the street, but Alan wondered if I wanted to drive to the museum.

'I don't think so. Where would we park? It's not that far away, and the rain isn't as bad today.'

'It could get worse rapidly. Island weather is capricious.'

'If it does, we'll head straight back to Belle Isle, where we can get into dry clothes.'

The museum building itself was interesting, being the old schoolhouse – really old; a plaque on the wall showed a date of 1790. The inscription was in French, but such simple French that even I could read the basic facts of the school's founding by one Jean Le Mesurier, governor of the island at the time.

Inside, the place didn't show its age. It was clean and bright, and the exhibits turned out to be far more interesting than I had anticipated. I was captivated by the display of artefacts from the Elizabethan shipwreck, which included several cannons in remarkably good condition. 'They've undergone extensive conservation, of course,' said another visitor in response to my admiring comments. 'Still, it is amazing, isn't it? All those years in salt-water, and here they are. Have you seen the muskets?'

There was, in fact, a great deal to see. Alan, who remembered almost nothing of World War Two but had lived as a child with the terrible aftermath, was drawn to artefacts from the German occupation he'd been reading about. 'Slave labour camps,' he murmured to me. 'Horrible.'

History can be terrifying or amusing or instructive, but it is almost never boring. I was amazed to discover that two hours had passed when an attendant came to us and apologetically announced that the museum was closing for lunch. 'We'll reopen at two thirty, and no one will charge you another admission fee if you want to come back then.'

'Goodness! It felt like five minutes,' I said to Alan when we were back on the street, where the rain had diminished to a fine mizzle. 'This business of shutting down over the lunch hour: so very continental.'

'We're closer to France than to England,' Alan reminded me. 'And France, or at least Normandy, ruled here for quite some time. Now, are you hungry, or shall we pop over to the library?'

'The library's closing in just a few minutes,' said the museum lady, who was just locking the door behind her as she left. 'They'll open at two thirty as well.'

'It's a conspiracy,' I said with a giggle. 'Let's get a sandwich or something and then have a nap.'

TWENTY-ONE

One need never go hungry in Alderney. There's food of one sort or another everywhere you look. We found a little takeaway in Victoria Street, P.J.'s Pantry, where we got a couple of jacket potatoes, in a waterproof bag so we could get them back to our lodging intact. Then we settled down to our accustomed nap. After a disturbed night, I was more than ready for a respite, and fell heavily asleep.

I wasn't even quite fully awake after Alan roused me and got me in motion toward the library. 'What's so important to see at the library?' I grumbled. 'I'm still sleepy.'

'You always say if you nap too long in the afternoon you won't be able to get to sleep at night.'

'I was making up for last night. And we bought lots of books. Why not just read them?'

'This isn't a book. You'll like it. Trust me.'

The rain had stopped, but the world was still very wet. We cut through the churchyard for what Alan said was a shortcut. I usually enjoy churchyards, but today this one seemed gloomy, the branches of its trees bowed down with rain, dripping sullenly onto the gravestones. I thought about the hard decision the church authorities had to make about whether to bury the remains of William Abercrombie in consecrated ground, and sighed as we splashed along the path.

The assistant greeted us pleasantly. 'I believe you may have visited before, yes? Christine told me about you. Did she say that you can borrow books during your stay on Alderney, if you want? We require a deposit, but it will be refunded when you return them.'

'That's very kind of you,' said Alan, 'but today I had something else in mind. I wanted to show my wife the Finale.'

'Huh?' I said brilliantly. 'What are you talking about?'

He turned me around and pointed. '*Voilà!*'

I looked. And looked again. And looked up, puzzled. 'But – what's it doing here? And where's the rest of it?'

'This *is* the rest of it,' the assistant said with a chuckle, and went on to explain. 'You've seen the original Bayeux Tapestry?'

'Yes, many, *many* years ago. My parents took me on a brief trip to Europe as a gift when I graduated from college – er, university.' It should perhaps be explained that the Bayeux Tapestry is not a tapestry at all, but a massive piece of embroidery, done on linen about twenty inches wide and well over two hundred feet long. 'The guide told us it was a needlework record of the Norman Conquest, done by William's queen and her ladies.'

'They used to think so. Now, they've decided they know really very little about it – who made it, or when, or even where.'

'Not at Bayeux?'

'No, it's been on display there for a long time,' she said, 'at present in a lovely museum built expressly for it, but experts think it was probably created somewhere else. At any rate, the original ends in a ragged edge, so it's obvious that part of it is missing. Books have been written about it, and a few years ago two of our residents decided to create what might be the missing scenes. In fact our own Kate Russell – she's on the library committee – started the project, and Robin Whicker, whom you've met, researched eleventh-century Latin for the inscriptions. It's lovely, isn't it?'

'It's amazing.' I looked at it more closely. 'I don't remember the original well. It's been over fifty years, for Pete's sake! But this looks exactly like it, as nearly as I can recall. I can hardly believe it's brand new.'

'We're very proud of it, as you can imagine. You would scarcely credit the research that went into making sure that the linen was the right texture and colour, the yarn dyed with the same vegetable dyes, the stitches matched to the original. Everyone on the island was invited to take a stitch or two, and quite a few did. We also had some guest stitchers, including Charles and Camilla! Look.' She showed us a small picture of the two royals sitting at the tapestry, studying it industriously. 'And this is my favourite detail.' She pointed to a small bit of the lower border of the last scene, where four stylized animals posed. 'These are for the Channel Islands, traditional symbols. The donkey for Guernsey, the toad for Jersey, our own Alderney puffin and the English lion with his tail arched protectively over all.'

I spent quite a little time studying details: the tiny, perfectly set stitches, the bright colours, and especially the little animals and symbols that decorated the top and bottom borders. I could have wished for more light, but I realized that textiles are sensitive to light, and the creators of this masterpiece wanted it to last – perhaps as long as the original, now looking good for its thousandth birthday later this century.

When we finally left the library at closing time, I gave Alan a hug. 'That was the perfect antidote to everything that's been going on the past few days. Thank you!'

'And the rain has stopped. While you were lost in admiration of the tapestry, I checked the online weather forecast for Alderney. It's set fair for the next few days, so tomorrow we can go exploring to our heart's content.'

'Lovely. Meanwhile let's stop at the supermarket and pick up some supper fixings. I don't feel like going out tonight. It's around here somewhere, isn't it?'

'Just down this way.'

Once more I blessed Alan's sense of direction.

As I was stowing our little cache of edibles in our temporary larder, my phone rang. Or rather, it played the first few bars of the *Toccata and Fugue in D Minor*, a favourite piece of music I had chosen as my ringtone. It startled me; I'd had no calls while on Alderney. I managed to find the thing in my purse just as it stopped ringing. I looked at the caller ID still displayed: Nigel Evans, our young friend back in Shrewsbury.

I felt that instant alarm occasioned by an unexpected phone call. What was wrong? His family? Our family of animals? Jane?

'Why on earth would Nigel be calling?'

'I don't know, darling,' said Alan calmly. 'Why not call him back and find out?'

I swear, sometimes I *want* other people to get into a swivet along with me, whether justified or not. I glared at Alan and punched the right buttons to return the call.

'Hi, Dorothy, stop worrying,' said a cheerful voice.

'How did you know I was worrying? What is there to worry about?'

'Nothing, and I knew because I know you. I just came across something I thought would interest you. Jane told me you've got yourselves mixed up in another murder.'

'I wouldn't have put it quite that way, and we're not sure it even *was* murder – but you've got the right general idea. We're embroiled in something distinctly unpleasant, at any rate.'

'Concerning an American clergyman named William Abercrombie.'

'Yes. But what—'

'I'm coming to that. After Jane told me the story, I started surfing.'

Nigel is the sort of computer guru to whom one turns when no one else can figure out what's wrong with the blasted thing. He works in IT services at Sherebury University, and if there's something he can't do on a computer, it can't be done. It's a good thing he's honest; he'd make the world's most formidable hacker.

'So you started surfing. And I'm assuming you learned something interesting, or you wouldn't be calling.'

'Too right it's interesting. Did you know that the man had a wealthy parishioner who just died and left him everything?'

'Heavens, no. What's "everything"?'

'A cool couple of million. That's in dollars, of course, not pounds. But still.'

'But still, as my southern mama used to say, that ain't hay. Wait a minute.'

I related the conversation to Alan and then switched to speaker mode. 'Okay, got it. Anything else? Although that's quite enough to think about.'

'This is a little less certain. I mean, I couldn't prove it, but I'm sure in my own mind. It looks as though, with that money and some other little bits and pieces he had lying about, he was planning to buy a big share of one of the computer gambling businesses in Alderney.'

Alan slapped his knee. 'I was right!'

'I don't know if he could actually have done it,' Nigel went on. 'The laws are fairly complicated, and I'm just a lowly geek, not a lawyer. But it looks as though he was setting up a holding company or two, to hide the connections. I rather delved into it, because it seemed a strange sort of operation for a clergyman.'

'He was a strange sort of clergyman,' I said tartly. 'Some of those other bits and pieces you mention came from money he embezzled from his parish. And that's not rumour, but cold hard fact.'

Nigel's whistle came clearly down the airwaves. 'Well. I begin to see why you think he might have been murdered. I might've wanted to have a go myself.'

'Oh, that's far from the worst of it,' said Alan. 'About the only sin he hasn't been accused of so far is paedophilia, and that may yet come.'

'If he was murdered, I sincerely hope you don't catch up with the – I hesitate to call him villain.'

'We feel a little that way ourselves, but still . . . Anyway, how are Inga and the kids?'

'All well. Inga's glad to be back at work. Staying home with those two was much harder work than tending bar, but the Nipper's settled down a good deal since going to school, and we've found a really reliable minder for them. Nigel Peter is spending most of his time this summer trying to read to Greta Jane, but he can't read all that well yet, and she's too young really to understand. I caught him the other day piling books on top of her so she wouldn't try to crawl away.'

'Oh, goodness, my sister and her best friend did that once to a cat, only it was bricks. They had dressed it up in doll clothes and were trying to take it for a ride in a doll carriage. The cat wasn't best pleased, but it survived to an extremely old age. I imagine Greta Jane will too.'

'To misquote one of your American authors, she will not merely survive, she will prevail. She picked up one of the books and shied it at him. Got him squarely on the jaw. He won't try that trick again in a hurry!'

We rang off with laughter, and I turned to my triumphant husband. 'Congratulations,' I said. 'Good hunch.'

'I knew I smelled a rat. Back when I was a copper I learned

to follow my nose. In this case it seemed there wasn't enough money, but with over a million pounds, he could have done quite nicely.'

'And don't forget the "bits and pieces". Unless he'd already spent that on travel and toys. Alan, I cannot grasp why a man with that kind of money would resort to nasty little penny-ante games like stealing from a church jumble sale.'

'You don't, thank God, understand the criminal mind as I came to do. There is a kind of sociopath, usually with a brilliant mind, who will commit crimes simply because he can. He's pitting his superior wits against all the other poor fools out there, and derives great pleasure when he wins, as of course he nearly always does. It's the victory itself that he loves, as much as the spoils, though of course he enjoys the spoils as well.'

I shuddered. 'A person like that would have to be completely amoral.'

Alan looked surprised. 'Of course, that goes without saying.'

'And he became a priest! What kind of a twisted mind could do such a thing?'

'The kind he had. Totally egocentric, totally without conscience. I'm not a psychologist, but I would say that such a man would be quite literally incapable of seeing anyone else's point of view, or of understanding why it mattered if an action of his caused harm to someone else. That would be simply irrelevant to him. Witness his reaction to the death of the little American baby, which touched him not at all. He probably chose the church as a profession because he needed to be admired, and because of the opportunity for drama. The Mass is a great drama, and a really fine actor can get a powerful response from the congregation.'

'What about sermons? How could he possibly preach the Gospel?'

'Acting again, probably. Such people are usually pathological liars. That is, they don't even know that they're lying. So he could, with a straight face, have made powerful speeches from the pulpit, while not believing – or practicing – a single word he said.'

'You've come around to anti-Abercrombie side, haven't you? What was the tipping point?'

'Nigel's revelations. With that kind of money, he could have helped the poor in his community, set up a small foundation, done lots of good. Instead he chose to come to a remote island and get into big-money gambling. And I have to say I'm driven to wonder how that parishioner died, and whether the family suspected undue influence.'

'Alan! Surely he wouldn't have . . . but if he was really the way you've described him, he might have, mightn't he?'

Alan looked at his watch. 'I think I'm going to walk down and have a little talk with Derek Partridge. I think the American police might be interested in the chain of events we've uncovered.'

TWENTY-TWO

Wednesday did, as promised, dawn clear and lovely. It was perfect exploring weather, so Alan and I planned at breakfast what we might do that day.

He had not made a lot of headway with the Alderney police. While they conceded that there was a convincing case against Abercrombie, one that might have been pursued while he was living, there was little point now. 'Yes,' Derek had said, 'the man sounds an out-and-out rotter. But he's dead. You can't prosecute the dead. And there are a fair number of people here who are already a bit unhappy about what we've found out about him. Think we're "desecrating his memory". Hah! Yes, I'll pass along your suspicions to the authorities in Ohio, but I doubt, sir, that they'll do much about it. With murders two a penny on that side of the pond, they've enough on their plates without casting doubts on the death of an elderly woman, a death that was never in question.'

'From his point of view, he's quite right,' said Alan. 'In this small community, it's wise not to make too many waves. We've stirred up a bit of a hornet's next, just looking into Abercrombie's background.'

'Yes, but . . . There's always a "yes, but", isn't there. A man who was that evil dies in what might have been an accident. I think we have – I think everyone has, for that matter – an obligation to know for certain whether or not it was accidental. It comes back to the coincidence question, but in a slightly different sense. Was it just coincidence that a man so dearly hated, for such good reason, a man who was an experienced walker, tripped and fell? Is it just coincidence that a man with some of the best reasons to hate him has disappeared?'

'I'm not any happier about the notion of coincidence than you are, love.' Alan cut a neat piece off his egg, secured it on his fork with a bit of bacon, and propelled the whole to his mouth. 'But they do happen. I saw a good many in police work through the years, some that beggared belief, but they were real.' He finished his coffee. 'Now, love, there comes a time in every difficult case when there are no apparent leads to pursue. One has come to what you Americans colourfully call a "dead end". When that happens, often the best thing to do is nothing. Set it aside, try to put it out of one's mind, deal with other matters. That is what I propose to do today. I'd like to do a lot of walking to work off some of the lovely food we've been putting away in such quantity. Then this afternoon I'd like to take the bus tour around the island. There are quite a few things we've missed, and we can see them in comfort from the minibus. How does that sound to you?'

'Perfect,' I said. 'You lead the way. Whither thou goest . . .'

'Right. Except when you prefer to goest somewhere else.'

Alan decided he wanted to see the old water mill, a ruin dating, originally, from the thirteenth century. 'The present ruins are quite new, though; the mill was rebuilt in 1796.'

'Good grief, that's young enough to belong to my country.' I grinned; he shook his head in mock disgust.

The water mill was a great success as an expedition for the simple reason that we were unable to find it. We went, map in hand, in what we were sure was the right direction. We chose forks as random when the map was no help, and when we ended up in someone's garden we retraced our steps and took the other fork. After this had gone on for a couple of hours we had seen a good many pretty gardens and a fair sampling of the north-western part of the island. We had several times caught glimpses of a Victorian fort and its German reincarnation. We asked directions of a young couple we encountered in passing; they were French and couldn't help.

'All right,' I said at last. 'I'll be the wimp and give up. I'm beginning to feel like poor old Charlie on the MTA.'

Fortunately my husband had also been a fan of the Kingston Trio back in the dear dead days beyond recall. 'And did he ever return?' he carolled.

'No, he never returned,' I responded. 'And his fate is still unlur-r-rned,' we chorused.

The French couple, returning from wherever they'd been, looked at us oddly.

'Too young,' I said, and got a fit of the giggles that lasted nearly back to town.

'Time for a pint,' said Alan. 'I'm dry enough to drink the barrel.'

'Me, too. Look, here's the Marais Hall. Let's do it.'

After a refreshing interval we ambled back to Victoria Street and walked toward our B & B. 'You know, Alan, I can't seem to walk as far as I could twenty years ago. Funniest thing.'

'Talking of coincidence – neither can I. Look, here's a bench. I know we're close to our room, but we've never come in here before.'

'In here' was a little garden with soft green grass, roses and some small marble monuments. 'It's a collection of war memorials,' I said, touched. 'Even so small an island lost a lot of men in the two big wars. And oh, Alan!'

I pointed. There on the wall was a marble plaque: 'Sapper George Onions, Royal Engineers, who gave his life on minefield clearing operations on Alderney 21 June 1945. In Grateful Remembrance.'

'That's what that little garden is about,' I said softly, 'the Sapper Onions Peace Garden. A living memorial to a poor man who died here after the war was over, when all the fighting was done and all the Germans had left. Died helping make the island safe again.'

I had to wipe my eyes, and we were silent the rest of the way back.

We decided to forgo our usual nap. We stopped at the Visitor Centre to book our bus tour, and then, after a leisurely and rather late lunch at Jack's, we crossed the street to wait for the minibus. We were there only a moment or two when the bus pulled up. 'You're my only two passengers, so far,' said the driver, an attractive woman who introduced herself as Annabel. 'If you don't mind, we'll wait for a minute or two to see if anyone else turns up.'

But no one did, so the driver said, 'Right, then. You can sit up front if you like, so I won't have to shout!'

'Suits me,' I said, and climbed in.

We did indeed see many parts of the island we hadn't visited before, some residential areas outside the 'town' area, some beaches we'd never noticed. We went to the structure called the Nunnery; the driver had no more idea than anyone else about why it was called that. Seen by daylight it was quite interesting. The most obvious remnant of the Roman site was a crumbling wall, but we were told that almost the whole outer structure is Roman, with a hodgepodge of eighteenth-, nineteenth-, and twentieth-century adaptations. Apparently a fortress for most of its long existence, it was now a residence, so we couldn't go inside. But the thought of all those centuries of defensive use raised in me the usual shiver of awareness of the past, of the rich history of a place whose habitation went back to the dim ages of pre-history.

'First the Romans against the rest of the world, then Alderney against the French, then the Germans against the rest of the world. What's next, do you suppose?' I asked rhetorically.

'There were a good many centuries in there when nothing much was happening. That's why the wall crumbled,' Alan pointed out. 'We seem to be in one of those periods now, touch wood.'

'Yes, here on this island, perhaps. But even here, a serpent got in, only weeks ago.'

'And has been vanquished. Annabel is beckoning us. Shall we go on?'

We saw nearly all the forts, of whatever era – and there were a lot of them. Some, like this one, had been turned into residences. We saw a house owned by Julie Andrews, one of my all-time favourite singers, and still used, from time to time, by her grandchildren. And we heard a story.

'Was your family among the ones evacuated during the war?' I asked Annabel.

'No, but I live in the house of someone who was. My husband and I bought it from a man who, as a boy, was sent to Glasgow.'

'I've read stories about that time, when the Germans burned everything they could – furniture, floorboards, everything – just to keep from freezing to death. Was the boy's house badly damaged?'

'Yes, he said it was gutted. With one notable exception.' She smiled a little. 'Apparently the officer who lived there had tried at first to keep the house in good order. I suppose he thought he'd be living there for a long time. The Germans thought they'd

win the war. So the officer had had the house painted, inside
and out. For some reason, when the painters got to the kitchen,
the officer ordered them not to paint over the children's growth
marks pencilled on the wall. And when the family returned at
the end of the war, with everything else torn up and destroyed,
that wall and those marks remained.' She smiled again. 'They're
still there. We've left them as a reminder that even an enemy
can have a heart. There's good in everyone.'

We pondered that remark as we sat in the garden of Belle
Isle having our tea. 'Good in everyone. I suppose she's right,
but . . . Abercrombie?'

'He made a lot of people happy, don't forget. All those ladies
who thought, who still think, he was wonderful. He brightened
their lives.'

'But it was all a sham.'

'We think it was. That doesn't change the fact that those
women loved him. Isn't the ability to inspire love a positive
quality, even if it's pretence?'

'I don't know. He did it for his own purposes, as part of his
con act.'

'Yes, but that brings us to another point. Derek Partridge is
not in favour of a full investigation of Abercrombie's crimes,
in part because it would hurt those devoted ladies to know they
had been used.'

I sighed. 'It would break their hearts. But they'll know, sooner
or later. Word will get around. Nothing stays hidden in a community this size. And Alan, they *need* to know. In this world of
woe, it's dangerous to be innocent and trusting.'

'You have a point. But do you want to be the one to tell them?'

TWENTY-THREE

I got a call that evening from Mr Lewison. 'I thought you'd want to know that Mrs Small has returned home. For a few days she'll have a full-time caregiver, until she learns how to get about safely on her crutches. She's in somewhat better spirits, and I think she'd enjoy a visit.'

'That's good news. I'm not sure I still have her phone number.' He gave it to me. 'Thanks so much. We'll go tomorrow, right after Morning Prayer.'

Alan looked at me inquiringly. 'Alice is home and wants visitors. At least that's what Mr Lewison says. Let's take her some flowers.'

We went to church at the last possible minute in the morning, and left as soon as the service was over. I wanted to talk more to some of the ladies, but not yet, and not in church. There was a nice florist almost next door to Belle Isle, so we got a big bouquet. After we'd phoned Alice and were assured by her caregiver that this was a good time to visit, Alan retrieved our car and we drove to her house.

Phil was there, which was no surprise. If the man had a job, his hours were obviously flexible. He looked pleased to see us. 'She's told me about her sister,' he said quietly as we came in. 'I think she wants to talk about it.'

He showed us to a sitting room, where Alice was comfortably installed in a recliner, her bulky cast up on the footrest, a pair of crutches leaning handy on a bookcase, water and a vial of pills and a book within reach. She looked tired but more peaceful than we had yet seen her. She thanked us for the flowers, which we gave to her caregiver to put in a vase, and asked us to sit down.

'You're feeling better,' I said with certainty.

'I am. They found a painkiller that doesn't make me sick, and it helps. You were so right, though, about getting around and doing everyday tasks. I can hardly even brush my hair without losing my balance. Grace is a lifesaver.' She smiled at the woman as she brought the vase of flowers back into the room and put them on a table in front of the window.

'I'm glad to hear you're able to ease the pain of your ankle, but that wasn't the pain I was talking about.' I glanced at Grace.

'It's all right,' said Alice. 'We can talk about it. Grace is the soul of discretion. And I've wanted to talk about it. Mr Lewison has helped me put it all in perspective.'

She shifted a little in her chair, took a sip of water. 'It's hard to know where to begin.'

'Would you like to know the rest of what we've learned about Abercrombie, or would it disturb you too much?'

'More than his thefts from his parish? Wasn't that enough?' She sounded bitter, and then sighed. 'I'm working on trying to forgive the man. Mr Lewison says I must. It's the hardest thing I've ever attempted. I'm not at all sure I can do it.'

Alan looked at me. I nodded. 'I think it may help you to know, Alice, that Abercrombie was probably not in full control of his actions. I believe that he was a sociopath, a man with no moral scruples, no conscience. When I was working in the police, we occasionally came across such criminals. They were almost always charming people, at least charming when they wanted to be. They could also be vicious, but it was an odd sort of viciousness, with no anger or spite involved, simply a cold determination to have their own way. We don't know what forces combine to create such individuals, though psychiatrists have their theories. What we do know is that, once a person has fallen into such a mould, his actions follow patterns as rigid as any laboratory rate in a maze, and he becomes less and less able to deviate from those patterns. Further, he can see nothing wrong with his actions.'

'You're saying he no longer has free will?' Alice sounded frightened, as well she might.

'My dear woman, I'm not a theologian. All I can tell you is what I have observed. I do believe that at some point the sociopath's mind and spirit have been so warped by circumstances that he can no longer make what we would call the "right" choices, only the expedient ones, expedient for him, that is. If that is a loss of free will, then yes, he has lost it.'

'Mr Lewison said he was in a hell of his own making.'

I cleared my throat. 'When Dr Faustus asks Mephistopheles why he is out of hell, Marlowe has him reply, "Why, this is hell, nor am I out of it." I'm not great at theology, either, but it seems to me that all of us can make our own hells. The thing is, most of us can avoid drawing everyone else in with us, and if we really want to, we can get out. I think what Alan is saying is that maybe Abercrombie couldn't get out.'

'And couldn't help wreaking hell on everyone he met?' The bitterness was back in her voice. 'I'm sorry, I can't accept that. And yet I have to try to forgive him for what he did to Aleta!'

'It wasn't just Aleta,' I said. I didn't know if I was doing more harm than good, but this tormented woman deserved the truth. 'He not only stole a great deal of money from his church in Ohio, and lied about it; he also refused to come to the bedside of a woman who was fighting to save her pregnancy. She lost the baby and can never have another, and her husband has left her because of it. Abercrombie showed no compunction over the matter, seemed not to think he had done anything wrong.'

'Then,' Alan went on, 'when things became dangerous for him in the States, he came to Alderney and began systematically defrauding the parish church. We can't prove it, but we believe he stole funds from the jumble sale and collected money for choir folders he never intended to order. Tiny amounts of money, senseless thefts, particularly—' he leaned forward – 'particularly since he had inherited something over a million pounds from a parishioner.'

'I think that's enough,' said Phil, standing. He didn't look happy with us. 'Alice needs to rest.'

'No, Phil, it's all right.' She drank a little more water. 'There really was no end to it, was there?'

'But there's an end to it now,' I said. 'Not to the damage he did, not to the lives he damaged forever. But he'll never hurt anyone again, and I firmly believe that he'll see justice in the end.'

'And yet I'm asked to forgive him.'

'Yes. For your own sake, not his. He's beyond caring.' I took her hand. 'Look, Alice, I know it isn't easy. It's almost impossible. But think of it this way. As long as you don't forgive him, your hatred of him will fester. Someone said it's like giving a

person permission to live in your head, rent-free, and mess it up
forever. If you can manage to off-load that terrible infestation,
you'll be the better for it.'

She fell silent, her eyes closed. Alan and I stood up to leave.
'No, don't go,' she said at last. 'I was thinking, not sleeping.
I must know. Do you still think someone pushed him down that
hill?'

I let Alan answer that. 'I would have to say,' he said after
some deliberation, 'that we're not at all certain what we think.
It's all too obvious that the man went through life making enemies,
some of them here on Alderney. It would have been easy for one
of them, perhaps one we don't know about yet, to have come
across him on that hill and given a push without much forethought.
I can see no way that such actions could ever be proven, lacking
an eyewitness – and presumably if such a witness existed, he or
she would have come forward by now.'

'Suppose that it happened. Would you want to prove it, given
the character of the devil he killed?'

'Yes, Alice, I would. I would feel every sympathy for the
murderer, but I would want to bring him to justice. We, as individuals, are not allowed to make life-and-death decisions. Justice
is a matter for the courts, and ultimately for God. If any man
starts deciding that this murder or that robbery or that sexual
assault was justified, we're not far from anarchy – or, to put it
another way, from hell.'

'Judges and juries make mistakes.'

'They do. The system isn't perfect. That's one reason why the
death penalty was abolished in the United Kingdom, and most
of Europe, years ago.'

'If someone killed that man, and he's discovered and tried and
sentenced to life imprisonment – a living hell – your cherished
system is no better than the man it would call the victim.'

'Don't forget that there are other possible verdicts, other
possible sentences.'

She gestured away the argument, looking suddenly very tired
and much older than her years.

I stood. 'We must go, Alice. I'm sorry we've troubled you.
Get some rest.'

Phil walked us – marched us – to the door and went outside

with us. 'If this is your idea of comforting the afflicted,' he began in furious tones, 'you needn't come back.'

I turned to him, suddenly sick of the whole thing. 'Phil, she has to talk about it. She has to get it out of her system. It isn't easy conversation, or pleasant, but sometimes things need to be said. You say you love her. You're not doing her any favours by trying to wrap her in cotton wool. Reality is what it is, and she's beginning to realize that she must face it.'

We got in the car and drove away. Without a word, Alan headed for the harbour. We drove until we reached a deserted beach, and then we got out and sat on a bench and watched the waves and the gulls and let the wind blow through our minds until they were clean.

I did a lot of thinking for the next couple of hours. 'Alan,' I said after we'd picked at our lunches, 'when is our return flight? I forget. Saturday or Sunday?'

'Monday morning, actually. I thought I'd give us a full two weeks of holiday. It hasn't been quite like that, has it?'

'Not quite. Did you have anything in particular you wanted to do this afternoon?'

'No plans. You?'

'I hope you won't mind, but I'd like to spend some time by myself. I need to get my head on straight.'

He stared at it. 'Looks all right to me,' he said with a grin. Then he kissed my cheek. 'I do understand what you mean. Take all the time you need, and go wherever you like. Just be sensible about it, and be sure your phone is handy. I don't want to have to rescue *you* off any cliffs.'

'No cliffs, I promise. Thank you for understanding.'

In fact, I was headed for the church, hoping it would be deserted and quiet. I had some serious thinking to do, and I do that best in an atmosphere of peace.

One of the many things I love about small English churches is that they're left open much of the time. In the dim reaches of the past, they were all left open, all the time, partly so people could come in and pray any time, partly because the medieval tradition of sanctuary still prevailed, if no longer in law, at least in the hearts and minds of many Christians. As society has changed, and violence has become ever more common, most town churches have conceded the necessity for locks and keys, but some of the villages still keep to the old ways. And as the lady at the Visitor Centre had said, Alderney was very like an English village.

What a blessing.

The church was dark and cool, and deserted. I slipped into a pew on the Gospel side, well away from the south door. For a few minutes I just sat and tried to quiet my thoughts. There were decisions to be made, decisions that could affect a number of people. When I'd achieved at least a transient calm, I knelt to pray, somewhat incoherently.

I had been on my knees for some little time, and had reached some conclusions, when a sound brought me scuttling back into the pew. Why is it that one feels foolish when interrupted at private prayer?

I had other feelings when I saw who had come into the church.

Robin didn't see me at first. He walked up to the chancel, bowed to the altar and began doing something in the book racks of the pews. Organizing choir music, I supposed.

He wasn't paying any attention to me. He had turned on the lights in the chancel, leaving the rest of the church in relative darkness. I could slip out.

I stood. The wood of the pew creaked loudly, and I dropped my purse.

Robin looked back, shading his eyes with his hand. I nodded and started on my way, then changed my mind. I walked up the aisle.

'You startled me, Mrs Martin. I thought I was alone in the church.'

'And I thought I was, until I heard you come in.' I took a deep breath. 'Alan and I had a long talk this morning with Alice Small.'

'Oh?' He wasn't going to help at all.

'We told her your story – Mr Guillot's story – about the woman who lost her child. We told her about the thefts from Abercrombie's church in Ohio, and the possible thefts from the church here. We told her something you may not know, about the large inheritance Abercrombie had from a parishioner.'

'Yes?'

'We told her all this because she's trying hard to learn to forgive the man.'

Robin's jaw worked. He said, 'You told her all this, thinking it might help her to forgive him? Madam, I must question your sanity.'

'Yes, I thought you'd say that. But you see, it makes his actions with respect to her tragedy less personal. Alan thinks he was a sociopath, unable for some time now to take his life in a different direction.'

Robin was the sort of man who wouldn't sit while a woman was standing. I sat down creakily in one of the choir pews, and went on. 'Each new success in some criminal endeavour, you see, would feed his enormous ego. He would begin to feel invincible. When his actions hurt other people, it simply didn't matter, so long as he remained untouched.'

'You're making *excuses* for him?'

'Not excuses, but a possible explanation. If we can understand why he did the things he did, it may perhaps make it marginally easier to forgive. And Alice needs to forgive, Robin. So does Mr Guillot. Hatred is corrosive.'

'And yet you are, I think, intending to continue a search for a murderer, if there is one. That hardly smacks of forgiveness.'

'Forgiveness is a personal thing, an individual thing. The law is the law, a community thing. There is a difference.'

'A philosophical one, perhaps.'

'And a practical one. When an individual decides to make himself judge and jury, civilization crumbles.'

'So – what are you saying? What are you asking of me?'

'I believe that no amount of conversation is going to uncover a murderer, if, as you say, there is one. I believe that a community meeting, the comparing of notes, is the only way we will ever know the truth. I'm going to ask Mr Lewison to call such a meeting, and I want you to ask Mr Guillot to attend.'

'And exactly what do you hope to accomplish by such a meeting, which will undoubtedly turn into a melee?'

'I hope it will not. That's why I hope we can hold it here in the church. As for what I hope to accomplish, I said before: I want to know the truth.'

TWENTY-FOUR

M r Lewison was dubious about the idea, to say the least. 'This is not my parish, Mrs Martin. These are only temporarily my parishioners. Great harm has already been done to them by that unscrupulous cleric. This – this public baring of souls could damage the congregation profoundly, perhaps irreparably.'

'I know you'll want to consult the vicar, and possibly your bishop. But consider, sir. Eventually the truth will be known, at least the truth about all of Abercrombie's wickedness. Wouldn't more harm be done by rumours and innuendo? This way people would get the truth, unfiltered by wishful thinking. I liken this to the tearing off of a Band-Aid – a plaster, I mean. You can do it excruciatingly slowly and prolong the pain, or you can rip it off, which hurts more, but only for a moment. And we might learn enough to put to rest once and for all the question of how the man met his death.'

'Yes, I see.' He paused, looking miserable. 'I will think and pray about this, Mrs Martin, and I will consult the vicar if I can find him. He and his family are in the Greek islands some-where, and I'm not sure he can be reached at all. When would you like to have the meeting?'

'We're leaving for home Monday morning. The sooner the better.'

'Yes. I will phone you.'

Alan wasn't easy to convince, either. 'Dorothy, I have to say this smacks of your favourite brand of reading material. Poirot assembles all the suspects and re-enacts the crime for them, in his own slanted fashion, and someone either confesses or tries to run away, amounting to the same thing in the end. A policeman shudders at the thought, and I'll be very surprised if Lewison allows it.'

'But there are big differences,' I insisted. 'For one thing, Poirot always knew who the criminal was. The big showdown was just to get a confession. In this case, we don't even know whether there was a crime.

'But more importantly, this thing needs to get out in the open. I told Mr Lewison it was like ripping off a Band-Aid, but actually it's more like lancing a boil. Painful and ugly, but necessary. The poison has to be released.'

I couldn't keep my mind on anything for the rest of the day. We went out to dinner. I couldn't tell you where, or what we ate. We watched something on television and then I tried to read, but gave up and went to a bed that gave me no rest.

My phone rang at eight the next morning. Bleary-eyed, I punched buttons just before it stopped ringing.

'I agree, Mrs Martin. Ten o'clock tomorrow morning in the nave. I will set volunteers to work calling the parish, and posters will be distributed all over town. And may God have mercy.'

'Amen,' I whispered.

Now that we were committed to the meeting, I developed a bad case of cold feet. 'So much could go wrong,' I said as I drank cup after cup of coffee and tried to eat a little breakfast. 'I was out of my mind to think such a thing was a good idea.'

'Good idea or not, it's on the books. You've often said, love, that there's no point in worrying unless you can change something. You can't change this; you can only prepare for it. And you know you don't think well on an empty stomach. If you don't eat more than that piece of toast, you'll have a caffeine high that won't let you do anything sensible.'

I ate the rest of the toast and a little cereal before I gave up. 'It's no use, Alan. There's a whole day to kill before this thing, and I can't think about anything else. I need something to do, and a good walk isn't going to be enough. Walking leaves you too much time to think.'

'Well, let's see. Daytime television is a waste of time. Some of those good books we bought?'

'I can't concentrate.'

'We've visited the library and the museum. How about one of the forts? I believe the Cambridge Battery is open to the public.'

'Just now I don't care about forts, or much of anything else about the history here. I'm concerned about the future. The very near future.'

'Well, then, I believe there's a weekday Eucharist at St Anne's at ten thirty.'

'Someone would want to talk to us, and I'll bet we wouldn't want to hear what they had to say.'

'You never know. Some will welcome this chance to air their feelings and ideas. Anyway, we could stroll in late and leave early. We'd be harder to buttonhole that way. And a little dose of liturgy wouldn't hurt us.'

I was reluctantly persuaded. The church was the very last place I wanted to be, but the alternative was sitting around the lounge stewing, and Alan had a point about the liturgy.

We had an hour to kill. Alan read the papers and continued with a book he'd begun. I paced and fretted.

We were successful in slipping quietly in to the church after the service had begun. The tiny congregation was seated in the chapel at the end of the south aisle; we took our seats in a nearby pew hidden behind a pillar. We couldn't see, but we could hear the service and follow along silently, secure in the knowledge that no one knew we were there.

The words were those of the old Book of Common Prayer, words I knew so well I didn't need to read them. They were comforting, so comforting that when the congregation went forward to receive Communion, I almost joined them. Common sense prevailed, however. Even if I didn't meet overt hostility, I would certainly disturb the communicants, and that didn't seem a proper thing to do.

We slipped out before the benediction, still unseen, and beat it back to Belle Isle before anyone on the street recognized us.

'That was a good idea, Alan,' I said when we had achieved the haven of our room. 'I feel much better. And I have in fact had an idea.'

'Oh, dear,' said Alan.

'All right, I admit that some of my ideas have been . . . well, not entirely productive. But this one will be, I think.'

'All right. Fire when ready, Gridley.'

'Did you know that Gridley was born in Indiana? I looked it up once. Anyway, my idea has to do with the presumed thefts from the church. I'd like to see if I can find some proof.'

'And how do you propose to do that, when you don't want to talk to any of the parishioners?'

'The business about the choir folders will be easy. I'm going to go to the library and do a computer search. There can't be all that many firms providing high-quality blue leather folders with gold stamping. I'll phone them all and ask what's happened to the order from St Anne's, Alderney. If they all claim there was no such order – bingo!'

'That's not a bad idea. Of course it would be easier if you could find the catalogue Abercrombie showed around.'

'Of course, but I can't think of a way to do that.'

'And the jumble sale funds?'

'That's a lot harder, but I'm relying on my experience with rummage sales, as we called them back in Indiana. It's going to mean talking to one parishioner, though, if I can find her. I need to ask some questions of "Lucille", whoever she is, who ran the sales from time immemorial until Abercrombie bulldozed his way in. I think maybe Alice will give me her name and phone number, and the best part of that is, I know for sure where to find Alice.'

'Poor thing,' said Alan. 'Homebound with an avenging fury about to bear down on her.'

Reluctant to leave my hidey-hole until I absolutely had to, I phoned Alice instead of going to see her. She was less than thrilled to hear from me.

'You're the one behind this community meeting, aren't you?'

I admitted it.

'I don't know what you hope to prove.'

'I don't know that we'll prove anything. I do hope we'll learn the truth.'

'And it will set us free?' There was no amusement in Alice's laugh. 'I'll go to your misbegotten meeting, because Phil wants me to, but for no other reason.'

'At any rate you'll be there, and I'm glad. But that isn't the reason I called. There's a woman at the parish church named Lucille. I don't know her last name, but she did a lot of volunteer work, especially with jumble sales over the years. I hoped you might have her phone number.'

'I won't have you upsetting Lucille! She's given her life

to that church. It broke her heart when that man shoved her aside.'

'Alice, I have no intention of upsetting her. We've a jumble sale coming up at my church in a few months, and they've asked me to help out. I have some ideas from the way we used to do things back in Indiana, but I don't know if they'll work here. I just want to ask an expert.'

'I don't believe you.'

A shrug couldn't be seen over the phone, but apparently Alice sensed it. 'Oh, very well. Her name is Lucille Crenshawe, and she'll be home. She goes almost no place now that her eyes are so bad. I'll ask Grace to find you the number. But you must promise you won't say anything to hurt her.'

'I do promise. There's been quite enough hurt already.'

'Yes, well, she can be . . . never mind. Just tread gently.'

Grace gave me the number. I phoned Lucille immediately, because I feared if I thought about it too much I'd lose my courage.

She answered promptly, and her voice was not the voice of a sweet old lady. Perfectly courteous, but with an underpinning of steel.

I took a deep breath. 'Mrs Crenshawe, you don't know me. My name is Dorothy Martin, and I've been visiting here on Alderney for the past two weeks.'

There was a chuckle on the other end. 'It's Miss Crenshawe, or just Lucille. And we may not have met, but I know who you are. You're the American woman who's trying to prove someone pushed that upstart clergyman down the hill. And high time, too, I say.'

'Um . . . well, I am American, or at least I was, and I am looking into the man's death, but—'

'You may fool the others, but you can't fool me. I'm old, and my eyes don't see well, but my mind can still tell a hawk from a handsaw. What are you up to with this meeting you've called?'

I debated saying that it wasn't my meeting, but gave it up. I also abandoned any idea of trying to get the information I wanted by little fibs. Alice's conception of this woman's character was, I thought, somewhat mistaken, or else I had misinterpreted.

'What I hope to do is get at the truth, the truth about a number of things. Abercrombie's character, for a start, and perhaps the manner of his death, though that's less certain.'

'Hah! And how can I help you do that?'

'I'd like to talk to you about the details of the way the jumble sale is run.'

'Want to catch him out, do you? It won't be easy. He was a devil, but clever, as the devil always is.'

'Nevertheless, I think I have an idea about how to do it.'

'Good. More than I do. You come and see me, and we'll talk.' She told me where she lived.

'Wait a second. Let me give my husband the phone. He's the one who has to find your house.'

She lived, it turned out, not far from Harold Guillot. I took the phone back. 'It's nearly lunchtime. Would one o'clock suit you, or one thirty?'

'Come now. I'll give you some lunch.' She rang off before I could protest.

'Heavens! Eye of newt and toe of frog, probably,' I said to Alan. 'She sounds exactly like a witch. Alice said I wasn't to upset her. I'd say we're the ones who might get upset. I'll bet people give her little gifts so their hens will keep laying and their cows' milk won't dry up.'

'Precious few hens and cows here in town, love. They more likely go to her to find out how to treat bunions and cure a persistent cough. But a gift or two, of the edible sort, might be a wise precaution.'

So we stopped at the little food shop in the village for some cheese, and the bakery for some lovely French bread, and then picked up a fresh lemon drizzle loaf from the stand in Victoria Street, and headed up to Miss Crenshawe's house.

TWENTY-FIVE

I t didn't resemble a witch's cottage in the least, but looked pretty much like all the other houses in the neighbourhood: small, with stone walls painted pale blue, shutters a darker blue and a faded red tile roof. The garden was neat but not pretentious. A pink rose climbed a trellis by the front door, which stood open.

'Come in, if you're who I think you are,' came a voice from inside. So we did.

The front room was exquisitely neat and clean, and so was Miss Crenshawe. She wasn't the frail little person I'd somehow expected, but tall, thin and nicely dressed in black slacks and a white shirt, with a colourful scarf around her neck. No pointed hat, no long nose or warty chin. Her laugh, though, approached a cackle.

'Not quite what you thought, am I? You'll be pleased to note that I do keep a cat. He's probably over there in the window seat; that's where he spends his days, the lazy beast. Lucifer, come and greet our guests.'

Her eyes were filmed and we could tell that she was able to see very little. We looked over at the window seat, where a blue cushion supported a very large, long-haired black cat. He half opened one eye, revealing a glint of green, stretched out a paw, yawned, turned over and went back to sleep.

'Clearly a dangerous animal,' said Alan, smiling.

'Ah, he's there, then? And wouldn't come when called? Well, that's a cat for you. Come and sit down. He'll come fast enough when there's a meal laid out.'

'We brought a few things,' I said awkwardly. 'I mean, we couldn't just turn up at lunchtime with empty hands.'

'And,' said Lucille with a wicked grin, 'you weren't sure what sort of witch's brew I might have prepared for you.'

'That was before we saw you,' said Alan, who was clearly enjoying himself. 'It's just bread and cheese and one of those wonderful cakes from the stand near the church.'

'Oh, Moray's the best baker in the town. Lemon drizzle, I hope?'

'Lemon drizzle it is.'

'I'll ask you to cut it for me, and the bread, as well, if you please. Cheese is easier; I can manage that for myself without cutting off my thumb. And there's chicken salad and ham in the refrigerator, and help yourself to anything else you might want. I'll set out the plates and cutlery.'

She moved around deftly, with no apparent difficulty in finding what she wanted. Yet she couldn't see the cat.

'You manage very well,' I said as we settled down to our meal, 'if you don't mind my saying so.'

'For someone nearly blind, you mean. I've lived here all my life, you see. I can put my hand on anything in the pitch blackness of a winter's night, at least anything that stays where it's put. Not Lucifer, of course. He's learned to stay out from under my feet, as he vanishes for me in any but the brightest light.'

'A vanishing black cat,' said Alan. 'How appropriate.'

She cackled again.

'How do you deal with meals? I'd think cooking would be a bit tricky.'

'Soups and stews are easy; just pop whatever I like into a pot and add water.' She shot us a look, and I felt uncomfortably sure that her mind's eye could see exactly what we were thinking. She confirmed it. 'Though frogs' toes are a ruinous price these days. I don't bake anymore, but friends bring me baked goods.'

She turned serious. 'The church has been good to me. There's hardly a soul who hasn't helped me in one way or another. They run errands, help me sort out my medicines, take me places I can't reach on my own two feet, take Lucifer to the vet when he has to go.'

Lucifer, who had crept close to the table and was eyeing the platter of ham, sprang away when he heard the word 'vet' and vanished, as Lucille had said, into a dark corner where even Alan and I could scarcely see him.

'Was that the cat?' she asked at our laughter.

'An intelligent animal who apparently prefers to avoid medical care,' said Alan.

'Oh, he loves the vet, actually. She pampers him scandalously.

He just hates his carrier. But enough of this. You came for information about the jumble sale, information that I hope will help
you prove that man's perfidy.'

'It's already proven in at least one other case,' I said, and
told her about the embezzlement in America. 'And I hope to
prove he stole the money for the choir folders. But the jumble
sale money is harder. Tell me, do you – did you, I suppose I
should say – keep a record of items sold and their prices?'

'Of course. Have you ever run a jumble sale?'

'I've helped, but I've never been in charge. What I remember
is a sense of mass chaos.'

'It's all of that, but good records can help. Until this year, I
managed the show. It's only within the past few months that my
eyes have got so bad. I could see well enough to set prices,
though someone else had to attach the stickers for me; the numbers
were too small for me to read. Then all the items and their prices
were entered in an account book, and copies made so every till
had one. When an item sold, it was checked off. Then at the end
of the day we could add up the prices to tell us how much money
we ought to have, and count the money to see if it tallied.'

'And did it, usually?'

'Not exactly. Never exactly. One couldn't expect it, what with
the rush, and some people much better at making change than
others. But it was always within a pound or two, so we never
worried.'

'Did it tally this year?'

'I've no idea. I was edged right out of the whole affair. All
done with kindness, of course. "Really too much for you . . .
time for you to relax and let someone else do the work . . .
you've carried the load all these years." Pah! That man just wanted
to manage everything.'

'But surely you would have heard some talk if the accounts
came up short.'

'Oh, they came up short, all right, in one sense. We didn't
make nearly what we usually do. Some said it was because my
friends didn't contribute goods, didn't come to buy. Which of
course is simply not true. That man made off with the money
somehow, but I don't know how.'

'I think I do, and I may be able to prove it. Tell me, what is done with unsold items after the sale is over? Back home, everyone was so tired by the end of the day that we just bundled them off willy-nilly into a storage room, and then sometime later when we'd all got a little energy back, we'd take them to the Salvation Army or some other charity.'

'We do the same. At least we always did. Sometimes it was weeks before we got all the leftovers packed off to Barbara's charity shop.'

'Good. That's what I was hoping. Now, where would this year's account book be kept?'

'At the vicarage, along with other church records. There's no proper office at the church.'

'And where would I be able to find this year's leftovers?'

That afternoon we divided our efforts. Alan went to the library to look for vendors of deluxe choir folders; I went to the church to rummage in a little storage room for unsold merchandise.

The room was actually a sort of shed. It was padlocked, but very little ingenuity was required to find the key under a nearby flowerpot. The lighting was bad, and the flashlight I'd bought wasn't very powerful, but my search didn't take me very long. The leftovers were much the sort of thing one might expect: books that didn't look very appealing, lamps that might have seemed a good idea once, mediocre pictures, rather drab clothing. There were also a few items that might have attracted buyers but for their rather high prices: a small table for forty pounds that I might have considered at thirty, a small framed embroidery (the frame slightly chipped) for fifty, when it was worth thirty-five at the very most.

I slipped the embroidery and a couple of small pictures into my purse and made my furtive way out of the churchyard and back to Belle Isle.

Alan wasn't back yet, so I phoned Mr Lewison. He was rather stiff with me, but yes, he was at home, and yes, he knew where to lay his hands on the jumble sale ledger, and yes, he could bring it to me.

'I don't think I want to know why you want it,' he said.

'Then I won't tell you,' I said agreeably.

Alan returned before Mr Lewison arrived. 'I was lucky,' he

said. 'I could find only five firms that supply the sort of folders Abercrombie said he ordered. I haven't phoned them yet.'

'No, of course you couldn't do it at the library.'

'Would you rather make the calls?'

'No, you go ahead. You can sound much more business-like than I. What I'm hoping is that one company will say such an order was discussed, but they're waiting for payment before they can ship.'

He hit pay dirt on the third call. His end of the conversation was enlightening. 'I see. But I was assured that had been taken care of a few weeks ago. Give me the final price again, and I'll look into it at once.'

Mr Lewison knocked on our door just then, and was surprised when I asked him to sit down. 'We've found another length of rope,' I said. He looked puzzled. 'For hanging purposes, if he were still around to be hanged.'

'The choir folders were never ordered,' said Alan heavily. 'I just spoke with a representative of the company from whom Abercrombie requested an estimate. I would be very much surprised if Abercrombie didn't quote a very much higher price to your vicar and choir director, to justify collecting more money.'

The priest sighed. 'I can't say I'm surprised, after all the other misdeeds that have been laid at his feet.'

'And I've another,' I said. 'I'm sorry. None of this is pleasant.'

'Truth is often unpleasant. What have you uncovered?'

'I'll know for certain when I've seen the ledger.'

He handed it to me. It was a simple spiral notebook with lists of items and prices, many with checkmarks beside them. I went through rapidly until I found what I was looking for. 'Framed embroidery, parish church, walnut frame, twenty-five pounds.' I read aloud. I pulled the item in question out of my purse. 'I purloined this from the storage room a little while ago. I'll return it, of course. Note the price tag.'

'Fifty pounds. Someone made a mistake.'

'Yes. The mistake was in not destroying the ledger or removing the tags. Here's another: "Occasional table, modern, round, chipped leg, twenty pounds." I didn't bring that with me, obviously, but it was priced at forty pounds. Here are some pictures, mostly photographs, of some value perhaps for their frames. I think if you'll look them up you'll find prices far lower than the ones on the tags.'

He glanced at them, still puzzled. 'Group photos, not very good. Whoever took them wasn't a photographer. The frames aren't bad, but they're certainly priced quite high. I don't understand. Are you saying that Abercrombie reduced prices to increase sales?'

'No, I'm saying just the opposite. I believe Abercrombie either tagged all the items himself, or more likely removed the price tags before the event and replaced them with much higher ones. He left the ledger entries as they were. On the day, he collected the prices shown on the tags and pocketed the difference. If he had removed the altered tags before the unsold items were stored away, no one would ever have known. He must have decreed a single till and served at it himself, or perhaps counted on the confusion of the day making others less careful about checking prices.'

'But it's insane! The amount of money would be so small, and you say he was a millionaire!'

'He was insane, in a sense,' said Alan, 'though perhaps not by any legal definition. He had to keep proving that he was so very much cleverer than anyone else, that he was invincible.'

Mr Lewison was silent, his face dark with sorrow. 'Such a waste,' he said finally. 'So much power for good, and he turned to evil instead.'

'And ruined several people's lives in the process,' I said rather sharply.

'I haven't forgotten them,' he said, 'but neither must we forget Mr Abercrombie himself.'

I sighed. 'I keep telling other people that they must try to forgive him. I should learn to practice what I preach.'

'We all have trouble doing that, don't we?' He stood. 'I presume you will add these latest discoveries to the information you dispense at the meeting tomorrow?'

'I think we must.'

He shook his head sorrowfully and left.

'Oh, look, he left the ledger behind. And I meant to ask him to take these things back to the storage room.'

'Tomorrow,' said Alan. He sat down on the bed and started to take his shoes off. 'Sufficient unto the moment is the evil thereof.'

Evil. Just dealing with it tangentially was enervating and depressing. I found I could, after all, summon up a tiny bit of sympathy for Abercrombie, who had been entrapped in its clutches.

And had perhaps died for that reason?

TWENTY-SIX

After our nap, we spent the evening planning the meeting. I was nervous. So many things could go wrong. What if the pro- and anti-Abercrombie factions got into a slanging match? What if all of them turned against Alan and me as the common enemy? What if, conversely, everyone simply sat in sullen silence, refusing to contribute or to listen to anything that contradicted their fixed ideas?

'Is this a really, really stupid idea?' I asked. I had been asking him some variant of the same question for hours.

'It's too late to worry about that now,' he said patiently, some variant of the same answer every time. And I went back to worrying.

I had a hard time sleeping, and woke much too early. Alan was still sound asleep, so I dressed as quietly as I could and went out for a walk.

The morning was fresh and cool, and almost nobody was yet stirring. The deafening chorus of birdsong from trees a few streets away somehow emphasized the essential stillness. The bakery was awake and at work, though, sending out tantalizing aromas of yeast and cinnamon, and a sleek ginger cat walked down the street on silent pads, bent on some important errand of his own and taking no notice of me. He paused at the door of the fish-monger's and sniffed it thoroughly, then flicked his tail and disappeared around a corner.

I walked up to the High Street, silent and deserted. In another hour or so it would come alive. Now it was sleeping, gathering strength for the day ahead.

The day ahead. Which might be productive or an utter disaster, and if a disaster, one for which I felt solely responsible.

The early morning peace deserted me. I plodded back to Belle Isle.

It wasn't even seven o'clock yet, and Alan was still asleep. I made some coffee. That occupied a few – a very few – of the endless minutes until the meeting was to begin. I was tired, but I knew I couldn't sleep if I went back to bed, and I'd wake Alan if I paced. I took my coffee down to the lounge and paced there.

Traffic in Victoria Street picked up. I watched as dogs were walked, merchants prepared to open their doors, delivery vans blocked the street. A few shoppers headed for the bakery, which opened earlier than the other shops.

A few minutes before eight, Alan came downstairs. 'I thought I'd find you here or out in the garden. Buck up, old dear. It's no worse than a root canal.'

'Yes, it is. The dentist gives you anaesthetic.'

'Well, when it's all over, I'll have some anaesthetic for you, if required. On my way back from the library yesterday I found a bottle of Jack Daniel's at the off-licence. I know you don't usually have anything stronger than wine at midday, but some circumstances may justify an exception. Now let's go in and dawdle over breakfast.'

'I don't want anything.'

'I didn't think you would, but you're going to have something, anyway. You can manage some yogurt, at least, and perhaps fruit. And proper coffee,' he added, looking at my half-finished cup.

I managed to eat a little, though I thought it would stick going down. And I drank tea instead of coffee. My nerves were jumpy enough; they didn't need concentrated caffeine.

The time dragged until about nine thirty, and then suddenly, before I was ready, it was time to go to the church and face the music. Alan remembered at the last minute to bring the ledger and the bits of evidence I had taken from storage, and held my arm in a firm grip as we walked through the churchyard.

'Maybe nobody will come,' I muttered to him, and I couldn't have told anyone whether the remark was hopeful or fearful.

It was, at any rate, not going to happen. The church was half full when we got there, with more people coming in a steady stream. I would have liked to sit in the back, but Mr Lewison had been watching for us, and gestured to a pew at the very front, just under the lectern. I felt every eye on us as we walked up the aisle.

The clock chimed ten. A silence fell in the church. On the last stroke of the hour, Mr Lewison stood.

'This meeting is not, strictly speaking, a religious occasion. On the other hand, since the subject matter is very serious indeed, and closely involves many members of this church, perhaps it would be appropriate to open with a prayer. The Lord be with you.'

'And also with you,' chorused most of the audience.

'Let us pray. We are gathered here, dear Lord, to seek the truth. We are in distress; heal us. We are confused; show us the way. We are groping in darkness; show us thy light and thy truth. Give us charity of heart and a spirit of forgiveness, O Father, and make us whole. Amen.'

In a few carefully chosen words, he set out the known facts. Mr William Abercrombie had been a priest of the Episcopal Church in America. He had come to Alderney with the apparent intention of settling here permanently. He had been an active volunteer at the parish church, though he could not take up clerical duties until the vetting process of the Church of England had been completed. He had enjoyed walking, and had been found lying dead on a steep path nearly two weeks before.

Mr Lewison cleared his throat. 'Mr Partridge is here with us this morning. I ask you, sir, to tell us anything you can about the circumstances of his death.'

Derek stood up. 'He was about halfway down the Blue Bridge path, which as you know is quite steep. He had fallen and hit his head on a large stone, causing a cranial fracture and haemorrhage. It was estimated that he had been dead less than an hour before he was found.'

He sat down. Mr Lewison took a deep breath. 'The death was an accident, then?'

Derek stayed in his seat. 'There were no indications that it was not.'

Well, everyone in the church knew that already, but there was a little flurry of whispers anyway. I was thankful now that we were sitting in front; if everyone was looking at us, at least we didn't have to meet their eyes.

'Now,' said Mr Lewison, clearing his throat again, 'we come to the part of this discussion that may prove painful to many of you. I am well aware that many of the people of the town and the church of St Anne had deep affection for Mr Abercrombie. It has unfortunately been proven quite conclusively that our affection and our trust were misplaced. I will call once more upon Mr Partridge to tell us what he learned from the American authorities.'

'In searching for any family Mr Abercrombie might have had, we asked for the help of the American Embassy in London, who contacted the church where he had been serving before he came to England and then Alderney. There the authorities learned that Mr Abercrombie, had he stayed in America, would have been arrested for larceny. They had certain proof that he had stolen a large sum of money from the church treasury. He would also have been stripped of his authority as a priest. The state of Ohio was about to apply for extradition when word came of Abercrombie's death.'

There were a good many present who hadn't known that. This time the whispers were punctuated by gasps, and here and there a stifled sob.

We heard someone get to his feet. Mr Lewison nodded. 'Yes, sir?'

'I'd like to ask just how much money was stolen.'

Derek replied, 'Something in the neighbourhood of one hundred thousand dollars American. That's around sixty-five thousand pounds.'

More gasps.

I felt the butterflies in my stomach start doing aerobatics. I knew what was coming. Sure enough, Mr Lewison looked at me. He spoke gently.

'Many of you know that our visitors Mrs Martin and Mr Nesbitt, by reason of their having been the ones to find Mr Abercrombie on the hill, have taken an interest in him and conducted some researches of their own. Mrs Martin, would you tell us what you've found?'

My knees were shaking, but I managed to get to my feet. 'First, some computer research revealed that an elderly parishioner of Mr Abercrombie's back in Ohio had died recently, leaving her entire estate to him. It amounted to over two million dollars. Close to a million and a half pounds.' I waited for the reaction to die down and then went on. 'Further, despite the fact that he had inherited a great deal of money and had stolen a great deal more, he still went about defrauding this church of small sums. Those of you who attend St Anne's will remember that he took up a collection to fund the purchase of new choir folders, with the understanding that if the monies collected were not enough, he would make up the difference. This was some time ago. The folders have never been ordered; we checked with the company concerned and they were waiting for payment. Finally, I have proved that he went to rather elaborate lengths to steal part of the proceeds of the recent jumble sale.'

A woman in the middle of the nave stood and said belligerently, 'That's impossible! The money tallied with the ledger. I saw that with my own eyes.'

'I have no doubt it did. He had repriced items. Perhaps all of them, perhaps only some of the more expensive.' Alan handed me the framed embroidery. 'This, for example, is marked with a price of fifty pounds. It is listed in the ledger at twenty-five. It did not sell, but if it had, Mr Abercrombie could have pocketed a nice little profit of twenty-five pounds with no one the wiser.'

'One item!' sneered the woman.

'Not just one. I have a few more here, and if you search the storeroom for the other unsold items, I think you'll find them all marked far higher than the entries in the ledger. Now if you're going to ask me why a millionaire would find it necessary to stoop to such tactics, I fear I have no reasonable explanation.'

I sat down, feeling as if I'd run an obstacle course. There were murmurings, but no one else questioned what I'd said.

'Thank you, Mrs Martin. Now it needs to be said that you have, I fear, heard only negative things about Mr Abercrombie. Sad as it is to tell, those things are all true, but we are not conducting a crucifixion here. We know, at least those of us here at the parish church know, that there was another side to the man. He did indeed work hard at several thankless volunteer jobs, and for that we owe him our gratitude. I knew him for only a short time, but in that time he helped me considerably with some mundane parish tasks, and for that I personally am grateful. I would like now to open up the meeting to anyone who has any comments at all to make about Mr Abercrombie.'

Dead silence. Then there was a little stir, and I turned around to see. Martha Duckett stood up. I gave a mental cheer. Brave lady!

'I–I have to believe everything that has been said this morning. If he really did steal all that money, when he didn't even need it . . . but there was another side to him. There really was. He was a pleasant man, with a good word for everyone, and he really did help so much with so many small duties. I suppose I'm just old and stupid, but I–I really did like him a lot.' Her voice broke and she sat down amid soothing murmurs. I saw the woman sitting next to her pat her on the shoulder and hand her a tissue.

Then it was Rebecca Smith. 'He supported the choir. I think we were all grateful for that. I'm not so happy about the folders. We need them badly, and no one has much money to spare. I'm still trying to deal with the idea that he took our money. I wouldn't have believed it. You're sure, Mrs Martin?'

Alan stood. 'At my wife's suggestion, I looked up possible suppliers and phoned them till I found the right one. There's really no doubt, I'm afraid. Abercrombie had talked with them and obtained a quote for the very nice folders he suggested to you, and then nothing further was done. They have kept the order open, awaiting payment.'

Robin stood. 'It's no secret to most of you that I disliked the man, for many reasons. He did, however, have a good idea about the folders. We need new ones, although perhaps nothing quite as elaborate as what he proposed. However, as a choir member, I will, if you will allow me, remit payment for them, if you, Mrs Martin, will give me the pertinent information.'

He sat down. A woman I didn't know spoke up. 'I think we need to know why you disliked him so much.'

Robin stood again, looking weary. 'It isn't my story to tell. I will say simply that I learned through a friend of a truly despicable thing he did at his old parish, something that caused a great deal of heartbreak, something wholly unworthy of a priest. After that, I could only despise him.'

Speculative murmurs, which were quelled when another voice spoke. 'I hope you can hear me. It's hard for me to stand; my broken ankle is still somewhat painful and I'm not yet quite secure on my crutches. I would like to tell you my story.'

TWENTY-SEVEN

I clutched Alan's hand. Mr Lewison said, 'Mrs Small, are you sure? You are not at all well, and this will be—'

'Painful, yes. But also necessary. It concerns my sister, my twin sister, who committed suicide because of Mr Abercrombie.'

The shock was so great that no one even gasped. The room was completely silent.

She told her story, simply, with no prejudicial remarks. When she had finished, she said, 'I very nearly followed my sister to the grave. If I had not been found, after falling on Longis Common, I would almost certainly have died of exposure. I have been persuaded, by Mr Lewison and others, that I must forgive Mr Abercrombie, not only for the sake of my own mental health, but because I have come to believe that my life was not saved so that I could nourish hatred for the rest of my life. I have not yet been able to forgive him, but I'm trying hard, and one day I will manage it. I hope that all of you who have been disappointed by learning the truth about him, or who have actually been defrauded, will also find it in your hearts to forgive. That's all.'

I doubt there was a dry eye in the house, but through the tears there were subdued cries of sympathy and support, and the occasional 'Well done, Alice!'

It was the equivalent of a standing ovation in America, and I was extremely touched – and extremely relieved.

I would have been delighted if Mr Lewison had chosen to end the meeting then, but he had still one thing to bring into the open.

'I am grateful to all of you who have spoken. I know it wasn't easy for anyone. There is one matter still unresolved. We may never be able to resolve it, but we need at least to talk about it. There has been some speculation that Mr Abercrombie's death might not have been an accident, that someone, though I hate even to say it in this sacred space, might have pushed him down that hill. You have heard that there are those who might have thought they had reason for such a horrific act, forbidden by the laws both of God and of man. If there is anyone in this room who has any knowledge about this, I urge you to speak now.'

Silence. It felt as if no one dared breathe.

The priest let the silence prolong itself. At last he said, 'Very well. If anyone has anything to say to me privately, I will remain here in the Lady Chapel all afternoon.' He gestured for us to rise. 'And now may the blessing of God Almighty, the Father, the Son and the Holy Ghost, be upon you and remain with you, now and always. Amen.'

The crowd dispersed with much less than the usual conversation. They had been too moved by Alice's speech to return right away to the everyday world. Once they got beyond the confines of the churchyard I suspect that a good deal of revisionist history would start developing. 'You know, I always felt there was something just a bit off about him.' 'Oh, I know. Just a little *too* nice, too smooth, if you know what I mean. I know I said to George when the man first came to town . . .' And so on. It was human nature. We hate to admit we've been wrong, hate especially to think we've been made to look like fools.

Alan and I didn't talk at all until we got back to our room, when Alan silently opened the bottle of bourbon and poured each of us a small tot.

I took a gulp.

'Better than you had feared?' asked Alan after he had done the same.

'Much better. I think even those who had loved the man came away feeling . . . I don't know, perhaps the word is "cleansed". Sad, of course, but not heartbroken. More than the feet of their idol was made of clay, but there was at least a little bronze, anyway. And I think Mr Lewison handled it beautifully. There's hope now for healing in the congregation.'

'Robin helped, with his offer to pay for the folders.'

'He really is a good man, just a little . . . prickly.'

'But,' said Alan, finishing his drink, 'we're no closer to knowing whether Abercrombie was killed or not.'

'No. And we're leaving on Monday. Probably we never will know.'

'Of course,' he mused, 'there was at least one person of interest missing.'

'Harold Guillot. At least we think he was missing. We don't know what he looks like.'

'True, but if he'd been there someone would have mentioned it. There's been a good deal of interest in his disappearance.'

'You're probably right. Oh, by the way, I need to put that stuff back in the storage room. And return the ledger to Mr Lewison.'

'I gave it to him just as we turned to leave. I left the other things on the pew; someone will look after them, I'm sure. Do you want some lunch?'

'Oddly enough, I do. I'm starving. Stress, I suppose. But let's drive down to the harbour. I'm too wiped out to walk that far, and I'd rather not talk to anybody here in town for a while yet.'

We didn't say much as we ate our meal. There were too many thoughts we needed to sort through, conflicting ideas and emotions screaming out for dominance. I presume the food was at least acceptable, because at one point I looked down to find my plate empty. I had consumed it purely as fuel.

Alan was of two minds about returning the car, which we probably wouldn't need anymore, but decided to keep it for the Monday morning drive to the airport. 'And you never know,' he said as he dropped me off at Belle Isle and went to park it. 'Something might come up.'

When he got back I was waiting for him in the lounge. 'Alan, we must go back and make sure someone's dealt with those pictures. Tomorrow's Sunday, and it would never do for the congregation to come in and find them lying there in the pew.'

'And you didn't want to walk over by yourself.'

'No.' I didn't need to say more. Alan understands that I hate confrontation and avoid it whenever possible.

'We may not find anyone there.'

'Then we'll put them back in the storage room. I know where the key is kept.'

As it happened, Rebecca Smith was there, fussing about in the choir stalls.

'Oh, dear, are we interrupting you?'

'No. I'm just changing the anthem for tomorrow. The one I had planned needs a strong tenor section. They know this one

by heart, so they can do it at the last moment. Did you need
something?' she asked. There was still some hostility in her
tone. Well, I had unseated her idol and destroyed her illusions.
Of course she'd still be a bit sore.

'No, it's just that I left those pictures behind, and I need to
put them back.' I looked around. The front pew was empty and
clean. 'Did you see them, by any chance? Or maybe someone
else put them away.'

'I put the embroidery away. It's a lovely piece of work.
Barbara's grandmother did it, and she cherishes it. It was noble
of her to donate it to the sale, and I intend to buy it, at the proper
price of course, and give it back to her.'

I thought about offering to do that myself, but quickly thought
better of it. No matter that I meant it as a conciliatory gesture;
it might not be seen that way. No, better just to leave this island
without too many hard feelings in our wake.

'As for the pictures, here they are.' She picked them up from
her music stand. 'They ought never to have been in the sale at
all; I can't imagine who put them in, or who they thought might
buy them. They're terribly bad, as pictures, but they're a part
of the history of this church and meant to be kept. This one is
a choir picnic from last summer.' She handed it to me. 'The
only face you can recognize is Robin's; you can't miss that
crooked smile.'

I glanced at it, picked out Robin, and then looked more
closely. 'And who,' I asked, my voice sounding odd even to
myself, 'is the man standing next to Robin?'

'Oh, that's his friend, the missing Mr Guillot. When he turns
up again I'm going to have a few things to say to him. Our choir
just isn't big enough that tenors can come and go as they please!'

I handed it to Alan without a word; my voice didn't seem to
want to function. He looked, then looked more closely, and
stared at me.

'What?' said Rebecca, looking from one of us to the other.

Alan cleared his throat. 'Nothing, really. It's just that he
resembles someone we saw once.'

'Hmph! Don't see how you can tell. I think Martha's grandson
took that picture with his mobile and didn't hold it steady.
Anyway, I'll see that the pictures get back where they belong.'

'Thank you,' I managed. 'We'll see you tomorrow, then.'

'Alan!' I said urgently, the minute we were out of earshot. 'The track suit.'

'Yes. Unmistakable, I'd say. Once seen, never forgotten.'

'Bright green stripes. That man on the Zig-Zag.'

'A few minutes after Abercrombie died. And now,' he said grimly, 'among the missing.'

TWENTY-EIGHT

'Talk to Robin first, or the police?' I asked. I didn't want to do either.

'It would be a courtesy to see Robin first. There may be some explanation we haven't considered.'

But we couldn't find Robin. He didn't answer his phone, and we didn't know where he lived.

'Derek, then,' said Alan with a sigh. 'I truly hate to do this, but I don't think we have a choice.'

We trudged to the police station. Derek wasn't there. 'He's off duty,' said the friendly stranger who greeted us. 'He's hardly had time off these two weeks, and his boy has a football match this afternoon. What can I do?'

There was a long pause before I finally said, 'It wasn't important. Would you ask Derek to phone us when he gets back?'

The man looked at us quizzically, but took down both our phone numbers. We left the station, dispirited. 'I'm going to try Robin again,' I said finally, as we neared Annie's bookshop.

'Wait,' said Alan, his hand on my arm. He pointed.

Robin was coming out of the shop with a bag full of books. He turned our way and then stopped, his face blank.

I bit the bullet and moved toward him. 'Robin, I'm sure we're the last people you want to see right now, and I'm sorry to intrude, but we need to talk with you. It's urgent.'

He looked up the street. 'You've just been to the police,' he said.

'No. Well, yes, but Derek wasn't in, and we didn't want to talk to anyone else. We did try to call you first, but you didn't answer.'

'No.' His silence spoke volumes, and lasted some seconds. Then he sighed. 'Very well, then, come with me. I live just up here.'

Not a word was spoken as we walked to his house in a street near QE2 Street.

He lived, as I would have expected, in a very old house. At another time I'm sure he would have wanted to point out the details of how it had been modernized for comfort without destroying the essential character of the structure. He made no attempt to show us anything, and we probably wouldn't have had the attention to spare anyway. He gestured us to a couple of chairs and sat down in another, putting his bag of books on the floor.

'Now. What is so urgent?'

'We happened to see a picture of Mr Guillot,' said Alan, going straight to the point. 'We both recognized him at once as a man we saw on the Zig-Zag, just a few minutes before we found Abercrombie's body.'

Robin said nothing.

'We had forgotten all about it. He was just one of several people we encountered.'

'Yet you remember him now.'

'It was his clothes. That track suit is unmistakable.'

No response.

'You see why we wanted to talk to you first,' I persisted. 'We must take this to the police, but if you know anything about this, we'd like to hear it.'

'I have nothing to tell you.'

'Or to tell to the police?'

Silence.

Alan stood. 'Very well. We will have to act without your information, then. But if you should happen to see Mr Guillot—' he looked hard at the bag of books – 'you may want to tell him that we intend to go to the authorities as soon as Derek Partridge is back on duty.'

'That is understood.' He walked us to the door. 'I will not try to prevent your doing what you think to be your duty. Nor do I bear you any ill will for doing so. I would ask you to remember, however, that things are not always what they seem.'

After which he closed the door firmly and I thought I heard the snick of a lock.

'Harold is there, isn't he?' I said when we had regained Victoria Street.

'Two hearts that beat as one, my dear. The books were for

him. He must be getting frightfully bored, shut away in there, afraid to see or talk to anyone.'

'You think he killed him, then?' I asked with a fine disregard of pronouns.

'I see no reason why an innocent person should hide.'

With that gloomy thought, we went back to Belle Isle and had a badly needed nap.

My phone woke me, long before I wanted it to. My eyes felt sandpapered. The phone stopped before I could reach it, but the number displayed was an Alderney one. I called back.

'Mrs Martin? Derek Partridge here.'

That woke me up. 'Yes, Derek. Thanks for calling back. The fact is, we have something very important to tell you. Can you come here, or shall we come to you?'

'I need to be here for a while, if you wouldn't mind coming here. Important how? Will I need reinforcements?'

'Possibly. I don't like to say more on the phone.'

'Right. See you soon.'

The streets were crowded as we walked to the station. Somewhere blackbirds were singing to each other. No one we passed seemed to be paying any attention to us. My steps grew lighter.

It didn't take long to tell Derek the story. 'You're quite sure of the identification?'

'Quite sure. The photo's terribly fuzzy, but there's no mistaking those bright green stripes. And Rebecca Smith identified the wearer as Guillot.'

'You didn't mention this chap in your earlier report of finding the body.'

'I'd forgotten all about it. It seemed of no importance at the time. Everything else about that day was wiped out by what came later.'

'Right.' He sighed and stood up. 'We need to find the chap and bring him in.'

'We think we know where he is,' I said, somewhat reluctantly. 'We talked to Robin Whicker about this. They're friends, you know. And we believe Harold is hiding in Robin's house.'

'Or at least,' said Alan, 'he was.'

The look Derek gave us was not particularly friendly. 'And you waited how long to tell us this, sir?'

'We wanted to tell you personally,' I said. 'And how did your son do in his soccer match?'

'His team lost. Badly. Now if you'll excuse me?'

'He's right, you know,' said Alan as we left, more-or-less with our tails between our legs. 'We should have reported it at once, to the other man on duty.'

'But if we had reported it before we talked to Robin, we wouldn't have known Guillot was there. Which in fact he may not have been. We're just speculating.'

'On the basis of some pretty good evidence, especially that locked door. Nobody, as we've been told before, locks doors on Alderney. And even granting that point, there was no excuse at all for us not to have gone right back to the station and reported what we believed.'

I linked my arm through his. 'No excuse, except that we're both confused about what the right thing is in this case. I refuse to feel guilty. What will be, will be.'

Alan muttered something.

'My dearest love, we have only one more day on this lovely island. And it is still lovely, no matter what. The actions of one man, no matter how dreadful, can't affect this place for very long. It's been here for many millennia, with people living here, they think, for at least the past five. We've been here for two weeks. A heartbeat in the history here. Less than a heartbeat. Yes, bad things have happened and yes, we have played a part in some of them. Parts were pretty awful, and some of our memories of this place will be dark. There are some people living here who will be glad to see us go. But there are other memories, too. Let's try to put it all behind us and enjoy our last proper evening.'

'You've suddenly become frightfully philosophical. A few hours ago you were wringing your hands over this whole tangle; now you're ready to put it behind us. What changed?'

'I'm not sure, but I think it was when Robin forgave us. You remember, he said he had no ill will. And then there were the blackbirds. I don't know. Maybe it's just getting the whole thing off our shoulders, or knowing that it's almost over, or that the ones hurt the worst are beginning to deal with it all. Anyway, I'd like to have a drink at the Georgian House and then a really good dinner somewhere, and then I'd like to drive out to the golf course and see if we can't find some hedgehogs.'

'You're sure you want to risk the Georgian House? It's pretty popular.'

'You're saying there will be people there who know us. I just don't care anymore. It's over, Alan. We'll be fine.'

The pub was crowded on a Saturday night, but a couple of people made room for us, and we had our drink in peace. No one made any reference to the troubled proceedings of the morning, which made me grateful again for the innate courtesy of the islanders.

I did tense up a bit when Derek walked in and saw us, but he simply shook his head and shrugged. 'He was gone,' I murmured to Alan.

'As we expected,' he said, and finished his pint.

As we left in search of dinner, Suzi the hedgehog (and train) lady walked in the door. 'You know, I still feel badly that you didn't get to see any of our most famous critters.'

'We're going to drive out to the golf course tonight to see if we have better luck. I hope we can find some; we're leaving Monday morning so it's almost our last chance.'

'Oh, look, I have a better idea. Why don't I pick you up in my car and drive you around? I know most of the best spots to find them. I don't want you to leave Alderney without seeing them. They really are sweet.'

'That's very kind of you. Are you sure? You must have better things to do with a Saturday night.'

'I love hedgehogs, you see. I love to show them off. You're staying at Belle Isle, aren't you? I'll stop for you at about ten, if that's not too late. It'll hardly be dark enough any earlier.'

We found an excellent meal at a little French restaurant we hadn't tried before, and dawdled over it until after nine. Then we went back to our room and changed into warm clothes for the chilly night, along with hiking boots. Taking our sticks, we went downstairs to wait for Suzi.

Walking through dark fields and along remote roads, keeping an eye out for rabbit holes and the natural hazards left by grazing animals, may not sound like a riotous way to spend a Saturday night. In fact, we had a wonderful time. The countryside was full of the sounds and scents of summer, and the sky was full of stars, more stars than we could ever see at home, what with city lights. The evening wasn't so very dark, though, once our eyes got used to it; midsummer twilight lasts all night in these climes.

Suzi led us confidently through parts of the island I don't think we'd visited before, though in the confusing dimness it was a little hard to tell. She shone her flashlight under hedges (a good place for the animals, as one might expect). We were quiet, not wanting to frighten them away, though she said they weren't easily frightened. And after about twenty minutes of wandering . . .

'There! And there's another!'

They stopped as if transfixed by the light of her torch. They were smaller than I'd expected, and sure enough, their fur was a lovely pale blonde. Suzi picked one up; it didn't try to get away, though it did tuck its nose and tail under defensively. 'Would you like to hold it?'

I took it in gingerly fashion, expecting a prickly handful. But the fur on its belly was soft; it had quills only on top, and they weren't so very harsh. I was enchanted. The little animal lay quietly in my hand. Alan picked up the other one, and I could see his face well enough to see the same doting expression I could feel on mine.

'And remember, they have no fleas, so you don't need to worry. Aren't they sweet?'

It was a delightful way to round out what had been meant as a holiday.

TWENTY-NINE

W
e planned to attend church at eight o'clock, when the congregation would be smaller and we would see fewer people we knew. I was still a little nervous about a possible backlash. Yesterday had gone far better than I had feared, but sometimes people change their reactions after they've had time to think.

However, we got to bed late Saturday night and slept, after a stressful day, like a couple of rocks. I woke only when the bell began to chime for the early service.

'Oops,' I said to Alan, who yawned and turned over.

He was awake by the time I'd showered and dressed, and we went down to breakfast and ate a huge meal. 'It's our last chance,' I said in justification. 'We're leaving too early tomorrow.'

Our waitress heard me. 'We can arrange an early breakfast for you,' she said with a smile.

'No, it's all right. It's just a short flight to Southampton, and then we'll be home soon.'

'At least take some fruit with you. I'll set it out a bit early. You can't travel on an empty stomach!'

I thought that if the Trislander encountered any rough air, I might be better off with an empty stomach, but I simply thanked her and asked for another cup of coffee.

Alan paid our bill, since we weren't sure if anyone would be about when we left in the morning, and then we walked to church. It was another of Alderney's perfect days, sunny and crisp. It almost made me wish we could stay longer.

Almost.

Our reception at St Anne's could best be described as mixed. There were smiles as we walked in; there were also heads turned aside, to avoid our eyes. We chose a pew on the Gospel side, far enough forward that we might not have anyone beside us. (I've never known a congregation, in any variety of church from Roman

Catholic to African-American Gospel Baptist, that didn't fill up the back of the church first.)

I was stunned, then, when a couple came up the aisle and stopped at our pew. Alice Small slowly pushed her walker; Phil Cooper assisted her into the pew.

There was no time for more than an exchange of glances before the organist launched into a prelude, we all stood and the procession started up the aisle.

The service proceeded in its usual order until the time came for the homily. Mr Lewison asked us to be seated for a moment.

'First, I want you all to welcome back your vicar. He is still officially on holiday, but he returned to Alderney late yesterday, and I'm sure we're all happy to have him here. He has kindly allowed me to preside for this, my last Sunday with you all, but he asked to say a few words. His remarks will serve in lieu of a homily this morning. Mr Venables.'

He had been sitting in the front pew, wearing a clerical grey suit. With his back turned to us, we had not seen his collar. He stood, bowed to the altar and turned to face us.

He was a small man with sparse grey hair and a kindly face. I imagined I could feel the wave of love passing between him and his congregation. He spoke simply, without preliminary.

'You have been having a difficult time, and I'm sorry it happened while I was away. I'm sure Mr Lewison did not anticipate such troubles when he agreed to serve as locum, and I, personally, owe him a great debt of gratitude, as I know you do, as well. I want to speak to you for a few minutes this morning about one of the most crucial doctrines of our faith, the concept of forgiveness.

'When Peter asked our Lord how many times he should forgive, Jesus replied "Seventy times seven." He wasn't saying that the four-hundred-and-ninety-first time we were allowed to bear a grudge.'

Small chuckles rippled through the church.

'He meant that forgiveness must be extended over and over, endlessly. He made it clear that our own sins would be forgiven only as we forgave those who sinned against us. Again and again, Jesus stressed forgiveness. And then, on the cross, he gave us his own example when he forgave those who put him there and tortured him.

'That wasn't easy for him, and forgiveness is never easy for us – but it is necessary. Necessary for our relationship with God, and with each other.

'Many of you have been deeply hurt by a man whom I mistakenly welcomed into our midst. I hope you can find it in your hearts to forgive me for that terrible mistake, but it is essential that you forgive him. *Why?* you ask. He'll never know or care. Well, I'm not at all sure you're right about that. We do say we believe in eternal life. But even if it were true that he will not know, you cannot and must not let bitterness and hatred remain in your heart.

'Some of you will remember the phrase in the Litany where we pray to be delivered from envy, hatred, malice and all uncharitableness, and from all assaults of the devil. You know, God is an excellent psychologist. He knows all about the damage hatred can cause in your soul, and he commands you to root it out – with his help, of course.

'I hope you will feel free to come to me when your struggles to do this seem impossible, and I'll try to help.'

He sat down, and Mr Lewison stood and continued the service with the Nicene Creed. I looked over at Alice and saw the tears trickling down her cheeks. I rummaged in my purse and handed her a tissue.

When the service was over, Alan and I were minded to leave promptly, avoiding the usual gathering for conversation, but Alice put a hand on my arm. 'We were wondering if you would like to join us at my house for Sunday lunch? It won't be anything very elaborate, but we'd like you to come if you can.'

'We'd like that,' I found myself saying, not at all sure that we would. 'I hope it won't be too much trouble for you.'

'I can hobble about, and Phil's an excellent cook. He's done most of the work. In about an hour, if that's convenient?' She left, assisted by the devoted Phil.

'What did I just let us in for?' I asked Alan in an undertone as we threaded our way through little groups in the churchyard. 'I mean, I had to say yes – there was no way I could compare notes with you.'

Alan shrugged. 'We had no other plans for this afternoon. At any rate, I don't think we'll be bored.'

'I think that a little boredom would make a nice change!'

We read yesterday's papers in the lounge, as the Sunday papers wouldn't be delivered until tomorrow, and fidgeted. I thought about starting to pack, decided there wasn't really enough time and had a sudden unpleasant thought. 'Oh, Alan, we forgot to ship our books back home, and they weigh a ton! We can't possibly take them with us, and we're leaving tomorrow before the post office opens.'

'Why don't you put them all back in the bag, and we'll take them with us to Alice's. Perhaps Phil would be willing to take care of that little chore for us.'

'If he's over his snit. He wasn't very happy with us there for a while.'

'He heard that sermon on forgiveness this morning, don't forget.' Alan grinned.

I went upstairs to gather our scattered books.

We walked to Alice's house. It wasn't far, and of course there was very little parking space. Today the house looked very different. Curtains blew gently in the breeze. The front door was set hospitably wide open, and a large black-and-white cat sat on the stoop licking a paw. He paused in his grooming long enough to give us a thoughtful look and then began to wash thoroughly behind one ear, ignoring us completely.

'Well, and hello to you, too, Sammy,' I said.

Alice appeared in the doorway with her walker. 'He's the Cat That Walks by Himself,' she said. 'If he decides he likes you, you won't be able to fend him off, but he prefers to take his own sweet time about making a decision.'

'Like any proper cat,' said Alan, stepping carefully around Sammy.

'Did you give Grace the day off?' I asked, looking around for her.

'Yes, until this evening. I'm needing less and less assistance as I learn how to cope, so it's just . . . personal care . . . that I need her to help me with.' She looked a little embarrassed and changed the subject. 'Phil did all the cooking for our meal. He roasted a chicken and made potato salad and a green salad, and a trifle that looks quite perfect. And there's a bottle of white wine on ice, and more in the fridge. You didn't drive, did you?'

'No,' I said. 'So yes, thank you, we will have some wine.'

'Then do come and sit down, and we'll eat.'

When we had expressed our admiration of her house, which was bright and airy, with clean lines and no clutter, and had complimented Phil on his cooking, conversation petered out. I tried desperately to think of some more small talk, but nothing came. I took another sip of wine.

Alice cleared her throat. 'You're wondering why we wanted you to come.'

'We were, rather,' said Alan calmly. 'You have some reason to associate us with unpleasantness.'

'Yes,' said Alice, 'but it was none of your doing. And you saved my life. I wasn't at all sure I was happy about that at the time, but as I said earlier, I've come to be grateful. You and Mr Lewison helped me see that I had a great deal to live for.' She glanced quickly at Phil and then turned back to us.

'You see, my sister's suicide made me desperately unhappy. I was barely stumbling through life for a few months. But gradually I began to heal. It was partly Sammy, who is a perfect love when he wants to be, and my flowers – I do love flowers – and my friends. Alderney is a friendly place, and everyone was very kind. And maybe it was something about the very air of this place. It does feel like home to me, even though I wasn't born here.

'I was learning to live again. The sun seemed bright and warm; food tasted good; music sounded sweet. And then That Man came.' Her voice had become ragged. She stopped.

Phil was sitting next to her, the better to assist her. He put his hand over hers and took up the story.

'It was as if she'd been turned to stone, that first time she saw him. I don't know if you're familiar with the legend of the Medusa?'

'Vaguely. We don't study the classics in America as you do here.'

'As we used to do; not so much anymore. So you know she could turn to stone anyone who looked into her eyes. It didn't even take that for Alice. When she came to church that morning

and the vicar introduced him to the congregation, she actually
went rigid in her seat. I was sitting next to her, and I could feel
every muscle tense.

'She and I had been seeing a good deal of each other. We
have a lot in common – both widowed with grown children,
both lovers of flowers and good music and cats. We . . . well,
nothing had been said, but we were both . . . at least *I* had a
notion . . . but then he came, and it was as if Alice . . . simply
wasn't there anymore. I had driven her to church that day, but
she walked out before Communion, even, and disappeared,
without a word to me. Of course when I got home I tried to
talk to her, but it was like talking to Sammy. No, worse. You
always get some response from Sammy, even if he just yawns
and walks away.'

Alice looked at Phil, a look full of love and apology. 'You
had it right. I had been turned to stone. All the grief, all the
bitterness, all the hatred had come back, with such force that
. . . I think I nearly had a stroke, or a heart attack. Well, in a
way it was a heart attack; it attacked my heart. You said, Mrs
Martin, and Mr Lewison said, that hatred is corrosive. You're
quite right. It was eating away at me. I was becoming nothing
but a walking lump of bitterness. I wanted nothing in life
except revenge. I turned my back on everything and everyone,
even Phil.'

'You still came to church,' I observed.

'Only because it gave me the chance to see him in action, to
feed my misery. I wanted to keep the flame burning at white
heat, because I intended to do something about it, though I didn't
know what.'

I put down my wine glass and came to full alert. Were we
about to hear a confession?

THIRTY

Alice interpreted my look and smiled. 'No, I'm not going to confess to murder. Although I murdered him over and over in my heart. That's supposed to be just as bad, isn't it?'

'Not in the eyes of the law,' said Alan. He sounded grim. I can sometimes read Alan's thoughts, though not as often as he reads mine (I'm told I have an expressive face and should never, never play poker). I knew now that he was wondering if Alice was being completely candid.

I thought she was. I didn't know her well, and that always makes it harder to assess a person's words, but she was being remarkably open about her deepest feelings. I nodded encouragingly.

'And then he really did die, and I went to pieces. I had wished for his death, had even tried to pray for it, knowing all the time that I was wicked and no one would listen, or care. I thought maybe I'd somehow made it happen, and I was glad and miserable at the same time, and – well, you know most of the rest. I just wanted to stop the pain, and I never thought that if I . . . that there might be people who would be unhappy if I died.'

'Idiot,' said Phil in an affectionate growl.

'That's all, really. I just wanted you to know the whole story. I haven't forgiven him yet. I don't know if I'll ever be able to. He did so much harm to so many people. But I'm trying to understand that he was a sick man, who cared only for money and power. He could have done so much good, but that devil in him kept pressing on for more, and more, until . . .' She had to stop again.

Phil sighed, not happy, but resigned.

'And I wanted to tell you both,' she went on, having regained control of her voice, 'that in the end I'm grateful to you. And I–I think if someone did kill that man, then I'd rather he weren't found. It might be wrong of me, but I know how I'd be feeling now if I had done that, and I do believe that he's suffering enough.' She looked directly at Alan. 'You're a policeman. I don't expect you to agree with me. I do know that it's a terrible thing to take a life. That Man took Aleta's life, as surely as if he'd handed her the bottle of pills, and now he's paying for it. If I'm sure of anything, I'm sure of that. And I don't see how more suffering, suffering imposed by law, could balance the scales of justice. Am I making any sense at all?'

'I think so,' I said. 'You believe that, if someone did push Abercrombie down that hill, he or she is suffering now from guilt, and needs no further punishment.'

'Yes.'

'You do realize,' said Alan, 'that any punishment he might receive would be merciful, when all the circumstances were understood.'

'It might be. It might not.'

I looked at Alan. There was something in her voice . . .

'Alice,' he said gravely, 'do you know who that person might be?'

'No!' she and Phil said together. Loudly. Definitely. And then they closed their mouths firmly.

Phil stood up and said, 'There's trifle for pudding. And would you like coffee?'

Discussion closed. Silence. Then Phil stood and helped Alice with her walker, and we adjourned to the sitting room for our trifle.

'Now we've got that over, there was actually another reason we wanted to see you,' said Alice when we were comfortably seated. She smiled at Phil, who became very busy pouring coffee.

'I think I can guess,' I said. 'May we offer our congratulations?'

'Nobody knows yet,' she went on. 'It's too soon. But you . . . well . . .'

'We're leaving the island tomorrow and won't tell anybody, so we're safe.' I kissed them both, and Alan shook hands all round, and when we'd had our coffee and left our books, which they agreed to post for us, we took our leave.

*   *   *

'They know,' I said as we walked back to Belle Isle.

'Or they have a strong suspicion,' said Alan. 'And they're not going to tell us or anyone else who he is.'

'Certainly "he", don't you think?'

'I do. And there isn't a thing we can do about it.'

'No.'

We spent the rest of the day packing and wishing we hadn't left all our books with Alice and Phil.

The alarm went off at seven. I hadn't slept well; I never do when I have to travel. I showered and dressed and opened the curtains.

The fog was so thick I could barely see across the street.

'Alan, look at this!'

Alan's phone rang. He said 'yes' and 'no' and 'yes' again and clicked off. 'Our flight has been cancelled. Nothing is landing or taking off. There's another around noon, if the fog clears, and one more at four or so. We'll just have to wait and see.'

There are few things that irritate me more than getting all ready to do something and then not being able to do it. We now had an unknown number of hours to fill and no productive way to fill them. We couldn't even read, as the newspapers hadn't reached Belle Isle yet. I suppose they came by the plane that couldn't land. We couldn't go for a walk, even if we'd wanted to in the dense fog, because we didn't dare get too far from the car; we didn't know when we might get a call to go to the airport. It was too early to call Jane and tell her to expect us when she saw us.

'Well, we can have breakfast, anyway,' said Alan.

Small comfort.

We went down at eight to find our usual places set. Our wait-ress smiled when we came in. 'I knew you wouldn't be going in this fog. So shall I cook you something lovely?'

'Porridge for me,' I said. 'It's that kind of a day.'

She nodded. 'Disgusting for holidaymakers, isn't it? It's good for the gardens, though. It's been far too dry. And, Mr Nesbitt, you'll have . . .?'

He opted for porridge, too, and when our meals came we ate them very slowly. I was trying, with no success at all, to think of something, anything, to occupy an indefinite amount of time.

'Would it be a good idea to turn in the car here in town? We can get a cab to the airport, and we certainly won't need it for anything else today.'

'The trouble is, we don't know how much notice we'll have of the flight. It would be sickening to be told the flight was ready and not be able to get there on time.'

'True.' I asked for another cup of coffee.

We managed to kill an hour over that fifteen-minute breakfast, and then went glumly back up to our room, where we sat and looked at each other.

'We could go to the museum,' I said listlessly. 'Or the library.'

'Neither of them opens till ten.'

'How about the charity shop? I wanted to browse in there.'

'I don't know when they open. And we've packed. I don't think we have room for any purchases.'

'We could unpack the bourbon and sit here and get ourselves quietly pickled.'

'Now there's a truly productive idea.'

At least it made us laugh for a moment.

I looked at the clock on the bedside table. 9.17.

I stood. 'Alan, this is absurd. We'll go stark staring crazy if we just sit here and look at each other. We can at least walk to the shops and see if any of them are open yet. If we buy anything we can post it home, from the airport if necessary.'

'Dorothy, consider the size of the Alderney airport. I seriously doubt they have facilities to post anything, much less a parcel.'

'Then we'll give it to someone to post for us. This is Alderney, remember? Where people are kind and friendly. Anyway, I have to do something or I'll start to scream.'

'We'd best stick together, then, in case we get a call and have to move fast.'

I looked out the window. 'I don't think anything is going to be moving at any speed for quite some time.'

We had packed our rain gear, and it took a little doing to free our jackets from their tight confines. 'I'd almost rather get wet,' I muttered as a button caught on something and wrenched itself off.

The fog was thick and penetrating. My hair had frizzed up into untidy ringlets before we'd been out five minutes.

'Is this like the pea soup London used to have?'

'Heavens, no, thank God! That stuff was lethal, quite literally. It was half fog and half smoke from the millions of coal fires, and people died in the thousands from breathing it. I got caught in it once, the notorious Great Smog. I was a boy, up with my parents for the day, and it was one of the worst experiences of my life. I was terrified! I couldn't see, and I could scarcely breathe, and I knew if I lost sight of my parents I might not find them again. It wasn't too long afterward that they banned coal fires in London, and not before time. This fog is cold and raw and you can't see a lot, but you can breathe it.'

'If it weren't for the mess it's making of our travel plans, I'd actually sort of like it. I've always had a secret love for fog. It's mysterious.'

Alan sneezed. 'And extremely wet. Here's the charity shop, and it does seem to be open. Let's get in out of this.'

We were the only customers. The volunteers were busy folding and pricing, tidying and sorting, and of course chatting. I recognized Sylvia Whiting, looking efficient, and sweet little Martha Duckett. Oh, dear. We were in a nest of Abercrombie supporters.

Or at least they had been. Had the events of the weekend made any difference to them, or would we find ourselves more comfortable back out in the fog?

They looked up and saw us. Little Martha turned pink and went back, with trembling hands, to pairing socks. Sylvia was made of sterner stuff. She put down a fluffy child's sweater that she was pricing and came up to us.

'So you were right and we were wrong. I suppose you're satisfied, now that you've made fools of us all.'

And then sweet, gentle little Martha came to our defence. 'Oh, no, Sylvia, it wasn't they who did that. They simply showed us what we had been too foolish to see. We mustn't kill the messengers.'

If one of the socks on the counter had sprung up and bit her, Sylvia couldn't have looked more surprised.

I had to bite back a nervous giggle. 'Martha, we both feel very sorry about the people who are feeling betrayed right now, especially for you, because – I hope you don't mind my saying so – you're such a sweet person.'

She turned pink again. 'Too trusting,' she said sadly. 'My dear sister always told me so. But it's better to know the truth.'

'So nothing would do but that it had to be blurted out in front of the whole island,' said Sylvia, still belligerent, and I suddenly knew what her problem was.

'I'm sure you could have thought of a much better way to do it, Sylvia. You're so good at organizing. But there simply wasn't time. We were leaving the island. We had meant to go by the first plane this morning, but . . .' I gestured out the window. 'I'm very glad we ran into you, though, because I lost your phone number and I wanted to talk to you. Do you think it would be a good idea for small groups of people, mostly parishioners I suppose, to meet and talk out the situation? I'm not sure whether it would work or not, and you know all these people so well . . .' I let it trail off.

Actually, I thought it was a terrible idea. Much better to leave it alone, let time do its work and the hurts start to heal, but it had popped into my head as a way to make Sylvia feel important again. The only hurt she had sustained, I thought, was to her ego.

Alan, at the back of the shop pretending to look at a rack of shirts, seemed to be in some bronchial distress. He had to keep coughing into his handkerchief.

Sylvia cocked her head to one side. 'It's worth some thought. I think it would be better for the groups to have some other purpose, clothes and food for the refugees, perhaps. Yes. We could meet in people's homes, and Barbara could donate anything we can't use here, and many of the women sew . . . I'll ask her about it right now.'

She bustled off, and I thought I could detect a hint of a smile on Martha's face.

'I think you are a very clever woman,' she whispered.

After that we had to buy something, so Alan chose a shirt that wasn't too bad and I found a book that would fit into my purse. We paid and left before Sylvia could come back.

The fog was no better, and there was no wind that might drive it away. 'What are you going to do with that shirt?'

'It'll do nicely for when I paint the shed.'

'It looks too big.'

'It is. That's why it'll make a good painting smock. My dear, you might warn me the next time you plan an act like that. I thought I was going to do myself some serious harm, trying not to laugh.'

'I didn't plan it. It just came out. I was tired of being browbeaten.' I looked around me. 'What now? It doesn't look as if this stuff is ever going to go away.'

'Here. The general store is open. Let's pop in, and I'll see what sort of forecast I can pull up on the mobile.'

We were entering the shop as he spoke, and the man behind the counter heard him. 'You'll not find anything good, if you're trying to fly. Where were you making for?'

'Southampton.'

He shook his head. 'Doubtful you'll get there at all today. Even if it clears here, the whole south coast is fogged in.'

I sagged back against the door. 'Alan, maybe you'd better call Aurigny.'

'They said they'd call me.' His phone rang. 'Right. Yes.' He turned to me. 'All flights to Southampton cancelled for the rest of the day. They'll put us on the first flight in the morning, but they don't know when that will be. Even with a small airline flying from a small airport, delays cause major problems. We'd better go back to Belle Isle and book one more night.'

'And I'll call Jane.'

'I gather,' came a voice from behind a shelf, 'that you are stranded here for one more day.'

Robin.

It seemed we were to spend the day being haunted by people with whom we had crossed swords. At least Robin had been anti-Abercrombie. But also anti-us, at least with regard to our hunt for a possible murderer.

Alan recovered before I did. 'Yes, so it seems. At least one more day. Apparently the pattern of fogs in these parts is rather unpredictable.'

'Yes.'

There was an awkward pause. Robin cleared his throat. 'Since the weather isn't conducive to outdoor activities, I wonder if you'd care to come to tea this afternoon.'

I opened my mouth and closed it again, and finally managed to say, 'Thank you, we'd enjoy that. Very much.'

'Around four, then? You remember where I live?'

'More or less, but you'd better give us directions.'

I almost volunteered to bring something, but I wasn't sure how formal this man would be. Better not.

THIRTY-ONE

I bought a few magazines to while away a long day, and then we picked up some groceries, enough to last us through the day and into the morning, in case that proved necessary. When we had stowed everything in our room, we found they hadn't changed the sheets and towels.

'When there's a fog like this, we know no one's leaving, and no new guests are coming,' the chambermaid explained. 'Of course we'll give you fresh linens if you wish.'

'Of course not. They were changed just yesterday, or at most the day before. At home it's once a week. No need to make extra work for yourselves.'

When we had unpacked what we needed for the day and phoned Jane, it was after ten. 'Library or museum?' asked Alan.

'Library, I suppose. These magazines don't look terribly interesting. There's sure to be something better to read there. And you can surf the Net if you want.'

We walked. It wasn't all that far, and now we'd unpacked all our wet-weather gear it wasn't too unpleasant, though the cobblestones were slippery and a bit treacherous.

The town looked strange. In two weeks we'd learned our way around fairly well, with the help of familiar landmarks, but those landmarks appeared now only when we got very near, and all the colour was faded. It was slightly eerie.

'I used to have the feeling, when I was a child, that things might disappear entirely in a fog. Or maybe that other things would be there, other houses and trees and even people.'

'I expect you liked *Brigadoon*.'

'I loved it.' And for the rest of the way we hummed the theme song from the old musical, a haunting tune.

The library was warm, bright and quiet, a haven from the raw weather. There were several other patrons, but no one was using the public computer, so Alan settled down to see if he could find something interesting, while I searched the mystery shelves until

I found one of my favourite Dorothy Sayers novels, *The Nine Tailors*. I'd read it many times, but it didn't matter. I immersed myself in the wintry world of Fenchurch St Paul, a perfect escape from the foggy and slightly hostile world of Alderney.

'Excuse me.' A whisper at my elbow brought me back. I had reached the story about the stolen emeralds and couldn't, for a moment, remember where I was and who was speaking to me. 'I'm sorry to disturb you, but might we go outside for just a moment, you and your husband?'

It was Mr Lewison. I couldn't imagine what he wanted with us, but I was getting stiff with sitting, anyway. He had already spoken to Alan, and the three of us stepped outside the door to shiver in the forecourt, where the fog looked as though it might have settled in for all eternity.

'As you see,' Mr Lewison began, 'I am also marooned here until the fog lifts. I had intended to go home yesterday, but there was a good deal I needed to discuss with Mr Venables. Now that none of us can go anywhere, I wondered if I could treat the two of you to morning coffee, and we could have a little chat. I brought my car,' he added. 'It's a bit of a walk down to Jack's in this weather.'

'That,' said Alan, 'sounds utterly delightful. Let me get our coats.'

Hot coffee and a pastry were precisely what I wanted, along with the company of someone who wasn't going to berate us for anything concerning the late unlamented William Abercrombie.

'Was this your first visit to Alderney?' the priest asked when we'd had our first sips of wonderful coffee.

We nodded.

'What a pity it turned out the way it did! I'm sure you'll be very glad to get away.'

'Yes and no,' I said, considering. 'Yes, there was a good deal of unpleasantness. And to be honest, my refusal to stay out of it made things worse.'

'For both of you, I'm sure it did. For the islanders, I think your intervention was a good and necessary thing. You opened a good many cupboards and let out a good many secrets, secrets of the kind that needed to be aired. Never blame yourselves for that.'

'We made a lot of people unhappy.'

'No, Mrs Martin. William Abercrombie made a lot of people unhappy, indeed miserable. You can't take the troubles of the world on your shoulders, though I suspect you constantly try.' His smile robbed his remark of most of its sting, but it was nevertheless a reprimand, and one I deserved. I shrugged, exchanged glances with Alan, and drank more coffee.

'I wonder: did the two of you ever come to any conclusion about whether the "accident" was really that?'

'Oh, dear, that's the piece of unfinished business that makes us wish, in a way, that we weren't leaving.' I looked at Alan, who nodded. 'There are so many indications that someone might have pushed him, or at least had reason to push him, but there's no evidence. I had hoped that someone might come forward at the meeting, but that didn't happen.'

'There are people here,' said Alan carefully, 'who know or believe they know more about it. But they have been unwilling to talk to us, and quite honestly I'm not sure they're wrong. I'm a policeman. You're a priest. In my profession causing the death of a human being is not always a crime; in yours I believe it is not always a sin. There is always the question of motive, isn't there?'

'Yes, a complicated enough question in a court of law, and far more complicated when one considers the inmost workings of the heart. There are thoughts and motives that may be unknown even to the doer of the deed, let alone to anyone else. I don't envy the police their job.'

'Much of the time it's simple enough. Most crime is thought-less and committed by thoughtless, not very intelligent people. This sort of thing, however, when the victim is one who, most people would say, richly deserved whatever he got – well, I don't envy *you* the task of sorting it out.'

'Fortunately it's not my job now, strictly speaking. I've dumped it in Mr Venables' lap, poor man.'

'He'll handle it well, I'm sure. I wish we'd had a chance to get to know him better. He seems to be an excellent priest.'

'He's a saint,' said Mr Lewison. 'Not an easy man to fill in for, even temporarily.'

'Oh, dear, it's like replacing a dearly beloved rector who retires, isn't it? I've often said that if Jesus himself came to take the position, many in the congregation would say it was all very well, but he wasn't a patch on Father So-and-So.'

Mr Lewison laughed, but ruefully. 'What are your plans for the rest of the day? It's a pity about the wretched fog.'

'Of course, if it weren't for the fog, we'd be home by now,' said Alan. 'As it is, we'll do a lot of reading, probably take a nap, and we've been invited out for tea. I only hope the fog clears by tomorrow morning.'

'As do I. We may find ourselves on the same plane, but if not . . .' He stood. 'I'll say goodbye, and God speed.'

We walked – carefully – back to our room for another dreary few hours of doing nothing.

By three thirty I had nearly reached screaming point again. I don't tolerate inaction well. When I'm frantically busy with the thousand chores of housekeeping, or volunteer work, or some problem I've become embroiled in, boredom seems desirable. When I'm actually mired in it, I long for something to do. Thus is my contrary nature. I often wonder how Alan puts up with me.

However, he was restless, too, mostly for lack of exercise. He's an active man, and we'd walked only a few cautious steps today. 'Love, let's walk to Robin's,' he said, getting up from his chair in the lounge and stretching. 'It isn't cobbled all the way, and we can take it slowly.'

'And there's no place to park, anyway. But I'm going to put on my boots. They're not going-to-tea wear, but they have a better grip.'

'Robin won't notice.'

'You want to bet?'

'Is it maybe a little thinner?' I asked when as we were picking our way up Victoria Street.

'We're just getting used to it.'

But the fog was thinner, I was sure. I could see things I hadn't before, and there was just the slightest breeze, so the mist swirled and eddied a bit. Confusing, but promising.

Robin was waiting for us, a cheerful fire crackling in the sitting room. 'A bit warm for a fire,' he said, 'but fog is nasty, depressing stuff. I see you wore sensible boots, Mrs Martin. Good for you. The cobbles are attractive, and of the right period, but they can be treacherous when they're wet.'

I shot Alan a look that said, 'Told you so!'

Robin had laid out an elaborate tea: scones, and assorted tiny sandwiches, and lemon drizzle cake. 'All courtesy of someone who can cook,' he said when I exclaimed over the bounty. 'The scones and sandwiches are from St Anne's Guest House down the street, and you know where I found the cake. I understand it's one of your favourites.'

Of course he'd know that. The Alderney grapevine.

'Robin, tell us about your house. We love old houses. We live in one, but it's positively modern compared to this one. I can't begin to guess its age.'

'Fourteenth-century, parts of it. I won't take you down to the cellar, but that's where you can see the old foundations. Of course it's been altered and added onto and generally mucked about over the centuries, so it's sometimes hard to tell the date of any particular bit. I've thought about digging in the walls to get down to the original layers, but it's a fearful expense.'

'And a dreadful mess! Our house is only early seventeenth-century, not long after the Dissolution. Yesterday, in your terms. But just keeping it in proper repair has entailed pots of money and plaster dust everywhere. And of course planning permission, as it's a listed building.'

We all groaned in mutual sympathy about the coils of the planning permission bureaucracy.

'If you'd like to see over the house, I'd be happy to show you after tea,' he said, somewhat diffidently.

'We'd like that,' said Alan. I'm sure we were both thinking the same thing. We would find no sign that Harold Guillot had ever been there, or Robin would not have made the offer.

Robin was a charming host. While we ate he chatted about historic preservation, and that led to the history of Alderney, especially during the war years. 'Some of it was horrific, of course,' he said.

'The labour camps,' said Alan. 'One can scarcely believe it, even of the Nazis.'

'And it was all so unnecessary. England had far too much to

worry about to expend time and money and men on retaking a
small island of very little strategic importance.'

'Hitler was paranoid, of course.'

'Hitler was mad,' said Robin flatly.

We moved on to the more congenial topic of his house, and
when we had eaten virtually all there was to eat, and drunk all
the tea, he stood. 'If you'd like a tour, I'm at your disposal.'

The tour was a treat, of course. The house was amazing, not
big, but with fascinating little details all over the place. Odd
corners here, steps up and down there, niches that seemed to
have no purpose until Robin pointed out that they had been
created when walls had been moved or added. As one would
expect, none of the floors were quite level and none of the
doorways quite rectangular, and all of the doorways were quite
low. Alan was told to mind his head. 'People were smaller then,'
said Robin. 'When I first moved in, my head was covered with
scars until I learned to duck automatically.'

It was all very interesting, but we were waiting for the other
shoe to drop. Robin hadn't invited us here just to give us pleasure.

We repaired back to the sitting room, where the fire was
burning low. Robin put on another log and poked expertly until
it was burning properly, and then bade us sit.

'I'd like to talk to you a little more about Abercrombie,' he
said, not to our surprise. 'A pity to spoil an agreeable afternoon,
but there are a few things I've decided you should know. There's
nothing you can do about them, even if you weren't leaving
tomorrow. I think, by the way, that you may count on that.'
He nodded at the front window. The fog was nearly gone, and
here and there a faint shadow showed us that the sun was trying
to peek through. 'This has been a bad one, but it's most unlikely
to come back for a few days. You'll be safe by your own fire-
side by this time tomorrow. Would you like a little sherry, by
the way?'

Not knowing what lay ahead, we both accepted. Something
to take the edge off?

'I have told only one other person what I am about to tell you.
I trust you to keep it to yourselves unless – well, there is no
"unless". There could be no reason for you to reveal it to anyone.'

He sipped his sherry. 'When Abercrombie first came here, I

found him an attractive personality, as did almost everyone else. Alice Small shunned him, as did Harold Guillot, and I had no idea why.

'Then one evening when I was helping Rebecca tidy up after choir practice, Abercrombie propositioned me.'

Well, I hadn't seen that one coming!

'Rebecca had gone back to the robing area for a moment, and Abercrombie had just come in. We were alone in the chancel. I was kneeling in a choir stall, fishing for some music that had fallen on the floor, and he made a suggestion, in the crudest possible terms.

'I couldn't get to my feet fast enough! Rebecca was returning, so I kept my voice as low as possible, and told him in terms just as unvarnished as his that . . . well, let's just say I said I wasn't interested.'

'He thought you were gay?'

'I suppose he thought it was a reasonable conjecture. I am unmarried; I taught for many years in a public school; my tastes run to music and art and history. As it happens, I am not homosexual, but even if I were, I would have found his approach to be entirely unacceptable. To say such a thing in the church, in that language, was utterly disgusting. The fact that he was a clergyman made it that much worse.

'When I had got home and got over my fury, I realized that he had almost certainly been seeking, not sex, but control. If I had accepted, he could have blackmailed me on the strength of it.'

'But you could also have blackmailed him,' said Alan. 'Not that you would have, of course, but a thing like that cuts both ways.'

'Not if he told his story first. He would have made me the aggressor. It would have turned into a tale of rape, with himself as the innocent victim. And he might have got by with it, even after my rebuff, if Rebecca had been out of the way just a little longer. As it was, he had failed on two counts: he had not got his way, which was a deep affront to his ego, and he had lost the opportunity to dominate me. He was furious, and he missed no opportunity to make me aware of his wrath.'

He paused. Neither Alan nor I could find anything to say.

'A little more sherry? No?' He poured some for himself and continued. 'His next victim was Harold. He knew that we were close friends and again made the wrong assumption. Our friendship is just that, and nothing more, despite the fact that Harold *is* gay. He is also a sensitive, reclusive man, and celibate for many years. He wanted nothing to do with Abercrombie and tried to avoid him whenever possible, but like me, he sings in the choir and does a good many little chores at the church. I suppose Abercrombie saw and resented Harold's dislike. At any rate, he pursued him and finally caught up with him, out on one of the trails. They both liked to walk and run.'

I licked my dry lips. Robin saw, and refilled my glass.

'I don't know exactly what happened; Harold's never told me. I suspect it was no more than threats and intimidation; there are any number of ways a subtle man can bully a quiet soul like Harold. I only know that from that day on, Harold went in terror of him. He was utterly miserable; it took me a very long time to persuade him that suicide was not the answer. The church means a great deal to him, and now it was tainted by the presence of that devil. He told me the story of his friend's daughter, and said it was all too much to bear. He saw no reason to go on living. I couldn't get him to go to a counsellor, but had to try to do it all myself.'

'That wasn't easy,' I said. 'And it wasn't fair to you.'

'No. But one does one's best for one's friends. He was just starting to feel that life might be possible again when the man died. And of course I knew who the chief suspect would be.'

'Did Harold kill him?' asked Alan bluntly.

'I think not, but I don't know,' said Robin, just as directly. 'I haven't asked him. I think he would have told me if that were the case. I also think he would have confessed to the police. He's a painfully honest man. He is, I believe, on the verge of a nervous breakdown, and I'm very worried about him.'

'Do you know where he is?' I asked.

'No. He was, as I'm sure you've surmised, staying with me for a few days. It was a great strain; I feared for his life. Then when you discovered where he had been at the relevant time, he insisted on leaving my house. It was becoming dangerous for me to keep him, he said. He went away that afternoon, and I've neither seen nor heard from him since.'

'Do you have any idea of his whereabouts?'

'I do not. I would report them to the police if I did, in his own interests. But I do not.'

'It's a great worry to you, isn't it?' I felt great sympathy for this man, and even more for Harold.

'It is also a great frustration. If he would only talk to me!'

'I try to make it a practice not to worry about a situation I can do nothing about.'

'And you always succeed?'

'Well . . .'

'Exactly.'

The fire had reduced itself to embers again. We stood and shook hands. There was nothing more to say.

We walked home on streets that were nearly dry. The sun shone. Tomorrow would be a fine day.

I wished the sun would shine a little in me.

THIRTY-TWO

Alan had turned his phone off while we were with Robin. Now he found a message from Aurigny saying that we were booked on the 8.15 plane tomorrow, and no delay was anticipated. 'We'd better let Jane know,' he said. We were taking the train from Southampton to Sherebury, and she planned to meet us at the station.

I made the call. She caught the depression in my voice. 'Something wrong?'

'Yes, but it's nothing I can explain on the phone.'

'Not ill?'

'Not in body. Jane, I must go. We'll tell you all about it tomorrow.'

I put the phone away and flopped down on the bed. Alan pulled me back up, gently but firmly. I protested. 'We missed our nap.'

'Yes, but it's too late to nap now. You know you'll have trouble getting to sleep, with a plane to catch – we hope! – early tomorrow. We'll go for a walk instead, a good long one. Come on, love. There's a nice breeze. We need the exercise and the air.'

I grumbled, but changed into jeans anyway. I was in one of those moods. I wasn't happy and I didn't want to be coaxed into cheerfulness. Very childish.

Alan steered me up Victoria Street. 'This time we're not going to do a planned walk. We're just going to wander.'

'We'll get lost.'

'Possibly. There will be someone to ask. Come along, love.'

We turned left when we got to the High Street and walked for what seemed like a long way through a residential area. Presently the houses gave way, on one side, to a couple of neat cemeteries. I was surprised. There was no church in sight. 'Overflow, darling,' Alan explained. 'The churchyard is full, but people keep dying. Most inconsiderate of them.'

We passed a large (very large) wooden sculpture of a puffin, painted brilliantly in the proper colors. That jolted me out of my

sulks. 'Alan, it's simply not true! Why would anyone put something like that here, of all places, so far from the usual tourist
attractions?'

'Why would anyone create something like that, period?'

The golf course appeared on our left, and Alan stopped to look
at his map. 'Now, it's about a mile to the north end of the island.'

'Not a lot there, right? Except the lighthouse.'

'Which we've already seen.'

'Right.'

'Look, the Nunnery is much closer. We could walk from there
across the common and join up with the coast road to take us
back. Are you tired?'

'Not really. I hate to admit it, but you were right about air
and exercise. Let's do that, and then you could always call for
a taxi if I begin to fade.'

It was a long walk, but not a difficult one. Most of it was
level, and we were walking on paved paths and roads, not scrambling through brush. When we got to the coast, the wind off the
sea grew stronger and the sun warmer, as if to deny that fog had
ever clamped us in its grip.

I was ready to sit, though, when we got in sight of the Braye
Beach Hotel. 'Let's see if they have room for us for dinner. I
don't think I can get up Braye Road without sustenance.'

They could accommodate us, so we dawdled over drinks
and dinner and coffee and then, refreshed, went up the hill to
Belle Isle.

I paid no attention to the large envelope on the hall table,
but Alan caught the name and picked it up. 'Addressed to us,'
he said. 'Probably our receipt.'

It was not a receipt. It was a note with, folded inside it, a
second envelope, still sealed.

Alan looked at the signature and said, 'It's from Robin. We'd
better take this upstairs to read.'

'There's no salutation,' he said when we were in our room with
the door shut. 'It begins: "The post was late today, owing to the
fog that delayed the mail plane until late this afternoon. It's six
thirty now, and I have just received the enclosed from Harold."'

'From Harold!'

'He goes on: "There was a note with it asking me to post this to you if I knew your address in England. I do not, but as I knew you had not yet left the island, I took the liberty of delivering it to you here. I believe that if Harold had wished me to know the contents he would have told me, so I will ask you not to reveal them to me or anyone else unless you think it absolutely necessary. Perhaps it would be best if you did not open the letter until you are on your way to England." There's no closure, either, just a scrawled signature that I take to read "Robin".'

I sat for a moment, stunned, and then said, 'Well, there goes any possibility of sleep tonight. I wish Robin had waited and delivered it tomorrow morning.'

'And I wish neither of us had taken coffee this evening. It doesn't usually keep me awake, but . . . I wonder if we're justified in doing as Robin asks. This could be a suicide note.' Alan ran a hand down the back of his neck in his classic gesture of frustration.

'Or a confession. Or both. I'm sure Robin has thought of both those possibilities.'

'It could even be an accusation of someone else, which would mean we'd have to tell Derek, and the sooner the better.'

'I think,' I said tentatively, 'that he would have written directly to Robin if he knew someone else had killed Abercrombie. Or even directly to Derek. And why would he have left the island, if someone else were guilty?'

'How do we know he's left the island?'

'The post, remember? His letter to Robin wasn't mailed here, or it wouldn't have had to be delivered on the mail plane.'

'True. I've lost my edge, haven't I?'

'You're tired. And so am I. Let's think logically.' I patted the bed next to me, and he stopped pacing and sat down. 'If it's a suicide note, he's almost certainly dead by now, so there's no rush about reading the note. If it's a confession, he'll have to be found, but how much difference would a few hours make? It's awfully hard in this computer age for someone to disappear for long. The moment he uses a credit card or an ATM, he's on the grid. And Robin wants to respect his wishes. I think we should, too – even though it's almost killing me not to know what's in that envelope.'

Alan nodded and stood up. 'All right. It goes against all my instincts as a policeman, but you've persuaded me. Now what we need to do is pack. We'll leave out most of the food; some of it will do for breakfast tomorrow, and the rest we can give to the staff. And we won't pack the wine. There's enough of that left to give us a fighting chance at some sleep tonight.'

We did sleep some, though we were both restless. Every time I woke I looked out the window for any signs of fog, but the sky was clear, the stars brilliant. Dawn came very early, of course, with sunshine so bright it hurt my eyes.

I made myself stay in bed till six, but after that it was impossible. Alan was awake, too. We got up, showered and dressed, and packed the last few remaining items. Six thirty.

We breakfasted on cheese and biscuits, a banana each, some rather withered grapes and the rest of the lemon drizzle cake. The rest of our food was fit only for the rubbish bin, but we left the bottle of bourbon sitting on the little table. 'We can't take it on the plane, and someone might want it.'

Six forty-five.

'We've nearly an hour before we go to the airport. Shall we go for a walk?'

'Might as well. I hope we don't run into half the population of Alderney wanting to chat.'

'I'd think that unlikely, so early in the morning. You'd best put on your cardigan; it's chilly.'

We walked down to the harbour, where there was considerable activity, even so early. A container ship was offloading, bringing food and other supplies and magazines and books and, in short, all the necessities for life on an island. We had been told that it would then take on containers of rubbish for disposal elsewhere, there being no room for a dump on the island. 'It must be worrisome, living in a place that's so entirely dependent on outside resources,' I mused.

'Not entirely. Don't forget that meat and fish and a good many fruits and vegetables are produced right here.'

'Still, there's tea and coffee and sugar, and clothing and shoes and medicines, and of course lemons! How would the island survive without Moray's lemon drizzle cake?'

'You have a point.' He looked at his watch. 'Perhaps we'd best toil back up the hill.'

We took it at a quicker pace than we had managed before, a pace that left me breathless, but I pushed on. I wanted to get to the airport and on that plane and in the air, just as soon as possible.

So of course we got to the airport much too soon. I hadn't got used to a place where the airport was five minutes away, if that. Alan returned the car and then we went through security procedures which, though relaxed, were still thorough. I had to be patted down, as always, because of my artificial knees.

Then it seemed hours before we were led out to the plane, though it was actually only a few minutes. Alan and I asked if we could be seated next to each other, and they sized us up and agreed. The plane was full, since they were trying to accommodate both yesterday's and today's passengers.

I had the letter in my pocket, and the moment the doors were shut and the plane was trundling over the grass toward the runway, I pulled it out, tore it open and took out the several sheets. Alan leaned across, and we began to read.

THIRTY-THREE

'**D**ear Mrs Martin and Mr Nesbitt, I regret that I never had the opportunity to meet you. Robin was quite taken with you both, and tried to persuade me to talk with you, but I could not bring myself to trust you. I have made the decision to trust you now.

'Robin will have told you why I detested and feared Abercrombie. He was, in a word, a monster, and the world is a better place with him out of it. I have some regret that he was not subjected to justice for the many crimes he committed, but we are told that he will meet with perfect justice wherever he is now. I hope that is true.

'When Robin told me that you remembered seeing me on the Zig-Zag that day, I was afraid that you would tell the police. I knew that I was already suspected of having killed him, simply because of all the reasons I had to hate him, and because I had apparently fled. When you placed me near the site of his death at the critical time, I knew they would come after me.

'I have a friend with a good boat. He took me off the island. I did not want to fly; flight manifests can be checked. I will not tell you where I am. The postmark on the envelope in which I enclosed this will tell you nothing; I gave it to someone to post for me.'

'That sounds as though he's still alive,' I shouted to Alan over the noise of the plane. He nodded, and we continued reading.

'I did not kill Abercrombie, but I bear a great responsibility for his death, nonetheless. You will wonder how that could be; I will explain.

'I have always been an active man. Exercise is vital to my well-being, so I run every morning as part of my regimen. I used to run in the town, but I began choosing more remote spots in order to avoid Abercrombie.

'That morning I chose a path that brought me to the top of what is known as the Blue Bridge path, the place where you found him. I paused for some stretching exercises. How I wish I had not! For I looked down the hill and saw him just a few yards down – very close to me in a remote area with, as I thought, no one else nearby.

'I was terrified. I must have made some noise, because he turned around and looked up at me and laughed and started back up the hill. That was when he tripped on something and began to fall. He was facing back up the hill; he fell backwards, hard, and continued to fall, bouncing from one spot to another until he was out of my sight.

'I called to him, something jeering about not being as good an athlete as he thought he was. There was no answer.

'It was a very still morning. I could hear the gulls crying down on the beach. Abercrombie had to have heard me.

'I was torn. On the one hand, I feared him and wanted to run away. On the other, I felt I had to know why he didn't answer me. I was afraid he might be hiding, planning to jump out at me or some such ploy. I thought I could perhaps bear a face-to-face confrontation, especially as he must be hurt by his fall, but if he were to come around and ambush me, that I could not bear. Carefully, fearfully, I walked down the hill.

'He was not yet dead. He was unconscious, and bleeding freely from a head wound, but he was breathing.

'I stood there for some time, in a kind of stupor. It wasn't so much that I didn't know what to do; rather that I seemed incapable of any action at all.

'He stopped breathing after a time; I don't know how long. I couldn't touch him, but I could see no pulse in his neck. I was reasonably certain that he was dead.

'Then quite suddenly I began to think again, and realized the danger of my own position. I had not killed him, yet in a way I had. Certainly I had stood and watched him die, and had done nothing. If I stayed there, if I reported his death, I would almost certainly be accused of having caused it. I got down that hill as fast as I could. I don't know why I went down, except that the bottom was closer than the top. I then followed the usual path and went up the Zig-Zag; that's when you saw me.

'I have always been a churchgoer. I do not know if I am morally responsible for his death. The thought has tormented me ever since it happened. I think you may have seen me in the peace garden, trying to resolve my emotional state. I have left Alderney, perhaps for good, so that I may have a chance to come to terms with my own conscience. I hope you will believe that I would not have kept silence if someone else had been accused of his murder.

'I could not have hidden with Robin forever. I am grateful to you for providing the catalyst for action.'

It was signed simply 'HG'.

The flight to Southampton is a short one. We deplaned, collected our luggage and made for the railway station. There was a rubbish bin outside the station. We stopped, and Alan helped me tear the letter into tiny pieces and consign them to oblivion.